M. L. S.
from
R. C. B.

An Indian Day

By the same
Author

THREE EASTERN PLAYS

CITHAERON DIALOGUES

POEMS 1902-1925

KRISHNA KUMARI

ATONEMENT

An Indian Day

by
Edward Thompson

LONDON
ALFRED A. KNOPF
1927

First Published, . *25th May* 1927
Second Impression, . *May* 1927
Third Impression, . *August* 1927

PRINTED IN GREAT BRITAIN BY
THE EDINBURGH PRESS, 9 AND 11 YOUNG STREET, EDINBURGH

To My Wife

Preface

No living person is sketched in this
story, and if anyone in India finds his
name in it he must please accept my
assurance that it is because I never
heard of him.

An Indian Day

1

THE train jerked into another station, gave a few uncertain jolts, and stopped. For the last two hours it had dawdled along through jungle. Shrubs that rarely exceeded eight feet in height studded the interstices between the taller sal woods, clumps of light-green trees as stately as flagstaffs and as unstooping, islands against whose shores the waves of coppice washed unendingly. Over the crest of this bushy sea ran a delicate grey spume, the new winter leaves of a creeper; seen separately, these were white, like poinsettia in shape and contrast to their green setting, with an effect as of millions of butterflies perched and with wings still fanning from flight. *Simuls,* massively buttressed with the triple thrust of their mighty roots into the soil, towered beside pools. Where the red earth cracked into long fissures, snaky, writhing *dhak*-trees clustered, their glistening, black boughs bare except for a ragged handful of rumpled leaves. Another month, and these crowded clefts would be plumaged deep with their spring glory of ruddy blossom—the flowers a Mogul Emperor thought so lovely that a man might never weary of gazing on them. Date-palms, tamarinds, mangoes, bamboo-

3

copses fringed the occasional hamlet or the outlying fields of some settlement.

It was all monotonously and unendingly beautiful, Hamar thought, and peacefulness took possession of him in that fresh spring air. He was glad of every-thing—glad to have left Suriganj, glad to be going to Vishnugram. What was this station? What was the time? Past noon; it could not be much further now. Suryakonda; three stations more.

As he stood by the window, a flood of sweetness swept against him, from a mango grove in flower. Peacefulness quickened into ecstasy as he held his face full in the tide of that invisible fragrance. He was going to Vishnugram—"Vishnugram? A rotten hole. They haven't got a club, there's an Indian collector, during half the year you can't get a four at bridge. Good shooting, though; jungles, plenty of bears, snipe, and that sort of thing." Suriganj had been "the best station in Bengal, if you have to be out of Calcutta"; there had been a club, with abundance of drinks and enough men and women to make as many sets at bridge and tennis as you wanted. Within comparatively easy reach had been that *sine qua non* of British bliss, things to kill. But he had been glad to get away, in spite of all this. It had not only been the unhappy finish of his term there, his whole stay had been a disappointment.

We must digress, and explain this. The War had made the trouble, or—at any rate—had brought it out. It had come when Vincent Hamar was new to the service, and he was therefore among the few who had been allowed to take commissions in the Indian Army Reserve of Officers. A mixed horde, of every station in life, missionaries, engineers, shop assistants, planters, Civil Servants like himself, had been "attached" to a regular regiment for training, and had spent three months in the Khurree hills. The regulars treated these New Army men, "so-called officers and gentlemen"—to quote one of the ready-made phrases which fitted and expressed their stereotyped scorn and wit—with open contempt. Then—and for three years more—the War was not taken seriously in India; we should run up to Baghdad presently, and in Europe finance, if nothing else, would send the German mob scuttling back. Meanwhile, the educational chance was not to be missed; the proletariat might be taught their place, and some of them even given a veneer of manners. The Adjutant of Hamar's temporary regiment, a boy of twenty-three, in his inaugural address took it upon himself to give a deal of valuable advice not strictly appertaining to war—he told them when to open the door for ladies, and explained other duties belonging to their fortuitous status as "gentlemen." Misled by the attentive hearing given to his kindness, he had continued the course. When it had gone on for some time, there had been a gathering of the insulted, and two of them, one a professor in a Government college and the other a fellow-civilian of Hamar's, had been deputed to interview the Adjutant. "I say," said the professor, going straight to the point, "in peace time I suppose I should rank as your social superior, and so would my friend here. He's the magistrate in charge of a district as big as the Isle of Wight, I'm vice-principal of a Bombay college with a thousand students." The soldier thought a moment, then good-humouredly conceded the point. "I suppose you would," he said. "It seems funny, though. I'd never thought about it." Subsequent lectures had kept more closely to military matters.

A few months later, release had come. Hamar was attached to a Gurkha regiment; he spent two years in Mesopotamia, was invalided to Bombay, rejoined his regiment late in 1917, and went with them to Palestine. But he never saw Palestine, for, after a short sojourn on the Suez Canal, he had been sent to the Lowland Division as a staff-captain and had gone with it to France, where it was smashed in the dreadful fights of early 1918. He had been wounded, he had been down with deadly sickness, he had suffered all the sinking of heart which comes from knowing that one's name has gone forward for a decoration and from finding it omitted from the list of awards, he had been wretched in mind and body, he had endured shell-shock. It was to this last experience that the more charitable of his colleagues attributed his errors, which to the rest of his countrymen were merely a welling up from seething depths of natural turpitude. When he returned to India in 1921, he was out of touch with his former life and former colleagues. His experience had knocked him aslant from sympathy with official lines of thought, and he was hungering for an existence that had a real hold on the land where it was passed. As everyone knows, he came to grief over the famous Conspiracy Case of Lambertgarh; and the Secretariat, recognizing the fierceness of public opinion, had transferred him now to Vishnugram.

Even so, he had compensations. "You've been an ass, of course," he had been told by Headley, the Chief

Secretary to Government. "But you did your job in the War. I met your colonel, and he said you ought to have been decorated before half the chaps who got ribbons. That's good enough for me. I'd have gone as a sweeper, gladly, and been proud to do my bit." Headley meant this. The War had troubled him, and it came out irrelevantly and harmfully in his administration of peace-time justice. One man "had done his bit," another had not; it went hard with the latter, if Headley had anything to do with it. Hamar wished the War had been left out of the reckoning; he was not content to be acquitted on wrong grounds. He said so. Headley—no politician, but a man who genuinely loved the Indian people and was loved back by them; his fearless championship of their rights had lost him no friends even among his own nation— listened to him, and caught a glimpse of his point of view. "I daresay you're right," he said at last. "Anyway, I'd rather have you than the next nine men, who've never hashed a case. No, no, of course not"— he waved Hamar's protest aside, for he was rushed for time, and really could not argue the matter out— "I'm not saying you *have* hashed this case. You're right to stick up for Indians; it's their country, it doesn't belong to a clan of jutewallas from Dundee. Only keep your head next time."

Consecutive thinking was not Headley's long suit; but he prided himself on his ability to keep his head. His method sometimes involved violence to the heads of others; only the previous day, he had smacked his *durwan's* hard, in full sight of his crowded office. The most virulent daily of the province, a paper which specialized in leaders headed "Brutal Assault by an

Englishman," had passed the incident over with playful mention—the indulgence recognized as due to the fieriest, most generous, best-loved man in India. Possibly some memory of his most recent feat of self-control rose now from Headley's subconsciousness, and gave him the metaphor of his concluding admonition to Hamar. "We've got to clout *any*one who's in the wrong, Indian or British. Remember that. I'm putting you in the jungles for a bit, to think things out and get rested."

That was after things had gone wrong. But for Hamar they had never gone right. Suriganj was not Calcutta, where something was always happening; nor was it the jungle, where nothing happened except the eternal processes of God. It was just an untidy mofussil town, with a population bursting through its sleeves of streets and tenements. It was a place of half-baked babus, cringing, insolent, seditious, wholly unprimitive except in their personal habits and sanitation; and a European station that chattered and quarrelled, quarrelled and chattered. Hamar, even after three years of Suriganj, still hoped and sometimes longed to meet something that could be called the Indian mind—thought unembittered by eating of the fruit of the tree of political knowledge. There was a glamour about the name of Vishnugram. The shallow stream of pettish contempt passed him by. His countrymen tested everything by their own sterile pleasures, as a tourist tests Jerusalem by its hotels and Athens by its cocktails. "A vile little hole—a damnable place." Yes; but its forts and temples witnessed to centuries when it had been a wall against Mogul and Mahratta, and both shield and lamp to the simple folk of these uplands. He was going to get back calm and strength of spirit.

"Excuse me, sir. There's room in here, isn't there?"

He apologized, and stood aside. That mango fragrance had intoxicated him, and he had been apparently deliberately blocking the door. Two Englishmen wished to enter; the younger loudly justified his disturbance of Hamar's privacy.

"Sorry," he said. "But there are some niggers in the only other first."

"No, *I*'m sorry," said Hamar. He wondered what the niggers next door—one of whom he knew by sight, an Indian scientist with some reputation in Europe— thought of this reference to themselves. Obviously his new companions were in the Army; only the Army and the rougher, less-educated class of boxwalla referred to Indians as "niggers," and these men were not of the latter type. "I didn't notice I was stopping up the way."

The coolies were paid. As they looked at the coins in their palms, any discussion was foreclosed by an imperious wave of the hand, and an order to *jao*. "And *jao jeldily,* and be *choop* about it. Wonder what they're doing with all these stacks of wood?" the speaker continued, as he shut the door. "They don't look like railway sleepers."

"They are, though," the other drawled. "It's about all they're good for, these sals. Lord! what a country!"

He looked about him with a sulky fastidiousness which Hamar found faintly amusing and not unattractive; he had lived with the type once, and had got past initial dislike, to something like warm respect.

Having settled himself in a corner and taken a *Tatler*
which the younger man handed to him, the last speaker
gazed at Hamar thoughtfully. Then he spoke—again
as if he were probing a misdemeanour which the land
was trying to conceal.

"Do you know that place we've just run in to?" he
asked.

Hamar did not, except by name.

"Rummy corner, miles from any sort of decency.
Not a saheb within twenty miles."

"It's an out-of-the-way district," said Hamar
weakly. He was plainly defending the indefensible,
and by his action was drawn into complicity with a
very guilty place.

"I rather liked it, though." Hamar felt that
Suryakonda had been let off, but with a warning. The
judge proceeded to give the extenuating circumstances.
They were the usual ones. "We've just put in a week's
shooting here."

"*Jolly* good shooting," corroborated his fellow
justice. "I say, sir, it's a treat to find such a place
nowadays. It hasn't been shot out, and you don't find
every native running about with a gun. They oughtn't
to be allowed to have guns." He warmed to his theme.
"You can get stacks of peafowl and jungle-fowl. Up
in the U. P., where my regiment is,"—this to Hamar—
"you can't shoot peafowl. The natives make such a
row."

"Damned row," his companion agreed.

"You'll never get me to understand these people."
He spoke defiantly, as if he were up against a challenge. "They don't like you shooting monkeys. And
peafowl you mustn't touch." He ruminated. "I was

ort of lost, the first day here. Took some time to realize that you could pot as many as you liked. We bagged about thirty; and other things galore. Topping!"

How repellent and how attractive he was! Hamar, seated opposite, felt himself carried back to those first days of army training. How they had *loathed* that handful of regular subalterns who lorded it over them, and looked down the end of their supercilious long noses! How maddening their patronage had been, their ignorance and complacency! He remembered a scrap of talk he had accidentally overheard, about one of his own group—a man of thirty-five who had travelled through the heart of unadministered lands in Burma and beyond the Bhutan-Tibetan border, and had made himself a name in science and geography. "I say, you know," one child had told another, "I've been talking to that fellow Shelmerdine. He's quite an able sort of chap, in his way. Knows a lot of things." "What sort of things?" had piped back the voice of "Baby Roscoe." "Price of ribbons and things?" It was understood that the I. A. R. O. wallas had all been sacked from the millinery shops of Bombay and Calcutta. And here were those far-off memories of 1915 back with Hamar; clean-shaven— except for the light down of the caste moustache— clean-limbed, insolently handsome, the British Army in its bright, ignorant youth sat opposite him. But he had other memories than those Khurree ones. The comradeship of many a bitter Mesopotamian dawn returned, and he remembered how generous and patient had been the boys he had seen die at Hanna and Sannaiyat and in the hand-to-hand struggles for the

B

loops of the Tigris, when Maude struck for Baghdad. Shopwalla and regular had known one another better then. This youngster in the carriage——

"They've got some astounding *beels* here"—the elder soldier was speaking. "One must be a couple of miles across. The place must have had a history of sorts, if one could get at it." He looked inquiringly at Hamar.

"It had," said Hamar. "It was the frontier fort of Vishnugram, when it was an independent kingdom. I've been reading it up in our *Gazetteer*." He rose, and reached for the book on the rack. "It doesn't say much, though. But there are a lot of yarns about."

"Yarns?" The subaltern yawned. "About a tree turning into a bull, and that sort of thing?"

"Not that kind. There were battles here with the Portuguese."

"The jolly old Portugooses! I say, sir, that must have been topping fun! The Major"—he explained to Hamar—"had the Portugooses on the right of his crowd, when he was in France. *And* twice as many British troops as they needed to hold the line anywhere else." The Major nodded, smiling. "It must have been damn funny, seeing a battalion of Portugoose generals charging a fort full of babu M. A.'s!"

"They believe that Akbar himself came here once," Hamar interjected.

The Major, keenly interested, raised his hand as he bent forward to listen. But the gesture, like Hamar's remark, was merely a rock in a brook; it jetted the flood of full-blooded, healthy ignorance into another direction, that was all.

"Akbar! I've seen his Taj at Delhi. Why didn't

he do another here? I say, sir, that *is* a top-hole bit of work, isn't it?"

"Shut up, Tommy. You let the Raj down, every time you speak. A happy barbarian"—the Major smiled at Hamar—"he's not deep in anything but polo and shooting."

"Oh, I say, sir!"

Hamar joined in the general laugh; in that moment, all three men liked each other. Major Henderson, taking the *Gazetteer,* leant across—the train was jolting, and it was hard to hear—and introduced himself. His pose dropped from him, and his manner was pleasant and cordial.

He was about a couple of years older than Hamar —was thirty-four or so. His face, furrowed with quizzical lines, was attractively discontented. Keen on a score of things, and finding life full of interest everywhere, Major Henderson amused everyone he met by keeping up a slightly pained, querulous tone about everything. He spoke of Indians, and of everything Indian, as if their presence on the planet distressed him physically. Yet he bought every book about India, he read largely about Indian history, customs, religion, even literature, he patiently went on pilgrimage to even the lesser sites, and he returned after every furlough, in spite of offers of excellent billets at home. "No one has a steadier grouse at life than Henderson," said his colonel. "But I never met a chap who enjoyed it more. He's like our quartermaster-sergeant, who curses the canteen beer, but sups up all he can lay hands on."

Hamar looked at him, and then at the athletic Philistine opposite. He knew both types; the former naturally generous and sympathetic, but warped by long listening to mess politics and mess philosophy—the latter stupid, self-satisfied, energetic, and kind. Both of them impossible people, of course, whatever the Major had once had it in him to become—impossible in their talk, incredibly circumscribed in attitude and opinions, ill-informed, and bigoted in training and ideas. But in practice often queerly tolerant, and breaking out in unexpected ways. You never knew where they might not shame you by some instinctive decency, when your careful thinker and scrupulous official would be ineffably mean, in his just, righteous fashion.

"Warren, of my regiment, the Norsets," the Major continued. "My nephew. He's going back to Fort William, after he's seen me settled in my new quarters. I've been told off to inspect the I. D. F.[1] in these parts. Duties more exhilarating than arduous, I understand. Mostly peg-drinking. You don't take soldiering over-seriously in the mofussil, do you?"

"About as seriously as they do in the Calcutta or Bombay Light Horse, I expect," said Hamar. He had not told them his name yet.

"Ah!"

"We reckon to pass our shooting tests; and we always turn out for one sham fight during the cold weather."

"*Quite* so," said the irrepressible Warren. "And when the *real* fight comes with these damned swarajists, I suppose you'll all turn out then?"

He swore hard for a minute or two. Indian poli-

[1] India Defence Force—volunteers.

tics were a deep sorrow to him, as to most people of his sort. It was all so simple; a dozen rounds from a machine-gun, a few executions, and everyone would be happy again. And yet we went on talking, and, what was worse, letting these blighters talk.

"My name's Hamar," said Hamar, seizing his chance when Warren had finished consigning to hell all babus, swarajists, seditionists, C. R. Das, Mahatma Gandhi, C. F. Andrews, the late Mr. E. S. Montagu, and the Labour Party.

Major Henderson was startled from his languid annoyance, and looked actively vexed. "Are you the Hamar who's going as Judge to Vishnugram?"

Hamar nodded. In a moment, he was aware of his companions withdrawing a thousand miles away. The air in the carriage suddenly seemed to grow arctic, even in that warm afternoon of an Indian February. Warren was staring at him open-eyed; he became open-mouthed, too, before he knew what he was saying.

"Do you mean that you're the jolly ass who let off those swarajist scoundrels who were in that bolshevist plot?"

Hamar went hot. "That's a newspaper lie. No, it's a club lie. They daren't put it in the newspapers. There never was a shadow of proof that they had anything to do with it."

"You let 'em off, anyway."

"The prosecution broke down. Government couldn't prove that those letters were authentic. I did my job. I dismissed the case."

Major Henderson's good manners came to the rescue; they had no right to bait a man they had just met. Also, the way Hamar stiffened up in his own defence won his respect. And, in claiming that he "had done his job," the accused had, all unconsciously, flung up the one flag that an Englishman accepts; by using that mystic formula he had somehow got home. If he'd done what he thought was his job, well, hang it, he had done his job, hadn't he? It might be a rotten job, but a man had to do his job, anyway, whatever it was. You couldn't get past that; you'd have to begin again. "Of course, you had to do what you felt was the right thing," Major Henderson admitted.

But Hamar was too indignant to see that he had escaped. "The right thing! The legal thing as well, in this case! Excuse me, Major, but you wouldn't discuss your conduct of an orderly room with me, a man outside your service!"

This also helped him; he had claimed a place in the freemasonry of the Army, had appealed to its traditions and custom. For a moment the prejudice between the Army and the Civil Service broke down. The Major nodded.

"Then why've you been sandbagged and shipped off to Vishnugram? Everyone knows――" Warren caught his senior's eye, and subsided. Henderson spoke, hurriedly and soothingly.

"Of course, we have only the newspapers and common gup to go by."

"Exactly. And nowadays every European believes that all Indians have bombs in their *dhutis* somewhere —just as our newspapers tell us that all Americans carry whisky-flasks in their hip pockets!"

"Well, but *is* there a single nigger who's still loyal, anywhere?" Warren was not to be denied any longer. "There were two of them got into a first-class carriage in which I was travelling to Calcutta the other day. They refused to turn out. Said they had a right to travel there, and that the train was full up!"

Hamar waved his hand despairingly. He was about to speak, but thought better of it. What was the use? He saw now what he was up against—utter confusion of thought, a miasma of prejudice, false history, secondhand report, memory of personal annoyances or fancied slights. When such an argument began, men instinctively aligned themselves by nationality. Neither from Indian nor from Englishman could you expect sanity. Henderson offered him his cheroot case.

"It's too hot for politics," he said. "Anyway, what do they matter?"

He lit another cheroot for himself; as he did so, he allowed himself one bitter flicker of resentment. "If there's one good thing the War has done, it's this. It showed us once for all that a single company of white troops, if you give them a couple of machine-guns, can walk across India."

"That wasn't my impression, sir," said Hamar.

"You were in the War, then?" said Warren. The Major suddenly remembered Hamar's reference to the conduct of an orderly room.

Hamar nodded. Both soldiers looked at him with respect. There were far too many civilians in India, especially in the Government services, who had managed to keep out of the biggest mess of our time.

"I was with the Gurkhas in Mespot," he went on. "The crowd who got cut up when we crossed the Tigris and took Kut. The Norfolks got over, because we were shot down."

"Ah, Gurkhas! They're different." It was Henderson who spoke. Hamar felt disappointed and surprised. Yet why? Wasn't this what every regiment outside the Indian Army said? Why should he expect a man to be untinged by the orthodoxy of his own creed?

"In what way—different?"

Henderson reflected, doubtfully. Warren did not. "Why, the jolly little Gurk's a first-class fighting man," he assured Hamar.

"He's a better man than the Indian," said Henderson. "He's more dependable, he has self-respect, he can carry on when his British officers have gone."

"Exactly," Hamar snapped. "He comes from a country that's its own master. His crowd aren't under our thumb."

He realized his mistake as soon as he had spoken. As an officer of Gurkhas, he had risen to a plane where he was accepted as every inch a white man; they were even prepared to find that behind his errors were reasons which had some perverted decency in them. Now nothing that he could say would convince them of his essential sahebdom. He was "pro-native"; then, by easy steps of argument, he was anti-British, he was seditious, a public danger, a traitor, a socialist, a communist, an atheist, a bolshevist.

Major Henderson turned the subject, and then excused himself. For a while, nobody spoke; Warren studied the *Sketch,* Henderson and Hamar the scenery. The train rumbled along, the shadows of the forest lengthened. Cool, mango-fragrant breezes solaced Hamar, defiantly watching the waving scrub dance slowly by. Changing his sky, he was keeping his soul; unfortunately, he was keeping his reputation as well. Suriganj was still travelling onward with him. He had not escaped.

2

NIXON, Police Superintendent of Vishnugram district, was waiting at the station for Hamar's train; a tallish, slender man, with an air of decent but not extravagant efficiency about him. A quiet, patient face—it seemed to say: "There are fifty things to worry one. But it's no use talking. Better get on with the next job, and trust to getting through everything somehow." He had a small corps of coolies, whom he turned on to Hamar's kit. As the train was the mid-day express, it was in no hurry; it had the line clear to itself for the next half-dozen hours, and could hang about the station indefinitely.

Hamar introduced Nixon to Henderson, and heard him invite the latter to stay with him when he came to inspect the Vishnugram volunteers. Then Nixon handed the luggage over to a constable, and took Hamar to his car.

"He means all right, I dare say," said Major Henderson, as he watched Hamar leave the station. "Full of sympathy, and all that sort of thing—very keen to do what's just, and so on. Pity those chaps can't *see* straight!"

"It's just those fellows who do all the jolly mischief," said Lieutenant Warren sagely. He felt very statesmanlike, as he leant back and studied Blanche's letters.

3

TORTUOUS, dirty streets, flanked by a mixed architecture of mud, brick, wood, stone, stucco—size and shape of every variety. One side would suddenly seem to fall away, disclosing a superb tank; or a tawdry tiny temple of Siva thrust up, with a pair of parakeets clinging screaming to its dome. Dogs in the last stages of decrepitude, a horror to the sight, crawled out in front of their wheels. A blue bee-eater rose from the road. Two women far advanced in elephantiasis stopped, water-pot on head, to gaze at the car.

"You've not much of the magnificence of old Vishnugram left," said Hamar.

Nixon did not catch what was said; he was shouting at a child who ran without warning right across the road. He turned his face inquiringly.

"Where are all the temples—the forts—the old city?"

Nixon waved in front, to the right. "Buried in jungle. All this tumble-down rubbish is modern. Modern *and* ancient. I suppose there was always some sort of inhabited filth here."

"Is there no one left in the old town?"

"The Rani still lives in what they are pleased to call the Palace. She has a kid of sixteen with her, whom they call the Raja. They get a pension from us—sixty dibs a month."

"It doesn't sound very princely!"

"It pays for dusting a couple of rickety chairs she keeps for visitors. Supplies her with umbrellas. She needs them. Her roof leaks in a five minutes' shower."

"Good Heavens!"

"Well, she's not the real Rani. The line finished twenty years ago. They claimed the right of adoption; that's all the right this boy of hers has. And she's just his mother. I don't see that we've any obligation to pay her anything."

They had cleared the bazaar now, and were moving in what might almost be called wooded country. The trees were taller, and there were plenty of them. A magnificent banyan occupied half of a considerable *maidan,* hiding all but glimpses of large buildings.

"There's your court," said Nixon. "Isn't that tree a whopper? Fairly squats on the place. *He'll* always have a grip on India, whatever happens to us. My *thana's* to the left—there, behind that gold *mohur.*"

Hamar commented on a dampness in the air.

"All these tanks. They make the place reek with malaria. We ought to drain them."

Hamar was horrified. "India'd never forgive us. These tanks are like a Westminster Abbey to these parts."

"I wouldn't mind seeing them all buried in their Westminster Abbey, as you call it." Then he smiled at his own truculence. "Perhaps you're right. Not that what India'd think matters a damn. But they make too good snipe-shooting in the cold weather. Here we are! You'll stop overnight, of course. My wife expects you to."

They had entered a compound which seemed like every other compound in this land of repetitions. The only difference that Hamar could see was that a straggly cactus hedge took the place of the usual low white wall.

"My cowsheds," said Nixon. He pointed to some

stately erections on the left. "Used to be a *bibikhana*
in the good old days. The place belonged to *your*
predecessors then; the district has some fine yarns
about them."

They passed a couple of tennis-courts, where a
squad of servants were already fixing screens and nets
and taking out chairs and tables.

"Our tennis day," Nixon explained. "I expect you
know we haven't a club. It's the beastliest, dullest
hole in Bengal. Now, when I was at Dacca——Oh,
damn!"

A dog that had been lying under the porch limped
away yelping, a *mali* accelerating its escape with shouts
and stones. And Mrs. Nixon appeared on the veranda,
against the eternal background of crotons in pots.

Hamar was artist enough to feel, for the first time,
that the detestable plants might have a purpose. Their
polished leaves, dark and flushed as if with southern
blood into a sullen redness, were a foil for beauty that
seemed to spatter them with sunlight. But the Demiurge, in bringing to life this human flower, had been
hard, wasteful, unpitying. This entrancing brightness
was born of healthy youthfulness, and would perish
with it. The work had been done supremely well.
But the maker had been technician only, and had left
it untinted by his dreams. There was nothing here
that he desired to keep, nothing that would trouble
men's thoughts, once away from its vision—nothing
that would kindle tenderness long after the physical
splendour had dimmed.

"Oh, *why* did you come by that *dreadful, dull day*-
train?" Mrs. Nixon was lavish in emphasis. It gave
her speech a pleasing liveliness; a quick-flitting butter-

fly, speckling dull flowers with its evasive presence. "You must be nearly *dead*. Tea's ready, John. You couldn't get *any*thing on *that* train, I know."

They sat down to tea. But in a moment Mrs. Nixon had sprung up again. Clapping her hands, she ran out on the back veranda, while a squirrel scampered away. Returning, she said: "We keep the horse-feed there, and they're at the bags all day long."

Nixon grinned. "I got my wife a catapult, but she hurt her thumb with it. *And* hit the cook so badly that I had to give him five dibs compensation."

The recollection seemed to please Mrs. Nixon. "He was carrying a dish of absolutely *boiling* stew when the pellet touched him up. He smashed the dish, of course! You should have heard him *howl!* I thought I must have hit a jackal. I'd get a cat, but they grow so mangy. We're plagued with pests."

A dissertation followed on the meanness of a Government which squandered money on the education of natives and on pampering them in every way, but left its officials without a stone wall to their compound. Hamar thought the grievance slight but did not say so. Later on he modified this judgment, when he tried himself to raise a vegetable garden in a district eminent for its capriculture. All he said now was: "A wall wouldn't keep the goats out—or the squirrels."

"It would keep out the cows, at any rate," said Nixon. "And *some* of the goats."

Hamar changed the subject. "I saw a good many monkeys in the bazaar."

"Monkeys!" exclaimed Nixon. "This town, being holy, swarms with them. We never get a fruit off our mangoes or guavas. They even invade my office. I found one going over my confidential correspondence files last Friday week."

"How on earth did it ever get past your orderly?"

"By direct permission. If it wasn't invitation! *He* wasn't going to stop the blessed creature—he, a pious Hindu!"

Mrs. Nixon was thinking hard; her charming face grew grave.

"Mr. Hamar, I suppose these swarajists couldn't *train* a monkey, could they? To get at John's confidential documents?"

The men laughed. Nixon added: "Anyway, I put a bullet in this particular swarajist agent. I expect you heard about the row they made."

Hamar *had* heard.

"The brute brought down a whole heap of things with a crash, clearing when I came in. And then sat on that peepul, jabbering and ripping my letters to ribbons. They weren't things I wanted broadcast, by any means. So I fetched him down. I don't see what else I could have done."

"I don't, either," Hamar assented. His confidential press-excerpts had shown how much had been made of Nixon's alleged brutality, but had said nothing of the provocation received.

"These blighters didn't see that, though."

"Oh, they saw it, right enough."

"Then why've they been tearing me to shreds? That scoundrel Jeejeewalla was up in the Legislative Assembly about it."

"That's part of the trouble now," said Hamar wearily. "Whatever you do, you're in the wrong.

They say: All's fair in war; and politics are war. They believe it's what we do at home—pretend to be shocked when we aren't, and on principle make a row whenever an opponent does anything, no matter what it is. Even their best fellows believe that there's no room in politics for ethics, and that everyone everywhere so believes."

Nixon stared, as he listened to this sound doctrine from so unexpected a preacher. He looked at Hamar with the beginnings of approbation; after all, the man might not be so bad. He might have learnt his lesson —might now realize that you couldn't afford to play with all this swarajist nonsense. They didn't thank you, they slanged you just as much as if you had handled them with the gloves off.

"Quite," he agreed. "The poor old off*ish* gets it in the neck every time—gets it from Government, gets it from these swabs. It's best to have no friendly truck with them, but to go for them bald-headed. Then, when they do howl at you, you have at any rate the satisfaction of feeling that you've earned it."

"Another cup, Mr. Hamar?" said Mrs. Nixon brightly. "John, you can find Mr. Hamar a racket."

A *chaprasi* reported that the Aldens had arrived.

4

As they went out to the tennis-courts, long shadows were already falling from a row of catalpa-trees behind the chairs. That core of coolness which even at noontide lurks in the February air now came out from its hiding-place and became a definite tiny breeze.

It wafted sweetness from the mangoes, dainty wisps of fragrance from the deeply pollened frangipanis.

Alden, tall, broad-shouldered, physically indolent and powerful, greeted Hamar eagerly. It was nothing; and yet Hamar felt, for the first time, as if Lambertgarh had fallen from him, or were even something in his favour. Alden's indolence did not extend further than those superb limbs of his; he was an enthusiast where the people of the land were concerned, their thought and their life. Hamar knew him by repute, and rather despised him. His sort were commonly assumed to be good-hearted but woolly in their thinking. It did not please Hamar to know that, among the more generous of his countrymen, this judgment was current about himself. But he was grateful for Alden's friendliness now.

That friendliness in this instance was not due to any sentimental affection for the Aryan brother, but was merely Alden's reaction from journalistic abuse of Hamar. Newspaper criticism did not impress Alden. If it is possible to do this, he exaggerated the cynicism with which Indian papers, of both sides, are run, and assumed their dishonesty too much as a matter of course. He knew pretty intimately the editor of a Calcutta daily which frequently scarified him for his supposed encouragement of sedition; and he had often in private conversation heard opinions the exact opposite of those his friend was obliged to hold officially. He was prepared to believe that Hamar had done the right thing at Suriganj, though he knew little of the facts.

Mrs. Alden came of a line of West Country gentlefolk that had rarely failed to produce beauty above the common in its women. She lacked the air of mild distress and disappointment that often marks the more intelligent missionary lady—fretful, resigned bewilderment at the slowness with which the Indian Christian community picks up the ethics of the remarkably religious populations of England and America. Married less than two years, in those two years she had made little effort to adjust herself to a new life. Her own circle had been distinctly "worldly," in a healthy pagan fashion, and her training had been for the pleasures rather than the enthusiasms of life. Her movements showed this; there was nothing tense or rigid about them, they were graceful with a proud attractive languor. But in her husband's neighbourhood she became vigilant, for her sense of decency, which was strong, was constantly outraged by his irresponsible cheerfulness. There were few public occasions when she could be sure that he would not play the fool. A meeting convened by the Collector, a solemn religious service, a stately visit from the Governor—all such ceremonial events fed his too abundant sense of the absurd. The Alden who on occasion leapt so fiercely into the front of bitter controversy, at these functions, as a colleague complained, often "behaved like a kid at a pantomime."

But Mrs. Alden's watchfulness relaxed now, for nothing more serious than tennis was proposed. Her face was its normal restful self as she shook hands with Hamar, and saw her husband then draw aside in company with a man even more disreputable than himself. Leaning back in a deck-chair, she announced that Mr. Jacks would be along presently, bringing with him her sister. Douglas, the College principal,

could not come, he was going over the estimates for
the new laboratory.

Mrs. Nixon sniffed discontentedly. "Haven't you
spent enough money on these natives? Couldn't you
get your Christians at home to do something for their
own flesh and blood out here?"

"They ought to, I know," Alden agreed, over
Hamar's shoulder. "It's perfectly vile, the way we
have treated the Eurasians. We brought them into
existence, and then we tread them underfoot and
despise them. Missions ought to take their case up
more."

Mrs. Nixon shrugged her dainty shoulders. She
had not meant Eurasians, whom she by no means considered her own flesh and blood. This dreadful missionary had committed a *bêtise* by referring to the way
they had come into existence.

"We're building the lab with a Government grant,"
Alden went on. "Our Society has nothing to do with
it this time."

Worse and worse. More Government money
squandered.

"There's always plenty of money for anything these
people want. But never any for us. No wonder they
get uppish!"

"Well, it's *their* money, isn't it?" asked Alden good-
naturedly.

"Not if it's our country."

"Cut out a political wrangle," said Nixon. "It's just
politics all day long in this damned country. As if
there were nothing else that mattered! I'm sick of
politics."

"That's sense, Nixon," said Alden. "The dullest

thing in the world; and yet people out here will chatter about nothing else."

Hamar partnered Mrs. Nixon against her husband and Alden, by the conventions that assume a new-comer to be the best player and a lady to be necessarily weaker than any man player. The latter convention had worn thin in Vishnugram. The lady was beyond comparison better than her husband, and the set fin-ished with swift ease. During it Neogyi—the Collec-tor—arrived, and Alden's colleague Jacks and Mrs. Alden's sister.

Hilda Mannering was twenty-two, five years younger than her sister. There was nothing in the least languid or cultivated about the air of proud aloofness which she shared with Frances. Her eyes gave the arrogance away; they were charged with a straightforward and most engaging friendliness. Hamar's attention was caught by the attractive, boyish swing with which she walked up. He lost a point—his partner, disapprovingly, noted the cause. Her carriage, both in repose and action, was not the least ensnaring charm of Miss Mannering's very competent and feminine person. But she was popular with her own sex, who forgave her her conquests.

She insisted now on standing down for "a men's four"; and a set followed which Hamar always remem-bered as a revelation of how closely matched two men can be in quite differing styles of badness. Nixon at the net would leap to incredible heights and bring down everything within reach, always on the wrong side of the net. Jacks, who was short but richly endowed with blundering activity, operated laterally instead of perpendicularly, and balls that were well outside he managed to scoop within the court. Neogyi, a quiet, accurate player, fought a separate and disconnected duel with Hamar. It seemed to be the custom to leave Jacks and Nixon to neutralize each other, while a simultaneous set was played on the same court.

The players returned to find the spectators in high good humour. Hilda Mannering looked up with mischievous anticipation as Alden, in his blandest manner, addressed Nixon.

"Have you a copy of the rules for entering your service, Nixon?"

"Why?" Nixon mopped his brow, and looked benignantly and incautiously at him. "Do you know anyone who's thinking of entering? For God's sake, tell him not to. Tell him to coal-heave, to chauff, to buttle or burgle, to be a missionary, to take on any soft job that's going—but to keep out of my show."

"Oh, no. Only my sister-in-law was wondering——"

"What, Miss Mannering? If he's a friend of yours, I say all the more, keep him out of it. But I'll gladly tell you anything I can."

Miss Mannering hesitated. It seemed mean to throw chivalry away. Even so Solomon might have paused before kicking silver aside, and then have reflected that, after all, it was the cheapest thing he possessed. And Gloriana must have known that the print of her shoe was worth all the ruined splendour of Raleigh's cloak.

"It's a shame for Rob to put it on me," she said. "We were simply wondering if there was anything about candidates having to be bad tennis-players."

"Quite likely, you know," said Alden. "Troubled times, most important service, the police. You can't

afford to have men who are likely to waste their time
playing games, rushing off to this and that championship competition."

Nixon liked Alden—a good fellow, if he wouldn't
be always sticking up for these swarajists. Too good
to be wasting his time as a missionary—not that you
could really call that silly college work missionary
work! And it was jolly to be chaffed by a girl like
Miss Mannering. Any man who had been the cause
of those mocking lights felt a benefactor to his kind.
Nixon had no illusions as to his tennis, and he grinned
agreement.

"Before you we had Hutchinson." Neogyi grew
reminiscent and pondering. "Funny thing, but whenever we spun out for a men's four, whoever else lost
he never did. We never had a decent men's four, all
the time he was here."

There was a lift of deprecating hands all round,
and Alden went through the pantomime of brandishing
his racket over an imaginary ball, which he smashed
down hard on the earth. Hutchinson's tennis was a
public possession, like Untermeyer's riding.

The last set was in fading light, between Miss
Mannering and Jacks and Mrs. Alden and Hamar.
Hamar was sportsman enough to put as many balls as
he could into Miss Mannering's court; but Jacks
bucketed about, poaching incessantly and furiously.
His play suggested a train of varied metaphors. Now
he was a toreador about to attack a bull; he held his
racket like a dagger, stoopingly. But the moment
the ball was over, he was a clumsy dog worrying a
rabbit round a tiny field. Hamar, watching the way
Miss Mannering kept her temper, admired her very

much. But her face reddened with something brighter than the mere glow of exertion.

"Hilda's a Christian." Alden was summing up the spectators' findings. "I'm not going to be a witness if she murders Jacks. She's entitled to. Let's avert our eyes."

As Hamar lay awake that night, he was conscious that the drabness of this Indian station had lightened. He saw the group sitting out after tennis, while a moon, full-globed and marvellous, rose orange-brilliant above the mangoes. The air was spiced with fragrances that exhilarated the tired blood; voices were speaking restfully and gaily. Alden was fooling and interchanging chaff with everyone. Mrs. Alden was friendly and charming; Mrs. Nixon, he saw, was exquisitely beautiful. His eyes were straying to Hilda Mannering, as she leaned back, her hands behind her head, her face tilted towards that climbing moon. She was not pretty; he was not the first man who had told himself that. It was her actions, he decided; they were quick and dainty, like the flutter of a bird or a startled wood-goddess. Then he wondered if it was her voice; for when she spoke the whole ghostly company in his spirit were silent, that they might listen.

He awoke in a rushing Indian dawn; the east in a hurry was flushing from white to gold, from gold to red, from red back again to gold. The mango groves were shaking to the mad laughter of *kokils,* the birds whose mirth brings in the morning. The sky rocked to the winnowing of wings, the wild pigeons striding to their business. A blue roller was absorbed in sun-worship; he would swoop up, up, up, as if he were going straight to the heart of that brightness, and then, dazzled and defeated, he would swing back to his perch. Across a sea of green forest, Hamar caught a glimpse of temples and of palm-bordered pools. If he had been a religious man, he would have praised God. Why wasn't there a God to thank? Almost for the first time in his life he felt he wanted someone to whom he could say, "Boss, you've done a good job." In default of other satisfaction, as he stood on the veranda beside a tub which was one sapphire magnificence with the flowers of morning glory, he saluted, as a man pays homage to beauty.

5

KAMALAKANTA NEOGYI, magistrate and Collector of Vishnugram, found life thorny. His family were Brahmos, with a long tradition of friendliness for England and English things. In happier days, that had passed with little comment. But his father's last years had been poisoned by the growing estrangements; and Kamala himself was serving the Raj at a time when such service seemed to most of his countrymen unprincipled selfishness and lack of courage and patriotism.

His father had been extraordinarily happy at Oxford, where he made friends who became distinguished in after-life and who never lost touch with him. With two of these he had written that volume, *Poems by Three Friends,* which had made some stir in the late seventies; the other two contributors had become famous. He loved English thought and literature passionately, and had hardly known his own tongue; his children were brought up in an atmosphere

of English-worship. In face of the increasing rancour
of his own people, he continued to believe in England,
and to assert that all evidence against the essential
justice and fairness of the British people was an accidental and temporary thing, without significance.
When that novel which so moved his countrymen,
Gilded Chains, appeared, he knew that everyone said
that he was Nilkamal Ghoshal, the toady who pock-
eted insult and humiliation for the sake of a few kind
words from a Lieutenant-Governor and a worthless
rai-bahadurship; but he pretended not to care. His
own brother, as English in thought and training as
himself—neither of them could speak Bengali, and
when Jatindranath Neogyi made his fiery anti-Partition tours his speeches, to the delight of the Anglo-
Indian press, were translated—swung over to extreme
hatred of the West, though he could never tear its
culture out of his brain. But Nilkamal kept his love,
a genuine love for an England which, not once or twice
but times innumerable, has won from Indians a passion
of loyalty and admiration surviving instances of folly
incredible and of scorn and wrong inexcusable. In his
last years, he was drawn more closely to his own
people, and felt their excitements, but to the end he
kept aloof from politics, he continued to teach in the
Government college where he was a professor, he held
up to his students' belief an England that was wise,
fearless, generous. It had been universally conceded
at last that he was honest and convinced and had kept
his honour. The rai-bahadurship had come his way,
and had been refused. Had Sir Charles Williamson,
who was at Oxford with him, still been Lieutenant-

Governor, the insult of its offer would never have been perpetrated.

Nilkamal was dead; and his son was Collector at Vishnugram. He, too, had been at Oxford, and at his father's college; he had happy memories of England and the English. Unlike the average Indian in the higher services, he understood his Western colleagues, he liked most of them, they liked him. One weakness he had, a delight in making long and pompous speeches; but, once away from the platform, he did not chatter, he had dignity, sense of duty, efficiency. If he had "an inferiority complex," he kept it from appearing or from influencing his actions. Nevertheless, the ties that bound him to the alien empire that he served were looser and more flexible than those which had bound his father. He had grown up with a knowledge of his own tongue and some acquaintance with its literature. The snatches heard on village roads were not a mere raucous barbarism to him, but had their tears and ecstasies. Also, the Oxford that he had known had been less friendly, perhaps because it had known many more Indians and those not all of a commendable sort, perhaps because the Anglo-Saxon, growing ever more uneasy, felt his ascendancy threatened. Or was it simply that the whole world, East no less than West, had grown suspicious? Both before and after his Oxford days, he cultivated closer relations than his father with Brahmo society; and, as everyone knows, the Samaj has moved far from its older enthusiasms. Puritanism still flamed in some of the survivors from the last generation; but Brahmo preachers were now anti-Christian, their unitarianism was linked up with Vedanta doctrine and was tolerant to the use of idols. There was little of religious feeling behind all this—the agnosticism and heart-break of the West occupied the mind of thinking Brahmos; there was not a rushlight of difference, except for the occasional flare-up of an irrational mysticism, which more often than not was merely a disguised nationalism. For Brahmos no longer kept aloof from politics. There might still be small sections of Indian society devoted to the foreign domination; the Brahmo Samaj was not one of them. Nor was political unrest the only source of wretchedness. The community was rich in intellect, in artistic ability the most gifted group in the world; and with all this went "temperament," an undue proportion of nervous disturbance, of unbalanced enthusiasm and unbalanced depression, often resulting in mental break-down. Discontent had settled on Neogyi's people; and it had left him, too, unhappy.

He frowned as he glanced at a card which his *chaprasi* brought him. This was a time which he would rather have free of all callers; he had been back from Mrs. Nixon's tennis hardly half an hour, and his dinner was due in a few minutes. And these callers were the last people he would have chosen to see. However—show them in. The Raja of Kendudi and his brother were shown in. They salaamed low, and sat down. There was silence. Both belligerents did a lot of hard thinking.

Neogyi's thoughts, summarized, came to this: "You blighters! You *utter* blighters! Again, you absolute, utterest sweeps and outsiders! What are you after now?"

Their thoughts were less clear-cut, more inchoate,

a mixture of nervousness and assurance. How far was Kamala Babu still Indian? Was his sahebdom merely a veneer? If it was, they could appeal to the instinct to be kind, always kind—to do the easiest thing, especially the least harsh thing. If the worst came to the worst, they might even throw out the shadow of a threat; fear shrank back from this, but hatred leapt at the possibility.

It was certainly a difficult meeting; in some ways, fantastic. Both sides were anachronisms. Neogyi—well, what was Neogyi? An Indian who was serving the British Raj, and serving it in the spirit of a generation that had vanished for ever; it was the ghost of old sentiment that functioned through him. The two Rajas were still more out of date—or ought to have been. They belonged to the eighteenth century; it was Warren Hastings who should have faced thcm, not Kamalakanta Neogyi. They belonged to the old bad zemindars, the robber-barons of Bengal—people who practised every kind of extortion on their tenants, and when they resisted suborned outcastes to burn down sheds or gather crops in the night. They kept a band of *lathials,* "club-carriers," ruffians hired from up-country, who beat and maimed at their masters' pleasure. Their estate harboured robbers, and they themselves were believed to be receivers of stolen goods. Kendudi was far from any centre of adminis-tration, and they had done evil safely for years, till this westernized Indian came. With him they had fought a drawn battle—it would have been a defeat but for assistance which they ought never to have received, from an Englishman who was over him.

They now wanted to exact a price for their casualties, which had been heavy.

Neogyi had been in a position to act, precisely *because* he was an Indian. Where there had been rumour before, he was able to gather evidence. Or he thought he had gathered it. But when it came to the point of action, some of it was doubtful, and the rest was withdrawn. Witnesses had ratted. Kamala Babu would not be here for ever—officials were constantly moved. The Rajas would remain, as the cobra remained in the roots of the village *pipal,* as the jungle demons remained who had to be placated with blood of goats. Then Kamala had changed his tactics, and had run them in under the Bad Livelihood section, a net with a conveniently general sweep, catching a great many fish that escape the slender rod and line of ordinary legal process. It was his artificial English conscience that made him persist in persecution. He knew only too well how more than easy it would have been for him to act as his Indian self urged, to have been "kind." "Ah, father, why be so angry?" the white-bearded munsiff who administered justice in Kendudi subdivision had asked him. But he "had to do his job"; he was there to see righteousness done, to prevent oppression, to protect the poor, and these men were notorious bad livers. Indignation helped him also; when he found that the Rajas had intimidated witnesses, sheer annoyance made him swing over to the "bad livelihood" method of assault, with as direct and unscrupulous a way of cutting to the point as any Englishman could have taken.

Fergusson, his commissioner, let him down. He motored over from the head-quarters of the division, and after some casual talk of a friendly kind he opened the matter.

"I say, Neogyi, what about this Kendudi business?"

Neogyi was annoyed. "I've run them in. They're bad people, and I can prove it."

"Are you sure you can?" Neogyi hesitated, and Fergusson went on smoothly. "Do you think it quite sporting, when you find you can't bring them down one way, to try another?"

So two cardinal points of the Englishman's code of ethics were jostling each other—an irresistible force was clashing against an immovable obstacle. What was to be done when "your job" and "what was sporting" involved opposing deeds?

"I don't quite understand you, Fergusson."

"Didn't you try first under Section 327? Assault and Robbery with Violence?" In Fergusson's voice was the fine scorn of an upright Briton confronted with an Oriental pretending to misunderstand.

"I did. But they got at my witnesses."

Fergusson very properly ignored this. "They've been to see me. They say no proof could be brought against them."

"I've told you, they got at my witnesses."

"Well, it doesn't seem—shall I say?—quite decent. You had your whack at them. And missed. Besides, they're not bad chaps in their own way. Look here—this district hasn't any hospital, and it needs one badly. They've taken the matter up—very generous of them, I must say—and they've offered me twenty thousand rupees for it. You must drop the case."

Neogyi had dropped it. He understood. An Englishman cannot be bribed, we are told. No, not in

the crude, straightforward fashion. Fergusson had no
high reputation with his fellows; but he would not
have touched a gift for himself. But the Rajas knew
his weakness. Centuries of servitude have made the
Bengali race trained psychologists where their rulers
are concerned. Fergusson had served on commissions,
he had once—for three months only—been a member
of the Lieutenant-Governor's Executive Council; and
now he was at the end of his service, about to retire
to England, to move in circles where "a K." was the
hall-mark of accepted achievement. At Cheltenham
or Tonbridge or Oxford, it would be wretched to be
plain Fergusson, instead of Sir William Beverley Fergusson. So he had persuaded himself into a passionate
philanthropic interest in the division's welfare; hos-
pitals, dispensaries, high and middle English schools
were shooting up, like cactus clumps in the Rains.
"There is a high school even at Taldangra," Neogyi
thought bitterly, "where there is no one but the jungle
bears to attend it." Pressure had been put on wealthy
Indians, cajolery and encouragement had been applied.
Money had come in.

The interview had taken place six months ago.
Government had added a grant to the Rajas' princely
offer, other Indians had subscribed, and the hospital
walls were now up. Fergusson in person had laid the
foundation-stone, while the Rajas, resplendent in gold
and crimson and conscious rectitude, stood by, hearing
praise of their munificence. Now that Sir William
Beverley Fergusson had gone to his own place, that
twenty thousand rupees rankled. It was a large sum,
to go for nothing. They decided to visit Neogyi.

Talk seemed likely to prove interminable, except

by direct rudeness. The weather was hot, but not unpleasant; both parties agreed that it was likely to get worse later on. Yes, the mangoes had blossomed well; it would be a good crop, unless there were very rough hail-storms presently. The local mangoes were not as good as the Bombay ones; Mandalay mangoes were said to be better still, better than any that grew in India. They had been troubled with leopards at Kendudi; the Rajas wished to arrange a shoot. Would His Honour come? The people would be very glad to see him. This Hamar Saheb who had just come as judge——

Neogyi cut them short, just as if he had been a brutal Englishman. He was glad to have seen them again, under happier auspices. He expressed the hope that they were now behaving themselves.

The Rajas were pained, and their countenances showed it. Such tactless directness was not what they expected from a fellow-countryman. They did not know what His Honour was referring to; certain slanders had been brought to him by evilly disposed persons, but there had been no proof, and His Honour, after the fullest personal investigation, had withdrawn the case. His Honour the late Commissioner had expressed to them his regret that they had been troubled.

Neogyi bit his lip. Damn Fergusson! He had done that, had he?

"Well, I won't keep you and your brother any longer, Jogen Babu. You'll be wanting to get back to Kendudi."

Oh, no. They were stopping at Vishnugram, with Satya Babu, the Government Pleader. They did not stir. How well Neogyi knew these methods, his countrymen's great gift of passive resistance! He felt kindlier towards the Englishman's bad manners; he must try a brusque vigour himself—courteous but firm.

"I'm sorry; but I must get at my files now. I have a lot of work to get done, for this election next month."

That reminded them. Satya Babu had suggested that Jogen Babu should stand as a candidate. What did His Honour think? Of course, a zemindar had other duties; he had the welfare of his tenants to look to. Perhaps he ought not to think of going to Calcutta. Still, Satya Babu said——

His Honour thought they would be very unsuitable candidates, both of them. One had to know English to follow the Legislative Assembly debates; the Rajas, excellently educated *in their own way,* did *not* know English. Or only a few words.

Jogen Babu reminded His Honour of the barber whom the local pleaders at Chhotagarh had caused to be elected. *He* did not know English.

His Honour with some annoyance retorted that, as they very well knew, that unfortunate case was not a precedent to be followed. The affair had been an attempt to make the Reforms ridiculous, and the Chhotagarh bar had since found the jest tiresome. The barber, in receipt of such a salary as he did not know that anyone in the whole world drew, as well as a daily hotel allowance of thrice his monthly earnings, had refused to resign, when the pleaders thought the joke had gone far enough.

"There's nothing else, is there?" he asked, as he rose.

They sat tight, like the now-famous barber, and

interchanged glances. Then Surya Babu spoke. They had wondered, he said, whether either of them— especially his brother, as the senior zemindar—was going to get anything in the next Birthday Honours. The Raja of Lokpur had recently been made a rai bahadur, the zemindar of Kesara a khan saheb.

Neogyi was so amazed that he fairly shouted at them.

"What? Why? What on earth have you ever done —except every sort of *budmashi* and *zoolum* you could think of?"

Here Jogen Babu spoke, quietly and with rebuking dignity.

"Your Honour has surely heard that we have given twenty thousand rupees to the hospital?"

There was a gentle emphasis on the "heard" which stung Neogyi to fury. Then he laughed outright at the absurdity of his anger. The whole thing was closing in comedy. Like most Bengalis, he had a keen sense of humour. He rose, and, good-humouredly but firmly, he fired them. As they went, Jogen's silky manner threw off a spark.

"His Honour the new Commissioner has promised to come to Kendudi for a shoot next month."

"He is *too* kind to me," said Surya Babu, breaking into English. "He love me bhery much." Then, in Bengali, "His Honour will surely hear us."

Neogyi thought it probable that he would. After Fergusson had come a worse, an Indian this time. Deogharia was the new Commissioner; Neogyi knew him only too well. He had heard him mentioned by an English colleague, with a snarl that was obviously habitual when his name came up. "That damned

D

swww-ine!" He *was* a damned swine. It would be hard to find any merit that Deogharia possessed. If Englishmen and Indians were ever to agree, it would be over their opinion of such men. But he was Commissioner now, and Neogyi was in his hands.

Neogyi was a bachelor, and his mother, who lived with him, was at present in Calcutta. As he sat down to dinner, his bearer handed him the *Asia Post*. There he read of a recent law-suit in London, in which an Indian of high position had played a part only less discreditable than that of the English men and women who had fleeced him, and made themselves rich out of his lechery. He read remarks of learned counsel on the extreme improbability that "a black man" could have attracted a beautiful Western woman, and statements that Orientals were naturally lustful and evil. His blood boiled. Which were worse—the men who wrote these complacent leaders and asked these impudent questions, who said these things and arrogated this chastity to themselves and their race? Or the Deogharias and zemindars of his own land?

6

HAMAR took over his bungalow and his duties. The latter began with a course of festivities and welcomes. By methods usual when money is collected in India to honour the Great at arrival or departure, the bar raised a sum which would have fed a thousand people for a week; it was gloriously flamed away in fireworks and squandered in refreshments for the Upper Ten. There were a great many sweets, especially the large super-saccharine balls of burnt rice and molasses for which the district was famous. There were European chocolates, dry even before the tin was opened, and crumbling into brown dust in the open air. There were meringues and confectionary from Calcutta, including a very expensive, very indigestible iced cake. The pleaders started the entertainment of His Honour the Judge; other departments of Government and private enthusiasts were to follow during the next few days.

The affair put Hamar in a bad temper. He wished they had been more discreet in their references to the event which had brought his name before the province recently; but the addresses all contained grateful allusion to it. Yes, he was their friend; but they need not line up racially, and ostentatiously draw him over from his own folk. He saw Mrs. Nixon shrug her scorn to her husband, and he started as if he wanted to get up and explain. It was what he had wanted to do very often these last few weeks. But there was nothing to explain.

He had entered on Vishnugram with relief, which had swiftly been fanned to pleasure. The evening of friendliness, the flaming, intoxicating morning, had set a new mood. At the pleaders' show he would of course meet everyone again; and until things went flat he did not admit to himself how much he had looked forward to the ridiculous tamasha. And the one person—apart from Alden, for whose opinion he did not care—who might have felt interest in him as the fearless champion of an oppressed—or, shall we say, misunderstood?—race was not present. He felt that Miss Mannering's absence showed a lack of even the normal interest that makes people turn up out of mere good nature and to see how a new man behaves. His manner disappointed those who did come. "Rather a sulky brute," Nixon told his wife. "A bit ungracious," Mrs. Alden said, "seeing the trouble and expense those pleaders had gone to."

His temper was not conspicuously better next morning, when he went the round of his office. His *seristadar,* Abdul Jubbar Khan, a Mussulman with a vast snowy beard, showed him over the court records, with the maximum of courtesy and the minimum of information. An Indian had preceded Hamar as judge—not a Neogyi, but an incompetent, good-humoured, sweetmeat-fattened incarnation of the spirit of laziness. Nothing was where it should be, nothing was in glass-fronted cabinets. Hamar disgustedly took up the files of an important case which had been hanging on since the preceding spring. Hornets had plastered the pages with mud, the shrivelled skins of grubs that their larvæ had devoured hung about them. A somnolent hornet was still there, sleeping the winter away. It was not too somnolent to rouse itself to sting him. In a land where snakes are a possibility, and scorpions a little more than a possibility, reaction to sharp sudden pain is prompter and more violent than in England. The file leapt from his hand, and he swore. Abdul Khan looked rebukingly at him. "Another irascible Englishman! O race uncontrolled, restless, undignified, extravagant in your passion over trifles!" Hamar apologized; Snowbeard by a look loftily gracious showed that the apology was accepted. Damn! a mental damn this time—he had been trapped by Fate into acknowledging himself in the wrong, and he could never

give this white-bearded father of slackness the wigging
he deserved. How on earth would he get this office
into decent order?

His chief copyist, Nilkantha Mukherji, a slender,
mild man with grizzled hair—he was about forty,
perhaps, but forty is old for the educated Indian—
brought up the dossier of work to be immediately
undertaken. He stood by meekly and submissively.
Hamar, trying with his imperfect knowledge of Bengali to read the appalling scrawl in which everyone
connected with any branch of Indian administration
writes the vernacular, lost his temper again. The
looks of the staff registered disappointment; Hamar
Saheb, then, was no better than others. After their
placid King Log, who had gone *multis bonis flebilis,*
were they to suffer from King Stork? "What the
devil does it say this woman is?" he asked, pointing to
a flourish of great but superfluous and confusing
beauty. Nilkantha peered over the script, then looked
questioningly at Abdul Khan, who shook his fine head
mournfully. "Why do you vex an old man with these
vanities?" his manner asked. "Saheb, saheb, let the
wheels of justice start revolving, but do not seek to
know too much about them. We shall be gone
to-morrow—what does it matter who or what an
accused person is? Let this woman be sent to jail—
or let her be acquitted. But have done with this foolery." The script passed from hand to hand, and outlying members of the staff sauntered up to discuss it.

Hamar repeated his question. "Doesn't *any*one
know anything about her? Good heavens! She's
been brought up twice in this court, and you have no
facts about her!" Nilkantha and Abdul both looked

round for support. Nilkantha's wife's cousin's nephew, Kshitish, a youth who haunted the office for occasional typewriting jobs, supplied a piece of irrelevant information. "She is a *bharjeen*," he informed Hamar. Hamar's interest in social matters was aroused, and he determined to know more about this new caste. His whole office, now almost a dozen persons standing round him, repeated the information. He grew ashamed of himself; he had passed his departmental examinations, and drawn the rewards, yet could not understand what was obviously a common Bengali word, since no one would do anything but repeat it. "I am sorry," he said at last. "I *never* seem to get hold of your language. Tell me in English." "But it *ees* Eengleesh," said Abdul Khan, rolling his eyes in surprise. Hamar handed him a blotting-pad, and told him to write it down. Abdul handed it to Nilkantha, who held it uncertainly. Finally, Kshitish, after some thought, pencilled the word *virjeen;* and Hamar, who had been trying to get at the accused's occupation, found that all the knowledge that ten minutes of exasperated questioning had brought him was that she was a virgin. Wasn't she married, he asked. "O-ah, yess"—this with doubtful looks all round, as each member of the group sought the corroboration of every other member. "But"—this very brightly and emphatically from the *seristadar*—"she has no kids." The occasional typist shook his head sadly. "Her husband," he said, "kicked the bucket before two years—at six o'clock Madras time." The company looked at him with respect; evidently he knew something about the accused's affairs. Nilkantha's heart swelled with pride and gratitude. A well-educated boy, precise in his statements and fluently idiomatic! Presently, when Hamar Saheb was still further impressed with his ability, a permanent place in the office would surely be found for him.

As a matter of fact, Hamar shared Nilkantha's gratitude to Kshitish, who had chased away for him the Englishman's besetting devil, ill humour. With good-natured sarcasm, so suave that it was lost on his listeners, he asked: "You will all be able to understand me even better in a short time?" Ten heads jerked in unison from left to right, in complacent agreement. "No doubt," said the *seristadar,* with a plump effect, as of a large stone dropping in a well. "But at present," said Hamar, "at present we seem to have some difficulty—not much, but a *little*—in following each' other." "Because we are not habituated to your Honour's accent," the occasional typist explained. This was a shock to Hamar, who had always prided himself on his freedom from accent.

7

THAT afternoon, Neogyi was holding a meeting of local notables, to discuss plans for the annual Agricultural Exhibition, due in two months' time. It was held in the Queen Victoria Memorial Hall, a superb building of the babu-Gothic school of architecture.

Hamar, who had declined a seat beside Neogyi—this was the Collector's show—sat on a chair to his left, half facing him. The Nixons and Douglases sat on chairs opposite, with Mrs. Alden and Miss Mannering next to them. Alden came in late—his invariable custom—and sat behind Hamar. His separation from his wife was perhaps not accidental. He regarded all public meetings as bores or bean-feasts; his particular chum Findlay had come in from his jungle station, thirty miles away, and was beside him, and Mrs. Alden realized with horror that this meeting was going to fall into the bean-feast class. The two were immediately behind Hamar, in high spirits; Indians were watching them with affectionate apprehension.

A local raja, in the second row of chairs opposite, was gorgeously and variously resplendent. He wore low shoes of a flamboyant orange, with scarlet stockings. His turban was a shimmer of gold and purple. All this, however, was but the foil to the chastely simple effect obtained by wearing what was apparently a blue seaman's-jersey. Findlay identified him as Sindbad the Sailor, information that Alden greeted with a peal of delight, which burst irrelevantly upon Neogyi's announcement that the Exhibition would be more expensive this year and that he was going to ask more of the gentlemen to collect subscriptions. Neogyi looked startled and annoyed, and began to fumble in his speech; Mrs. Alden bit her lip, and frowned; Findlay's face—which rarely expressed any sign of emotion—took on a look of surprise and grief. Miss Mannering alone seemed pleased. Alden recovered himself with difficulty, and kept his head down; for a long time Hamar could hear him struggling with suppressed enjoyment.

Neogyi continued. Last year's Exhibition, he said, had been encouraging; but it had come at short notice, and some of the outlying villages had been unrepresented. He was very anxious that *every* part of the district—every *thana,* every village—should have something to show this time. They all knew that this was the poorest district in Bengal. What was it the proverb said? That Vishnugram had rivers without water—he paused roguishly. There was obsequious laughter, recognition of His Honour's gift of humor, in dragging in the district's dullest and stalest jest, and of his condescension, in knowing it. Brahmins without learning—he must apologize for quoting so slanderous a statement. Here he saw learned friends of his who utterly disproved it. More obsequious laughter, especially from the learned friends referred to. Merchants without money—ah, well, he hoped to disprove this also, when the collectors of subscriptions went round to the generous *and wealthy* merchants of this town. Wry smiles from the two representatives present of the generous and wealthy merchants of Vishnugram. He ran—or, rather, limped with infinite tediousness—through the list of local paradoxes, to which Alden and Findlay made several ribald additions. Hamar heard with sympathy their groan as Neogyi caught by the ears and kicked in the other oldest jest about the district. Amid appreciative titters he quoted the rhyme alleged to have been made twenty years ago, when a native of the district had actually become a judge of the Calcutta High Court:

At Vishnugram they eat
Parched rice in piles, and think it sweet!
Now on the High Court bench one takes his seat!

The Europeans looked weary. So *that* was where the Indian came out in Neogyi! A good fellow—but he *did* love to hear his own voice, he did revel in the flattering ripples of silly, sycophantic laughter. But Hamar was not bored. His eyes, in spite of all restraint, kept straying to Hilda Mannering's face, set in calmest serenity while she watched Neogyi with well-bred interest as he rambled on and on. She was not pretty like Mrs. Nixon—Hamar had decided that at first glance again, and reaffirmed his decision from time to time. But that delight which flashed into her eyes when Alden's deplorable conduct disconcerted the assembly was the most teasing, intriguing thing he had seen since he came to India. Another glimpse of it, and his dreams would be troubled. He tried to keep his eyes from her, lest she should notice it. He told himself, very reasonably, that she attracted him only because he was in India, where one got so little of the society of charming English girls. How cool and dainty she seemed! That quick turn of her head when she was interested, that poise and carriage which made every other woman there seem asleep beside her! Her sister's air of pride seemed vulgar self-assertion beside this gracious aloofness which had no need to claim what none would think of refusing. But she was not pretty like Mrs. Nixon—Hamar repeated the assurance to himself.

Neogyi, having fully harvested the only two jokes that had ever grown in arid soil, returned to his theme, with a jerk that was almost a stumble. Yes, he wanted *every*one—every *thana*, every village—"seems to think he's got hold of a *mantra*," Findlay grumbled—to be represented. Every village, every *thana*, was to ask itself: "Now what do *we* produce? What is our *main* industry?" From Khaliara they expected wool— Khaliara was famous for its sheep, the universally used Ghariwal blankets were largely made from Khaliara wool. Sindbad the Sailor, who was Raja of Khaliara, hearing the name and recognizing it in the stream of talk in an unknown tongue, looked pleased, though ignorant whether Khaliara had been selected for applause or reprobation. From Kendudi—now what could they expect from Kendudi? It was certainly a difficult question; Neogyi began to wish he were not so fluent when once on his feet. The meeting looked up expectantly, as those about to receive infinite enlightenment. The obvious answer, "Rogues," was one which no one was likely to give. Neogyi repeated his question, swaying helplessly. Khaliara, Khaliara, he reminded them, toying with that musical and satisfying name, would send a flock of sheep, a flock of sheep. A flock of sheep. Yes, a flock of sheep. Hilda Mannering smiled across at her brother-in-law, remembering one of his stories of a sermon by a bishop, on the Prodigal Son. ("Now this prodigal, this prodigal, this prodigal, he went to his father, to his father, his father.") Hamar saw the smile, a sun-ray flashing unheedingly past him. What should Kendudi send? moaned Neogyi miserably. "A flock of *bears*," said Findlay, who knew the place and its products intimately. At this not very witty suggestion, Alden, who had been back in his schoolboy stage, struggling with internal jollity, guffawed insanely. Again that vexation on the faces of the Upper Ten, and of puzzlement on those of the

Indians; and again that gleam of delight on Hilda
Mannering's face. Hamar felt grateful to Alden.

Findlay saved the situation. Rising quickly, he
answered Neogyi's question. Kendudi jungles were
a home of the tusser silk-moth; and the lac insect fed
freely on its *palas* groves. These might be called the
town's *only* industries, since it had no wood-carving
or work in clay or metal, and no crops to speak of.
Even the children were employed guarding cocoons
and secretions, and warding off crows. The Kendudi
lac and tusser had never been developed as they should
have been.

There was low applause all round, at a first-rate
suggestion, obvious as soon as made. Neogyi was
relieved. These free-lance Englishmen—for so he
regarded missionaries, people widely and greatly
useful, though in quite other capacities than their
supposed effort and purpose—could help when they
cared. But, he pointed out, the place was very back-
ward, and there was no one who could organize the
collection of lac and tusser. At the back of his mind
was the fear that the two zemindars would collect it,
organizing only too well, and would harvest their
tenants' whole crop, using the Exhibition as a means
of selling it at a high price. Alden, with pain choking
down vast sobs of irrational laughter, rose and offered
to undertake the organization, if Douglas would
release him as soon as the College lectures closed, in
five weeks or so, for examinations. Douglas consented
gladly. The meeting recognized in Alden's action a
measure of *prayaschitta,* which partly appeased even
Neogyi.

After this, proceedings sagged. Neogyi felt disinclined to continue a speech which had cost him much trouble of preparation and had given him much joy of anticipation. The heart had been taken out of his simple pleasure of talking. Alden's inexcusable and childish fit still held him, and he sat in an attitude of prayer, with his hat before his face, but his devotions shook him terribly. As the meeting disbanded, Hamar heard Findlay take him to task before his wife and sister-in-law.

"You come to a serious meeting," he said righteously, "where everyone's busy thinking out what's for the good of the district; and you just treat the whole thing as a jest, and laugh and shout as if you were in an East-end music-hall!"

Mrs. Alden's outburst of annoyance swept rebuker and rebuked into one equal condemnation. It was hard for a woman to understand how pent-up men's spirits became from the long round of futile and footling duties which had to be taken seriously. The necessity for some relief from unbearable tension is at least part of the reason why Englishmen sometimes behave badly at public functions in India; natural bad manners, no doubt, is another part. Poor Alden always felt particularly light-hearted on a platform, and his evil angel made him see, in one ecstatic sequence, nothing but the abundant comedy of these meetings in which the Indian soul revels. When he was present, meetings were an agony to his wife; she invariably had a good deal to say to him afterwards. But in one thing she was mistaken. Indians did *not* resent his outbreaks. It was rude, no doubt, and Alden Saheb was laughing at them ("no doubt!"). But his amusement was infectious. He was generally watched more closely than anyone else on a platform; and more than one eloquent speaker had been put out by a sudden guffaw from his back, which had been answered by a volley of laughter from the main body of the audience in front.

Miss Mannering interceded for him. "You've got to forgive him, Frances. He's going to be punished for it."

Mrs. Alden pouted, between a frown and a smile. "Well——" she began irresolutely.

"Think of him in six weeks' time. When the weather becomes too hot for words. He's taken on that dreadful job at Kendudi."

"On a push-bike," Findlay added. "Thirty miles a morning, over strips of foot-path between paddy-fields, all burnt and cracking."

Hamar received a nod from Miss Mannering, and a smile whose radiance was merely the afterglow of her amusement. He was hurrying up when Mrs. Alden drew him into conversation; her sister walked on ahead with the two justified sinners. Presently Mrs. Nixon called to Mrs. Alden. The Nixons were giving her and Hilda a lift home.

8

ALEXANDER DOUGLAS, principal of the College, was usually referred to by Alden as "the most efficient missionary I know." His efficiency was many-sided. To begin with, he could make a rupee 'go as far as anybody could' (Alden); 'yes, but he never lets one go very far away from himself' (this was Findlay's addition). The College, the creation of his own sole energy, was now the best known and most influential outside Calcutta and won a grudging recognition of its general usefulness even from his evangelical colleagues. He was a huge Scot whose parents had been domiciled in Lancashire; his inherited energy and business ability would have made him wealthy, had he not been a missionary. He spoke Bengali, which he delighted in using, especially on public occasions, with a strong Lancashire accent and an utter ignoring of its numerous aspirates; he had a masterful way with grammar, and syntax was what he chose it should be. His stresses were as darting and irresponsible as humming-birds; his voice would soar aloft, to plunge down ruthlessly and swiftly on some trivial word. At meetings where the Indian speakers all used English, he would gratuitously provide low comedy, by speaking in what he alleged was the vernacular of the province. He did not impress people as a scholar, for neither inclination nor need had led him far into the more literary studies; but he was one, nevertheless. Scientific interests absorbed him. He spent nights on the roof, watching the skies through the College telescope. He kept lists of the birds, beasts, reptiles, insects, and flowers of the compound, much of which was still a luxuriant tangle. He had creatures under observation in strange places; there were stories of Mrs. Douglas finding scorpions in hat-boxes and cobras in cupboards. Further, his gifts as a talker were great. No man knew a swifter way to solution of most practical problems; but no man loved more to hold business up by hours of futile discussion, of absurd supposition or wanton objection. Suddenly, when everyone was exasperated and weary, he would

put, clearly and simply, the right solution, which had
been present in his mind from the first. He rarely
saw a joke, though himself the cause of very many.
He was generous in recognition of the gifts of others,
which was why he could use so different a man as
Alden, in building up the College's reputation in ways
that were not his own. If there was no deep intimacy
between these two, there was entire cordiality and
no glimmer of jealousy or mistrust.

Jacks, who with Douglas and Alden made up the
European staff of the College, was new from England.
He was a thoroughly good fellow, earnest in evangelical effort. The minds of the heathen, which he
understood imperfectly, distressed him; and he had
at his fingers' ends the various points of superiority
of Christianity to Hinduism, Buddhism, Jainism,
Sikhism, Confucianism, Taoism, and Mohammedanism. He got across his students from time to time,
by the frankness of his annoyance with their beliefs.
Alden's tolerance he regarded as almost disloyalty,
and his interest in Indian thought, philosophy, and
literature as apostasy. Worst of all, Alden had
infected Findlay, who was in directly evangelical work;
Findlay now read Indian books other than Christian
tracts, and found Hindu reform movements deserving
of sympathy. Christian women in Findlay's jurisdic-
tion were allowed, even encouraged, to wear the ver-
milion mark of Hindu wifehood at the parting of
their hair; and the notion that they all lived in irregu-
lar relations with men, once widespread throughout
the Hindu community, was being shaken. Indeed,
Findlay showed signs of becoming the worst heretic.

Hamar met Douglas and Jacks in the leisure of

the Aldens' home, where he dined the third evening after his arrival. That morning, idly strolling near the vast banyan by his court, he had seen Mrs. Douglas out walking with her two children. Mrs. Alden and Hilda Mannering were with her. Mrs. Douglas, kind and matronly, came across to the lonely bachelor. Would he dine with them on Sunday? And would he take this informal invitation, and excuse a note?

He walked back with her to the rest of the group. Mrs. Alden, also apologetic for informality, asked if he could spend that evening with them. It was all very friendly and casual, pleasant after the stiffness of conventional invitations from ladies who, he knew, disliked him and had no wish to see him in their homes.

Despite his uncomfortable notoriety, Hamar was pretty much of an Indian Babbitt. Already, in the four years of his sojourn since the War, his interest in Indian matters was thinning out, and becoming coldly impersonal. His Lambertgarh action could be traced back, not to any strong pro-Indian feeling, as his fellow-Babbitts assumed, but simply to an almost savage sense of fairness. He would have acquitted Old Nick himself, accused of rebellion against the Almighty, if the evidence had seemed to him faked or inadequate. Probably those Lambertgarh people had been guilty. He conceded that, readily enough; but the idea that Indians were entitled to legal procedure and not simply to a rough and ready "justice" was too technical for his countrymen, outside his own service, to follow. The Indians with whom they dealt were employees or servants, and their decisions involved no complicated palavers. It was hard that events should have segregated Hamar, just when in

E

most matters his straying mind had been shepherded
back to the beaten path of Anglo-Indian thought. In
most matters. Not all. There were some well-
trodden roads which the War had closed to him for
ever.

He shared the general conviction that missionary
work was, at best, a well-meant waste of time—at
worst, humbug. Some officials—and Hamar was
liberal enough to be inclined to agree with them—
conceded an unreligious kind of usefulness to certain
aspects of missionary work, so-called. Medical missions were good, leper asylums were a genuine philan-
thropy. That was fine work which was being done at
Gnarratong, where Europeans might send their half-
caste children, to be taught trades that would save
them from beggary in later years. Or individual
missionaries were singled out for strong approval.
Findlay was one of these. In his first year, which had
been spent in Calcutta, he had been a magnificent full-
back and a cricketer of almost county form. It was
a pity that an evangelist of this calibre was thrown
away on the jungles. He was understood to be still
a decent fellow—he had filled an emergency gap in
the three-quarter line for "England," in the annual
"versus Scotland" match, only two years ago, and,
though obviously stiff and out of form, had been
worth his place—and he had been useful in the famine
of three summers ago. But missionary work, as such,
was not praised. Discussion of it always reached the
same point of agreement. With men, it didn't matter
what religion a man had, so long as it was honestly
held—so what was the sense of trying to persuade
these people into a religion quite unsuited for them?

With women, the whole missionary enterprise was damned by the fact that it had produced so few good, cheap servants. Hamar, a reasonably competent thinker when he was interested, on this question had been shallow enough, had accepted the usual arguments and had chimed in with the common conclusion. He had no particular religious beliefs himself.

But the Vishnugram missionaries were educational missionaries. About these there was a division of opinion. Average European judgment condemned them more decidedly, if that were possible, than evangelical missionaries. If the latter were fools, the educational missionaries came very close to being knaves. Opinion did not hold with educating natives and making them above themselves. All this sedition was due to education, especially to missionary education. But the official world did not see things in quite the same way. A certain number of Indians *had* to be educated by someone—apart from any other necessity, there was that for an adequate supply of English-speaking subordinates. Missionary institutions, on the whole, provided these as well as any. Their students were less discontented, and were often tinged with Western morality.

So Hamar was interested in meeting educational missionaries in the flesh. At the Aldens' he sounded them—at first, very tentatively and carefully.

"Do you think the people of this country will *ever* become Christian—the better classes, I mean?" he asked, after the conversation had exhausted the authorized preliminaries.

As soon as he had spoken, he felt that his question sounded jaunty and shallow. The topic was obviously

one that struck the more intelligent of his companions
as funny. Jacks looked grave, Mrs. Douglas sweetly
pensive, her husband uninterested; but Miss Mannering and her sister smiled, and Hamar reddened and
cursed himself inwardly. Alden scented disapproval
in the query; his voice was light and playfully ironical,
as he asked: "You don't believe in missionary work?
These people have a religion which suits their simple
minds—why change it?"

"But their minds are so *dark*," said Jacks. "When
one gets a glimpse into what they *really* think——."
It was his favourite reflection. He left the sentence
unfinished—a stone flung into depths of unplumbed
gloom and never recovered.

At this solemn moment Miss Mannering laughed,
and then looked so charmingly apologetic that even
the speaker could not feel ruffled. But Hamar felt
hot and foolish. Alden burst in hastily.

"You feel that Christianity spoils them? The
Indian Christian, now—he has all the faults of the
Westerner without his merits."

Hamar admitted that he had often thought so.
But the discussion, with Alden's grave undertone of
urbane mischief and the merriment of the girl beside
him, made him feel that the missionaries were not
taking an I. C. S. official as seriously as his command-
ing intellect and position entitled him to be taken.

"Ah," said Alden, "I know what happened to you.
When you first came to Calcutta, you had a Christian
servant, and he didn't do your boots properly."

Miss Mannering bent mocking brows upon him.

"Mr. Hamar!" she said. "Before you asked your

searching question, you were silent for a couple of minutes."

"Well?" he asked defiantly.

"You were thinking—thinking hard—now what on earth am I to talk to these missionaries about? Then your trained intelligence saw it! I know, I'll ask them about the prospects of Christianity in India. It's the only subject on which they can be expected to have any ideas."

He was beaten, and threw up his hands. "Miss Mannering," he began piteously. Grey eyes softened a moment, then hardened brilliantly.

"Yes. Your face was all excitement as the notion came to you."

"We know the signs," said Alden brutally. "Whenever a chap's brooding for a minute or two, we know that he's beating the bushes for a topic. And he always starts the same hare. Nixon asked your question, nine months ago."

"But if you are *really* interested—" said Miss Mannering.

"I am," he said eagerly.

"You should ask Mrs. Nixon about it," was the disappointing conclusion.

"Why Mrs. Nixon?"

"Because she has had *two* Christian servants." It was Alden who supplied this information.

"And therefore knows *twice* as much about it as the people who have been satisfied with one," said Miss Mannering.

It was an unfortunate beginning. Hamar felt that behind the mockery was a touch of contempt and resentment. Alden did not seem to be quite the gushing, kindly fool that the province supposed him to be. Hamar knew at once that he cared greatly about his work; he felt the close friendship that existed between Alden and his sister-in-law. These two, firmly and not altogether courteously, had declined to let him talk about anything that mattered to them, and had relegated him to the outer frontiers of acquaintance-ship. He was, they reminded him, just an official, a person to have to dinner, to play tennis with. His humiliation was not the less, because he knew he "had bought it."

The evening settled down to dullness. Jacks had some invaluable thoughts on the missionary problem raised by Hamar, but Douglas swept them aside with an interminable story of what a coolie had said to him that morning. The labouring classes—and they alone—were of absorbing interest to him. The educated classes he affected to scorn, with all their mental furniture. "Books!" he used to exclaim. "I despise books! What I believe in is *Life!*" No fount has ever possessed capitals large enough to express the emphasis with which Douglas believed in *LIFE*. "And I told him," the tale concluded, "if you bring that darned cow of yours into this compound again, I'll send it to the pound at Huluberia—that's sixty miles away. I'll send it, if it takes my *mali* a week to get the brute there. So he went off in high dungeon." Most of Douglas's colloquists went off "in high dungeon."

He was put in excellent spirits by his story, and after they had risen from dinner continued to enter-tain the company. The evening was saved. Alden passed into his mood of irresponsible happiness, and

the whole heathen world, revealed by his comments
and interpolations, was seen as one vast troupe of
superbly endowed comedians. He interjected helpful
fact and interpretation, of a sort that threw their
witty ways into relief; the thunderous flood of Douglas's reminiscences accepted these light-flung pebbles
unnoticingly, but shimmered with the spray that they
tossed up. Miss Mannering abetted Alden; Mrs.
Douglas and Mrs. Alden were good-humouredly
tolerant; Jacks listened weightily and from time to
time shook his head. It became an experience of
infectious cheerfulness. Hamar never remembered
having laughed so much since he came to India, yet it
was hard to say why one laughed.

But at first he listened gloomily enough. When
the ladies went into the drawing-room, Douglas, who
was in the midst of a complicated story—a pause for
dramatic effect had been misunderstood as its conclusion—was unwilling to lose any of his audience, and
the men had not stayed behind for the customary
smoke. Jacks secured the chair next to Miss Mannering's. It was dull, ineffably and inexpressibly dull,
Hamar thought; dull and exasperating. Alden was
playing the fool—did he never do anything else?—
Jacks, with huge, bushy-browed head thrust down and
forward, was sipping his coffee and looming through
his glasses. Hilda Mannering—then he noticed that
she had risen to put her cup of half-drunk coffee down,
and had come over to him. She sank into an empty
chair beside him. He was aware of her shoulder
turned towards him, and a low voice speaking to him.

"Mr. Hamar, you are sulking because we chaffed
you!"

"I'm not, honestly. I only——"

"You deserved it, you know. You might have done us the justice of speaking from your own mind, and not passing on second-hand twaddle of which we are weary. Be just, and you won't be angry with Robin or me. Was it friendly of you?"

"I didn't deserve it, Miss Mannering. I don't mind the chaff——"

"No, of course not. No man ever does! But——?"

"Well, if you want me to be frank——"

"We'll find you out if you aren't! You may as well be!"

"What hurts is to feel that you and Alden think me a fool. There was contempt behind the chaff."

She did not deny it. "Well—no man has the right to offer patronage to my brother-in-law."

"I didn't. I was merely——"

"Merely bringing here the mentality of your club at Suriganj. Alden the pro-native missionary—a sentimental fool, a woolly-thinking humanitarian. Not a man of any brains or education." She brushed his denial aside. "You don't think that? All right. *Don't.* For Alden hasn't taken you at second-hand, by the things that other Europeans say. Now let us forget things, and be friends. I want to listen to Mr. Douglas. I like his stories."

She remained beside him, while Douglas continued his tales, walking to and fro, as was his habit. During these perambulations he frequently disappeared on to the veranda, returning to complete a sentence or a statement a few minutes later. These absences were generally for the purpose of emptying or filling his pipe; but he had been known to disappear for half an hour at a time, to return, after having done some work at the College or a hostel, with a comment or correction which had occurred to him. Sometimes, especially when his wife was away, he would vanish for the evening without leave-taking; his host and hostess, after waiting an hour or so, would reluctantly conclude that Mr. Douglas had finished with their hospitality for the time being and would be seen no more that night. Like royalty, he made his own conversation always, and any topic started in some temporary absence was consciously held on sufferance. When he returned—*if* he returned—it was understood that the talk would go back abruptly to the status quo.

This evening, his stream of narrative meandered widely. It was well past ten o'clock before it washed the shores of missionary experience or problems. That it did so at all was due to Hamar, who brought up the question of customs duties and their hardship. Douglas was reminded of an earlier missionary, who had smuggled a great many drugs in free of duty— for medical work, of course—by labelling them "Wearing Apparel." It was a story which Alden would rather not have heard told, and he intervened anxiously. But he knew it was little use trying to deflect Douglas, far less to stop him. He had to be satisfied with comments that modified the unethical view that Douglas apparently took. Douglas now resented these interruptions as irrelevant. He glared through his glasses, his voice booming angrily.

"The worst of it was," he said, "Tomlinson bragged about it afterwards, and told everyone how smart he'd been. And of course it got back to the customs people, and they were wild."

Alden got really nervous. "You mean," he said, "the ass ought to have had the decency to know what a rotter he had been, and to keep it to himself."

Douglas ignored him. "And the worst of it *is,* the Mission has had a wretched time with them ever since. They went through my last lab order from London piece by piece, and smashed test-tubes and bottles. They never take our word for anything, and they open every bally box we have and every parcel that's sent to us."

He disappeared, and they could hear him knocking the ashes out of his pipe. He thrust his face in at the door again, as if about to speak, decided he had nothing to say—an unusual occurrence—and withdrew. His heavy tread sounded down the steps.

"The worst of it *was*—and the worst of it *is*—" said Miss Mannering, in an aside to Hamar. "You notice with what precision Mr. Douglas distinguishes former evil and lasting bad result. I'm afraid, Mr. Hamar, you will now be sure that you understand why Christian servants do your boots so badly."

Hamar could think of nothing in reply. His look was so brimmed with forgiveness and gratitude that she turned away.

They waited a few minutes in hope of Douglas's return. They heard his voice raised in shouted expostulation with the driver of a bullock-cart, who had impudently taken a short cut in the darkness, through the Aldens' compound. His bellow alternated with the peasant's abjectly inarticulate appeals, or made a crashing and plaintive duet with them. The bullock-bells tinkled an accompaniment. Then there was silence. Douglas had evidently gone for the night. He had forgotten Mrs. Douglas.

"Rob will see you home," said Mrs. Alden. Mrs. Douglas, who had risen and was peering into the outer darkness, was persuaded to sit down again for a few minutes.

"Mr. Hamar," asked Miss Mannering, "have you done your duty by the station, by bringing us some new books? No one has a thing to read."

Jacks, who was studying Professor Macinlaye Macintosh's great book, *The Missionary Imperative,* and had daily been offering it for her perusal, looked reproving and disappointed. Alden leaned forward. Hamar begged the whole company to come to tea to-morrow, and to see what books he had.

The ladies considered the matter; a favourable reply seemed certain. But Alden reminded them that it was Neogyi's tennis day. Hamar felt that he understood why it was undesirable to have Indians in the services. Why must Neogyi have a tennis day at all? It was ridiculous, having every day someone's day, tying you down for all your spare time. Or, if he must have a day, why slap it down for to-morrow? It was just the sort of thing an Indian would do.

"We can't come to-morrow," said Mrs. Douglas.

"The only time we *might* be able to look in," said Miss Mannering, "would be just before tennis, on our way round to Mr. Neogyi's. But that would be no use, as we couldn't expect Mr. Hamar to leave office so early."

Mr. Hamar assured them that they could. In fact, he could be home by three; there was very little to do at court to-morrow.

Alden blundered again; Hamar began to dislike him. "I thought you said the office was in the most ghastly mess."

"Yes, you did," said Miss Mannering, checking symptoms of denial. "You said you doubted if you could get away a minute before six, for weeks to come. You were going to have tea every day in your court."

She gazed thoughtfully on his face. Its dumb reproach touched her, and she wavered, full of penitence. But as she started to speak, Douglas entered unexpectedly. His lips were pursed in disapproval, and he shook his head.

"It isn't worth it," he announced. "Getting the Mission a bad name for the sake of a few rupees."

No one gainsaying this pronouncement, the party broke up.

9

AT Suriganj, tennis had been a social duty. In Hamar's later days there, a bad habit had grown up among the ladies of taking it in turn to give tea at the club, and absence had been made lese-majesty. Mrs. Watkinson-Jones would remark to Mrs. Wilkinson-Smyth: "I don't know *what* Mr. Peterson has taken offence at, but I notice that he never comes to *my* tennis tea now"——the dreadful truth being that Peterson had been kept away once, by a sudden spate of office work. So tennis had taken its place with bridge and dining out and the other things that promoted good feeling; and the year was more than ever divided for the masculine world into warfare and peace. When May heats drove away most of the ladies to the hills, a vast forgiveness——not merely born of physical exhaustion—descended on their husbands. Men who had been scarcely on speaking terms met together for compact "men's fours" and to drink the quiet peg of peace. The truce would continue unbroken until the cool breezes of October reunited families, and etiquette again became rigorous. By Christmas bickering and aloofness would be in full swing once more, to flourish through the spring and increasing sun. Then May would wave her magic wand of burning wind, and they would sleep with the quarrels of yesteryear.

Hamar had been an offender at Suriganj. Though he played a decent game, he did not care for tennis; and in the cool of the day he haunted the jungles. He usually did this without a gun, and the charitable, therefore, had grounds for considering his offence as partly due to a weak brain. But a criminal's presence is none the more acceptable because he is imbecile as well as wicked. But now at Vishnugram he had eagerly taken on a tennis day of his own, and was diligent in attendance at the other courts of the station. He established friendlier relations with his own race than he had done since that Lambertgarh Case— his dependableness made an evening game something that could always be counted on. The Nixons were grateful, Alden liked him, Douglas approved. But he had an experience which warned him that even here there were possibilities of social estrangement. There was an evening when only Hilda Mannering, Jacks, and himself had turned up at the Nixons'; Nixon being away, they played only two sets. Hamar partnered Miss Mannering, and they won with grotesque ease; Mrs. Nixon, chafing under Jacks's assistance, thought

that Hamar played with unsporting carefulness. She
had a not unreasonable feeling, shared by most of
Jacks's lady partners, that her man opponent ought
to play left-handed, with broom instead of racket.
Her crossness perplexed Hamar, who had forgotten
that there was a second lady on the court; and after
the game she talked diligently to Hilda, and tacitly
assumed that the two men preferred their own conversation. Jacks, who was in the mood for serious
discussion, found Hamar scatter-brained and shallow,
incapable of consecutive argument. The evening was
teasing and inconsequent. It brought Hamar no
nearer to friendship with his partner, but it shattered
the remnants of his peace of mind. It became not the
slightest use his assuring himself that Hilda Mannering was not pretty. Every movement stirred in
his memory, every glance of her changing face was
vivid. Mrs. Nixon, he kept on telling himself, was
really lovely—yes, replied his subconsciousness, good
to look at, difficult to remember. Now Hilda Mannering—— It was not Mrs. Nixon's face that troubled
his dreams and came between him and his files.

March was on its striding way; the mango bloom
was dust, the jungles were fragrant with sal, lifting
its green-white plumage of blossom. The scarlet
trumpets of the *simul* were crowded with birds sucking
their honey-sweetened dews, the ground beneath was
strewn with the tossed-down bowls of blackening red.
Palas groves were glorious with their white-and-pink
parrot-beaks of flowers. The wind, a myriad tiny
goblins, was dancing and careering in little geysers of
dust. "The *bhuts* going to drink," said the Bengalis—
"an instance of defective observation," Douglas ex-

plained. "They have noticed that these eddies always stop at a tank. But if they watched the further shore they would presently see them begin again." "Aren't their minds *dark*?" asked the more spiritual Jacks. "They believe in *bhuts* everywhere, they are terrified of evil spirits, just as the people in the Roman Empire were when Christianity came." He offered to lend Miss Mannering Dr. Glover's book on the *Conflict of Religions in the Early Roman Empire;* it would explain the parallel to her much better than the rubbish that she had borrowed from Hamar. Hamar's library had been a disappointment to him.

In northern lands we can *feel* the earth gathering herself together to "go through it," steeling herself for the freezing grip of winter. In India this happens in spring, when the hot weather sends out its first heralds. The fields were withdrawing into themselves in dread—"Now for it!" they seemed to say. "It will be awful—our only chance is to sleep through it." The *kokil,* beloved of Indian poets, became a burden, with its demoniac laughter and its mocking hysterical shouts. Educated Indians identify this bird with the cuckoo, about which Wordsworth—who made some "nice poems" for Calcutta University—wrote, and they find therein augmented cause for rejoicing in its "sweet song." Alden was looking up Hamar in his office one morning, when a chorus of *kokils,* for no discoverable reason, lacerated the air from a mango outside. A look of ineffable peace flooded the *seristadar's* face, and he asked:

> "O cuckoo, s'all I call thee bahrrrd?
> Or but a ooandering bhoice?"

A ribald answer was on Alden's lips, but he remembered how disappointed an Indian friend had been in
England when, his mind filled with Shelley, he went
to hear a skylark. He told of this; and Hamar knew
an American girl who complained that the nightingale
"tinkled like a piano," and cherished a grievance
against the dying poet who alleged that he heard it

> *pouring forth* its soul abroad
> In such an ecstasy.

And did not an American poet—a modernist, of
course, and a great ornament of "the left wing" in
poetry—climb Boar's Hill to hear the Bagley Wood
nightingales, with the inevitable reaction for which
his whole being confidently yearned? They "sang
flat."

"Next time we hear the beastly bird," Alden suggested, "let's try and hear it as Indians." They had
done so; putting himself where Indian minds were,
withdrawing for a moment from his own herd-
psychology, with cool, sweet, unprejudiced mind each
had listened to the *kokil*'s shouts at dawn, and had
admitted their exhilarating quality. They were the
power of that rushing time, flinging itself up in foun-
tains of noise, as in the sky it flung itself up in cascades
of changing colour. Hamar knew that never again,
in any land, would dawn be fully dawn for him, with
that acclamation silent. The *kokil*'s "singing" continued
the process of enslavement to the land's beauty which
the mango fragrance—to our anæmic tastes as over-
rich as the *kokil*'s cry is over-loud—had begun, the
day when he first came to Vishnugram. The steady
croon of the doves through the hot day rejoiced him,

also; and the kite's keen of utter abandonment, the screaming of the sky's desolation far aloft, as the bird circled and hung in the dazzling fires. Only the coppersmith's *tonk, tonk,* beginning with the first light and never pausing till the stars came, never changed for him—never became other than a present distress to the brain and a clanging warning of wretchedness to come.

The days were still tolerable, and the mornings wonderful. "Get the most out of it while you can," something warned the world. The Europeans were out of doors in both twilights, the dawn and the sunset; and one morning Hamar had the happiness of riding with Mrs. Nixon. He had been provided with a country-bred from the police lines, a beast showy rather than efficient. Mrs. Nixon on horseback was Mrs. Nixon at her best; the riding took away the necessity for talk or companionship, and all that was apparent was a pretty woman who rode divinely. Having that, no man at the time would ask for more. Hamar's consciousness of the contrast between her powerful and absolutely controlled waler and his incompetent brute, with its absurd airs and prancings, increased his feeling of humility. He proved himself a very perfect squire, by his manner aware of his good luck.

Dawn was not over when he joined her where the old Vishnugram highway led to the buried temples. These, though they had filled his imagination when he first came, he had never seen. The fields and paths showed the Indian world already busy with its labours; men and women were hurrying along them, shrinking aside in terror of the horses. A mongoose crossed

F

the road, stopped to look at them, and shot into a cactus clump; a blue kingfisher leapt into sight from a nulla, curved over the bridge, and dived into darkness again. They reached the jungles, and cantered beside the Lal Bund—the "Red Lake," made by Raja Hambir Singh when Elizabeth was on the English throne. A few hundred yards of fairly good going gave way to ground broken by irrigation channels and a drying swamp. Their horses picked their way, till they reached an impassable quag. Then their riders sought higher ground, which after a sweeping detour, a monstrous cantle through rat-holes and scrub and ant-hills, brought them beside the Red Tank again, and on to a lengthy beach of sand. At last they could let the horses out! But it ended in a narrow ravine, enclosed by steep banks shagged with mimosa. Here it was single file, and Hamar for a full four hundred yards had the vision of the negligent ease with which Mrs. Nixon guided her great waler through rocks and stubs. Now the "path" became a steep declivity, and the mighty limbs and steel-clad clattering hooves paused, instinctively seeking an easier road; it was magnificent, the insolence with which their tiny rider sent them forward. The huge straining haunches, having crested the mound, backed from an unexpected cleavage; they cleared it, and were moving in strength of freedom and release, down smoother ways. Hamar's own mount was already showing signs of distress, which was almost as well, he no longer had to apologize for silly capers and cuttings in, nearly collisions. He must be spectator and worshipper, rather than Beauty's companion.

At the top was the famous temple built by Bi

Singh, Hambir Singh's father. Its sides were embossed with carvings that told of a time when these
deserted *beels* knew a crowded and illustrious life,
when they carried the pleasure-boats of kings and
their shores saw terrible funeral pomp and heard the
cries of "Blessed Sati!" as queens rode on horseback
to their pyres. These carvings showed—unless the
artists lied—that Gandeswari's paltry stream had
borne a navy in those days, and that in these jungles,
empty now except for hares and an occasional bear or
leopard, the Rajas of Vishnugram had hunted nilgai
and elephants, sambur, tigers, even rhinoceroses. The
temple was a small one; the jungle had gathered round
it, and *pipals* were splitting its sides and roof, but it
was in excellent preservation still. As the two riders
checked their horses, the morning breeze shook down
wave after wave of fragrance from the sal forest, till
they were almost dizzy with sweetness. Hamar's
mind was a storehouse of fragrances, and his most
tenacious memories were entwined with them. Whenever his guardian spirit wished to hammer some
moment into his consciousness for ever, he nailed it
with a flower scent. This glory of an Indian morning,
a glory ebbing even while it flowed round them, mantling them to their throats with splendour and fragrance, would have been for ever dedicated to the
lovely woman at his side if a scarlet-headed woodpecker had not suddenly shot by them. Hamar's
glance, following it, fell upon the temple's topmost
terrace. There, leaning against the *pipal* rooted in
the fissured stones, stood the Spirit of the spring morning, looking abroad over that empire of buried greatness on which her sal-drenched winds were blowing.

"It's only Hilda Mannering," said Mrs. Nixon, in a low tone. "Say good-morning, and let's get on. There's nothing here but a few old temples. Good morning, Miss Mannering!"

She lashed her horse almost viciously, and he bounded into a canter. As surprised as he, Hamar had to follow. Looking back, he saw Hilda Mannering, her cheeks bronzed with the breeze, following their course with shining eyes. He had forgotten Mrs. Nixon, when a mango bough caught him across the face, nearly sweeping his hat from his head and himself from the saddle. She was waiting for him the other side, her eyes angry and hard.

"What on earth have you done to your face?" she exclaimed.

"I rode into that mango. I didn't see it."

"I don't see how you could have helped seeing it. Do you always ride looking backwards?"

There was an air of constraint over their return. Mrs. Nixon was aware that she had ridden out a goddess, and was coming back a woman. Her husband was still on tour, but next morning she rode out alone. She did not offer to have the country-bred sent round for Hamar's use again.

10

FINDLAY had returned to his jungle fastnesses, the day after his deplorable behaviour with poor Alden. These occasional visits to Vishnugram were a refreshment to his spirit, for they meant a crack with his friend. The two were old schoolfellows, with a vast common store of jest and reminiscence, and their meetings were invariably hilarious ones. Findlay would lay bare his mind of every one of the petty, silly annoyances experienced from his Indian Christians, and for one brief hour they would appear solely comic, mists of iridescent folly in a world where nothing was serious. Alden in exchange produced college absurdities, full measure for his. Returning to Kanthala, Findlay would settle to his discouraging work again, and the saving laughter of it all would be denied to him.

Return, nevertheless, brought him deepened peace of mind and happiness. The station folk of Vishnugram wondered, with a touch of pity and contempt, whenever they heard that he had push-biked the long thirty miles from Kanthala or back to it; his missionary colleagues urged him to let the district apply to the home board for the grant of at least a motor-cycle. They did not understand how the slow miles as they unrolled smoothed out the wrinkled places of thought, and filled him with utter rest. To all solitude there is an outer solitude, more desolate yet; and as Vishnugram was to Suriganj, so Findlay's country was to Vishnugram. The river Gandeswari was the boundary; once across that, he was in his own country, whose wood-gods he knew. There was first the eight miles run through unpolled sal, with its glittering edges of jungle laurel and its superb swallow-tailed kites majestically circling above it. Then came open parklike country, with occasional sandy breaks leading down to tiny brooks, torrents in their season but now with hardly a trickle of water anywhere. There was one considerable village midway in the last twenty miles, but the jungle lapped its edges so closely that it fitted into the wildness and in no way disturbed it. It was but a five minutes' episode of plantain groves and palmyra-clustered tanks, and mango and *mahua* returned. And then? Through those last ten miles, Findlay passed with an exaltation of spirit that was sometimes almost unbearable; he loved this country with a passion that was very near worship. Yet it was nothing in itself—a scarred land cracking in the heat, studded with tall trees in isolated clumps, in whose boughs the leopards slept through the day, and trenched with ravines which the bears loved. Part of his joy in it was his knowledge that there was always a chance of catching a glimpse of these creatures. Six miles from Kanthala was a treeless patch, where a narrow sandy track ran through zizyph bushes, which he called Wolf Heath—he had names for every part of the district round his home. A pair of wolves lived here; at certain times, after dawn or just before sunset, he was almost sure of seeing them, and he had chased them on his cycle many a time. He would separate one from its mate, and it would slowly move before him till it stood at bay against a ravine. Then the chase ended; he would dismount, a few yards away, and wolf and man would gaze at each other for a few moments. Findlay would cycle on again, very cheered.

To-day he had even higher fortune. The *mahuas* were flaunting their large, fleshy, waxen-white petals; they were fast shedding them, to ferment as they lay in the sun. Jungle-dwellers were gathering them into baskets, to be distilled into sweet, heady wine. Findlay loved the *mahua*; its flowers delighted him, its thick succulent fruit, a glossy, polished white, was pleasant to see though nothing to taste, and the mauve orchids already festooning every tree—a sign of spring's evanishing—were the loveliest of the season's few glories. Since his glance took in every one of the thousands of *mahuas* that fringed his way, he went slowly. Leaving Vishnugram at five, he reckoned to reach Kanthala at ten, in time for a leisurely bath, with breakfast at eleven. The sun was not unpleasant as yet, so long as one was moving. He had plenty of time, he felt, to walk across Wolf Heath, pushing his bike and looking out for his friends there. Not seeing them, he left the track and turned towards a fine cluster of *mahuas*. While exploring its precincts, he heard a loud *woof;* he had disturbed a bears' picnic. The sickly-sweet, intoxicating petals will lure bears for miles; and two cubs with their parents were revelling in the abundant feast. Now cubbing-time is not the season to trouble bears; Findlay knew this, too many wood-cutters had come to his dispensary with torn scalps and terribly bitten limbs. He sprang to his cycle, as the mother bear dashed towards him. He never knew how he got away, skidding through sand and dodging rocks and thorn-masses. But the circuitous flight involved some delay for his pursuer also, and he had nearly twenty yards' start. He was not chased further than the main track. Short sprints are the Indian bear's specialty, and the sharp swerve necessitated to turn into the path made the animal overshoot him, and he was safe. He went on, laughing ruefully at himself; but examined no more *mahua* groves.

Kanthala had been a centre for growing and collecting indigo, fifty years ago. There was still a dak-

bungalow there, rarely used, since the occasional official was always Findlay's guest, unless he happened
to be a rigid Hindu. Findlay lived in a crumbling but
comfortable house, once the indigo-planter's, a spacious building with outhouses sufficient to harbour
four times his number of servants. The outhouses
were filled to overflowing with Indian Christians,
whose presence was a source of legitimate grievance
to his wife. His guavas, mangoes, and custard-apples
were stripped every year, and he had given up the folly
of trying to cultivate plantains or pine-apples or even
the winter peas and tomatoes which other Europeans
grew. He had effected a concordat with the school,
most of whose scholars infested his compound, by
which two small *lichis* immediately under his study
window were more or less unpillaged, and a precarious
supply of the fruit reached his table during May, the
month when no other fruit is obtainable; and by
bribery he got enough *bel*-fruit to make daily sherbet
in the worst of the hot weather for his wife, his child,
and himself. But the *bel* is not a fruit that many
care to eat. It is medicinal for its juice, which, as
everyone knows, keeps off dysentery.

It was fortunate that the compound was large, for
its corners were in an intolerable condition which
neither reasoning nor threats could improve. It
needed constant vigilance to keep even the well from
shocking contamination. When European visitors
asked him why he didn't "fire all this crowd," it was
hard for him to explain. If they were fired, where
should they go? They were a community gathered
by a predecessor, who with the stupidity that seemed
to have marked most of the proceedings of the older

generation of missionaries—men who now lived in England, and wondered why "the work" was not progressing as in their rosy memories it had done in their day—had collected them all from their homes and had amassed them round his own house. He had thus killed three birds with one stone—he had ensured their absolute and parasitic dependence on the missionary, he had taken away all chance of a strong Christian belief and practice growing up amidst opposition, and he had effectively prevented any further spread of Christianity in the villages from which they came. Homes had to be found for them, so they had filled the missionary's outhouses and slopped over into a specially created Christian hamlet, half a mile away.

Findlay's arrival was signalled to his dependents by their intelligence department; his wife's indignant vigilance with difficulty secured for him enough respite to bathe and have breakfast. During breakfast frequent coughing from a veranda reminded him of waiting clients. If publicity be the chief good of life, he was fortunate; for every minute of every day seemed to have shrewd eyes upon it. Life, for the most part, was an effort without relaxation.

It was hard to understand how amid such circumstances he found so much happiness. But his lonely journeys through the woods, his enthusiasm for their wild life and their wild flowers, his keenness, ever increasing, on Hindu thought and customs, his passion for others and their welfare, his busyness, his deep religious faith, the companionship of his wife and child, made him an exceptionally wealthy man. His wife's comradeship with him was perfect; her unselfishness was equal to his, all their thoughts and interests were in common. Their only child, a frail and delicate girl of six, made their happiness complete. He had that background of rest without which his wearing and intolerable work would have driven him to unbelief.

Breakfast was not a time for much talk; that would come later. "Anyone fresh at Vishnugram?" his wife asked.

"The new judge has come—Hamar his name is. The Hamar there was all that row about."

"He ought to be interesting."

"Ought to be. Apparently isn't. Alden says he was abominably rude and offhand when the pleaders gave him a show. We never seem to turn out anyone with manners—we're a race of efficient boors, seemly. I only saw him just to speak to—at Neogyi's meeting. An awful affair! Alden broke down laughing because of a silly jest we had."

"Oh, John! You and he are just as rude as these other men, when you play the fool publicly."

"I suppose we are. I can't help it, honestly. Getting away from these lambs of mine always seems to go to my head. Our Kendudi rogues were there, looking as pious as ever. Hilda Mannering's looking lovelier—the girl's a darling! I hope she's not going to marry that ass Jacks. She *can't* be such a fool! But tell me what's happened here."

"They want you to go out to Kleshtakul."

"What on earth for?"

"As far as I could make out, they've got some notion that they can raise the money from you to irrigate their *danga* land."

"I know that *danga* land. Everything streams and soaks away from it. The Ganges itself couldn't irrigate it."

"Then there has been trouble at Baranadi. Two of our Christians have been run in for having a still. They think if you square Nixon it will be all right."

"They're guilty, of course?"

"Of course. But they swear they are not. What happened was, when the police came they plunged all the stuff in with a lot of soap-suds. But the police carried the whole lot off, and had it analyzed."

Findlay smiled. "Poor untaught children of the wild! They don't realize the resources of modern science. It must seem like the black art to them, all this unfair analyzing and chemical hanky. And one can't regard their offence as a very shocking one, morally."

"But you do want to stop all this drinking."

"That's so. But Government's only aim is to raise a revenue. The people don't see why they shouldn't carry on as their forefathers did, and make the stuff they want instead of having to buy it plus excise and middleman's profit. Nor do I. It's like being in Ireland. Every one of these Sonthal villages has its private still. Oh, well, I'll give them a wigging, and then see what can be done. What is it, Marjorie?"

Marjorie had been whispering to her mother. "She wants me to tell you that the servants say there's a *bagh* about," said Mrs. Findlay. "It's been round our cow-sheds. Last night I daren't let her sleep on the veranda. And it was *so* breathless with all the doors shut! That's why she looks so seedy this morning."

Marjorie looked up excitedly. "Oh, Daddy, they say it's a big *bagh,* not a *nekrebagh* or a *hural.* It's been killing cows."

Findlay drew her to him, and fondled her hair. "Well, I'll have to kill *him*, if Mr. Bagh has been behaving in that way. We can't have him round here —we've got too precious people in this house."

He told them of his adventure, toning its danger down to a pleasant escapade.

After breakfast came the deputations. The school drew his attention to the fact that many of them had to cross the Kosai, and that its burning sands grew intolerably hot to bare feet by four in the afternoon. They asked for morning school—that is, school from six to ten. Findlay, recognizing an annual "try-on," recommended patient endurance for another month; he reduced this sentence to three weeks. Their looks registering profound disappointment, the deputation withdrew, rejoiced to have found Findlay Saheb in so complaisant a mood. The boy-scouts followed with a request for a feast. Feasts were the part of the scout ritual which stirred them to enthusiasm; Findlay, who was both short of cash and weary of the word feast, dismissed them briefly. Catechists and "workers" followed, earnest for advances of pay, loans additional to the large ones already owed, and with complaints about being underpaid. It was matter of common knowledge that the Mission possessed unlimited funds; all that the incredibly mean missionaries had to do was to send to *Bilait,* that land of fabulous wealth, for all the rupees they wanted. That the "workers," people of very slight qualifications, were paid salaries grossly in excess of what they would be worth as Hindus, did not trouble them. Deeply spiritual people, it had been left to them to discover the full implications of St. Paul's statement that those who sow spiritual things should reap carnal things. Findlay did not blame them; he knew that his predecessor, now legendary in England as a great pioneer missionary, had desired that all the Lord's people should become prophets, and had seen to it that most of them did. Mission employment had long been the accepted goal of every sort of ability and of no sort whatever. Findlay had wasted great part of his missionary career in pensioning off and firing his predecessor's horde of incompetent evangelists. As a result, he had made some diminution in the contempt with which the intelligent heathen regarded the community. But his heart was weary, utterly. He thought with despair of all the earnestness and unselfish enthusiasm that is squandered because of sheer stupidity, and of the compact and complex organization for preventing thought which Christendom has built up—meetings, rousing books on race and colour problems, books which after a great pomp and parade of "facing the situation" in the end say nothing at all, speeches, periodicals, articles. And clichés by the bucketful! "Christian statesmanship," "moral imperatives," "the Locarno spirit"—all the glittering emptiness that brainless well-meaning tosses up and up. Sand, sand, sand. He was bitter, as he reflected on the Christian leaders who showed "noble courage" by speaking frankly about matters which arouse no interest or opposition. There was magnificent outspokenness in England—about Armenia, never about Kenya or India; and in the United States—about everything except what hap-

pens in their own borders. When he had tried to focus
Christian attention on that scandalous state of things
in Central India last year, missionary "leaders" had
told him—privately—that his devotion and bravery
met with the greatest sympathy, but . . . "the time
was not ripe." We must be patient and make allowances. As Jesus Christ did, when He cleansed the
temple precincts of the money-changers and traffickers.

But he saw past the noise and foolishness, to the
love and heroism that are not noisy, not foolish, but
only wasted. All over the world the Kingdom had its
servants, men and women to whom life and all it can
contain were well lost if others could be saved. There
were countless humble people in England who were
praying and sacrificing that God's peace might come—
through him, their representative—to these imperfect
and childish minds, these jungle-dwellers who had no
earthly sort of claim upon them. Yet what was the
use of it all? He felt himself failing, falling. He
must stand aside from his work, he must think. He
stepped out to the veranda—not the one occupied by
the crowd who were coughing, but the one which
looked out on the bungalow's forest view.

It was noon. The brown turf shone, the aerial
space between the house and the woods danced and
quivered. Through the grey-leaved grove of custard-
apples to his left he caught the steely glimmer of two
large *beels* — "the eyes of the forest," the Sonthals
called them. They twinkled now as with somnolent
merriment; the high narrow ridge separating them
was like a nose between them, and the jungle, not for
the first time, seemed like a face that he knew. Suddenly the whole landscape was alive! That line of

scattered sals in single file, just before the land dipped
out of sight, were a jaunty procession to the water.
A tall lean tree was a wiry old man, with scrubby
patches of grizzled hair about his cheeks; he was
stooping down to speak to a pert, plump lady sal.
Behind them was a stout, middle-aged tree that had
caught the jest passing between them; his bushy head
was flung back in uproarious laughter. He was closely
followed by a tree apparently shivering in some imagined chilliness, for it had green arms flung across its
body in front, flogging itself into warmth and circu-
lation. A stunted shrub was running, a loutish boy
with head thrown forward. Findlay's heart grew
light, with that glimpse of living, eager activity about
him, the whole creation yearning into energy, even an
athlete's energy. He felt that exultant mood of which
the Hindu mystic spoke—when he saw the ever
welling, ever dancing waves of Hari, God sporting in
His creation, tossing up and taking back ever-new
forms of play, water flashing and leaping and sliding
at an Eternal Child's will. His own blood grew
eager; he had ceased to be a missionary, bound to an
austere creed and the ritual of stone sombre churches
in rain-swept northern towns. He was a young man
launching his boat on an inland sea, with a cool breeze
rippling down from the twin sentinel-poplars where
Jordan entered the lake. Ecstasy was flowing from
Hermon's snowy shoulders far aloft—the great white
throne that judged and condemned all the sorry busyness we call religion. God had ceased to be doctrine
or hymn or exhortation; He had become comrade and
playfellow, He was the voice of the oriole in the
mango, the shaking of the reeds on the shore; India

and Galilee had fused, all sweetness and loveliness were blossoming together. Another moment, and Findlay felt faint with fragrance of wild rose and honeysuckle; the oriole was a nightingale, that mid-day brightness had mellowed to moonlight. And then, from an infinite height above him, poised in the dazzling azure, rang out the kite's call—the voice of utter indifference, of aloofness crying in the wilderness, content to be there, motionless itself, and gazing out on a lifeless world. The wind shrivelled—had there been any stirring of this stagnant air?—the scents faded. The sals shed their sudden vigour, and were emblems, the faint scrabbles of a hand that had long ceased writing. The ever dancing, ever sportive Hari sank into the quiescent Immanence, his waves subsided into the dim, motionless expanse of unexpressive ocean, a face without vision. That cry would sound on for millions of years, while the phantom generations went their way. "No man hath seen God at any time"; and Findlay was content that it should be so. Nothing mattered, there was nothing to trouble about—it was all process, we were the shadows flung out by an unseen fire, which burnt only for itself and not for us, we were mists that rose from a hidden sea. And out of that Indian noon temptation came towards him, disguised as peace. Why not let things slide? Why not shut his eyes to the wretchedly unethical lives of most of this Christian crowd, why not take the easiest way, be kind, always kind, never vigilant? When one remembered the pit whence they were dug, the centuries of servitude in their blood and outlook—why not leave them as they were? God is love, God is leisure, God is peace. He sends the lethargies of the noontide, the slumber of slacker and of gorged python. He clamps the earth into its winter sleep or its summer swoon, He ordains fruitless years for the tree.

Marjorie came behind him. "Daddy, Mother says you must rest. Those people can come another time. We are all going to lie down. Come, Daddy!"

As he drew her to him, temptation was conquered. His mind and body were tired out, he knew; so he used the wisdom which saved him when beaten to the wall. He refused to wrestle with the question, he shelved it in the moment of its arising and before his mind was compromised. He went in, to sleep for an hour, knowing that he would awake an Englishman, whose duty is to be restless and to make all others restless. An ignoble way of overcoming temptation! But for his exhausted spirit and brain there was no other. As he often told himself, God wants no man to be a damned fool. Men and women fall from taking stock of themselves and their situation when things are at their worst; they despair because they face their problems when their whole being asks simply that these be put by for a while.

He went into his office again, to shut the glass doors, as a sign that the durbar was over for this morning. But as he entered a head dipped swiftly under the curtain, and a man glided into the room. Findlay automatically sat down, and spun his arm-chair round to face him. The new-comer was a young man, thirty perhaps, light-complexioned, obviously of the respectable classes but wearing the drabbest and poorest of cloth. He looked pinched and starved, his eyes were burning. Findlay's subconsciousness sent up a warning, for his visitor kept his right hand hidden

G

under the folds of his *dhuti;* men had carried revolvers so, in days hardly past. The man strode up to Findlay's desk, and began to speak in good English.

"I have written a letter to the United English Nation," he observed, in impassive tones. "It is here." His right hand uncovered itself, and swept a manuscript before Findlay.

"Why have not my clothing and fooding been delivered?" he asked. "I have only this." He twitched at his worn *dhuti*.

The document was an appeal to the United English Nation; it was dignified, stately, free from all trace of cringing or cadging. It reminded them that they had undertaken the charge of feeding and clothing the writer.

"I have written two letters before this. I sent them *bearing*. But I received no reply. Why was that? Does not the United English Nation answer appeals?"

It should be explained that *bearing* letters are a great feature of Indian correspondence. By the simple process of posting a letter unstamped, it is sent at no cost to the sender. This is called sending it *bearing,* and is an accepted technicality of the letter business. That the addressee pays double is an irrelevance; he can afford this, the system having obviously been established by a benevolent Government to facilitate relations between the rich and the poor. Findlay got a great many bearing letters. But the United English Nation evidently refused acceptance of such.

"You had better see the magistrate at Vishnugram," Findlay suggested, "or write to him. I am not a Government servant."

This quibble was pushed aside. "There is no need.

You are an Englishman. The voice of one is the voice of the people. You are the United English Nation here. The magistrate is an Indian."

The speaker paused, gazing into Findlay's blank face. "Three years ago," he went on, while at last a tremor entered his voice, "my wife and child died of cholera. It was the will of God. But my heart suffered *too* much. I could not live in my village, so I went from place to place singing the praises of God. But I had much difficulty to maintain my livelihood. So one day I went to the police *thana* in Calcutta——"

"What *thana?*" asked Findlay.

"That which is by the railway i-station," said his visitor, as if this made all clear. "On the left side of the road," he added helpfully. "Here I signed a deed giving myself to the United English Nation. They promised to provide my clothing and fooding. But they have not done so."

After some questioning, Findlay concluded that the man had actually been to some Calcutta police station, where a European sergeant had had a joke with him and had drawn up a bogus document.

"When nothing came—two months, three months, a year—I went to the post office here, and I was willing to send a telegram to the United English Nation. Bearing," he explained, lest it should be supposed that he had money to squander in this way. "But the postmaster said he could not send it, as he had received no instructions as to sending telegrams bearing. I have had nothing to eat for three days," he added indifferently. He stared at the flies and the ceiling.

"Well, it beat me," Findlay told Alden afterwards. "So, while I was thinking out what to do, I offered him a dib. And then, for the first time since I came into this blessed country, I had money refused. He shoved it back, and said: 'What am I to do with this?' So I saw that he was mad, and I asked him: 'Where do you live?' "

"I am putting up with Jayananda Sadhu," he had replied. "I have been away from him for three days, singing the praises of God. Now I shall go back. I shall tell him that I have spoken with the United English Nation."

Findlay twirled a paper-clip on the desk. When he looked up, his visitor had gone.

Jayananda Sadhu's name aroused suspicion; he was not a deeply trusted character with the European community. He was once in the I. C. S., but resigned under a cloud—rumour said that his T. A.[1] bills had been larger than the survey maps and their mileage warranted, and had included journeys to places he had never seen. This was denied by some of those likeliest to know, among them Headley. However that might be, he had left the service, and Ramsaran Chuckerbutty had suddenly become Deshabandhu Chakravarti —"and a damned nuisance besides. They might just as well have passed over what was nothing but a bit of bad arithmetic—oh, yes, and some technical mistakes that happened to be to his own advantage." Headley was right; he *had* become a damned nuisance. In the tempestuous anti-Partition[2] agitation, if with his magnificent presence, his flashing eyes and fiery words

[1] Travelling allowance.

[2] Bengal for administrative purposes was divided into two provinces in 1905. This led to angry protest. The Partition was annulled in 1911.

Rabindranath Tagore had supplied the blaze, Ramsaran had given the intellectual heat. His childhood and education had been in London, he understood Englishmen and the way to argue with them, to meet them in their own "universe of discourse." He could quibble and split hairs with any lawyer or journalist of them all, and while giving the maximum of annoyance keep well within the limits of what was legal and constitutional. And he had his own ways of rousing a flaming heat of anger, sweeping through myriads. Yet, suddenly, he had left all this; Deshabandhu had become Jayananda, "Bliss of Victory," and subsided into the forests, as fire sinks into ashes. Now, during fifteen years in which his former reputation had been fading out from the minds of men, he had been living with the bears and wild peacocks, a hero-king among ascetics. No, a bigger villain than ever, the United English Nation growled; every scoundrel and madcap resorted to his lair, and it was his unscrupulous brain that planned trouble from Chittagong to Peshawur. Findlay was inclined to think so, too. But Alden, whose intuitions and information seemed always more reliable, where Indians were concerned, than anyone else's, said he was mistaken. The man had genuinely chucked politics once and for ever; he was dreaming on infinity, withdrawing from existence into union with the *Paramatma,* the Absolute, that unconditioned, pulseless Silence over whose surface our brief lives flit and twitter for their imaginary hour. Findlay had not often, if ever, found Alden mistaken; and Alden knew Jayananda. And yet—here was this obvious lunatic in close touch with the Sadhu. It was such childish minds as this that could be worked upon for any deed of desperation. The Sadhu was understood to call himself a Saivite. But in practice, so far as he represented anything he represented the Ramkrishna Mission; and Alden himself had said that restlessness among the College students rose or fell according as the Ramkrishna Mission had a "worker" in the neighbourhood or not.

Well, he would look up the Sadhu, and judge for himself. But now—he might as well rest.

11

NEOGYI was wretched; his "mind had gone bad," as the Bengalis say. The miserable business of the elections was at hand—an unholy farce, a source of jeering to the English press and the European community. The matter did not interest him; he agreed with the swarajists that this was not the sort of representative government that India wanted. But it emphasized the loneliness of his position. The honestest of his Indian acquaintances, as well as many less honest, were holding aloof from the whole affair. He could not. He thought resentfully of the way Alden had openly laughed during his chairmanship of the Agricultural Exhibition meeting. That was the way the friendliest Englishman treated an Indian who served his Raj! He could guess how the others felt, under their self-control.

He might have foreseen that trouble would come from his Commissioner. But he did not.

Vishnugram returned two members, one from the head subdivision, the other from Suryakonda. There were originally three candidates for the Vishnugram subdivision; and Neogyi felt that the Guardian Goddess of his land must be weeping as she contemplated these sons of hers, now offering themselves as her representatives. One was the Raja of Kestanádi—a dullard, illiterate, destitute of any discoverable shred of morality, a drunkard, a leper. Findlay's injections of chaulmogra oil seemed to have checked his disease; but it was still there. He now proposed to carry his physical foulness into the national parliament, where he would sit through debates of which every word escaped him. A second candidate was Saratchandra Sarkar, a carpet-bagger from Calcutta, a fact which explained his temerity in standing against the third candidate, Jagannath Deogharia, brother of the Commissioner.

Neogyi, after a gruelling day inspecting a cluster of hamlets that were short of wells, was sitting very tired in his office, when the Raja of Kendudi and his brother were announced. They received his look of malevolence with disquieting composure, and settled down happily to chat about things at large. Neogyi, a man without a country or an ethos, was far too English in his training—also, far too weary—to be tactful.

"Don't let's waste time," he said. "You don't love me, and I'll confess that I'm not fond of you. You've got some business—probably dirty business. What is it?"

With a twinge of annoyed amusement he remembered that Alden always called this couple Moses and Aaron. The names were good ones. The Raja's massive, benevolent face, crowning his huge snowy beard, looked like a brooding prophet's. His role was dignified silence; he would have made a fortune in the West, as a touring Swami. He left exposition to suave, smirking Aaron, who was twenty years younger.

They saw Neogyi's bitter smile, and misunderstood it. Neogyi realized how intense was their hatred, when Aaron was stung into flinging aside all pretence of concealment and into hurling his dart at once.

"We have come from His Honour the Commissioner. He commands that his brother be elected for this subdivision. Thou"—yes, thou! Neogyi listened as in a dream—"wilt therefore see to it that all Government officers under thy orders compel the people to vote rightly."

Neogyi never understood how he escaped assaulting them. Nor did they, huddling terrified from the room. Once outside, shaking with fear and indignation, they wondered if an action did not lie, for such violence of manner and language. And yet—it was little enough that Neogyi had said. He had simply risen and rushed towards them. They had fled. That was all. It was useless to invent lies about the affair. Their business had been direct incitement of a Government officer to influence an election improperly; no case could be won on that. No witnesses could be secured by bribery, since the alleged assault had taken place in the Collector's private office, at his own bungalow. The Commissioner would certainly let them down, he would deny that he had authorized or suggested any such errand. On the whole, it seemed best to tell their lies all to him. They did so; and Deogharia swore hard, when he heard that an Indian subordinate had refused to put through a piece of jobbery for him.

The elections ended, as they began, in farce. The

Commissioner's brother, hearing, amazed, that Neogyi had refused to harass the constituency into returning him, was dejected to the point of withdrawal. In some places the police might have been used. But he knew that it was no use his brother's approaching Nixon with a request to put in action his still more effective corps of canvassers, after an Indian had dared to behave in Neogyi's scandalous fashion, showing unheard-of insolence. Nixon would do nothing but raise hell for them both. But the Commissioner would not hear of anything so unnecessarily pusillanimous as withdrawal. He merely transferred his brother's candidature, just in the nick of time, to the Suryakonda subdivision, which was under officials of the subordinate services, both civil and police, Indians who would do as His Honour instructed them. This spread dismay in the breasts of the two Suryakonda candidates already in the field; but one of them, Raichand Ghosh, receiving early warning from his intelligence department that the game was up, immediately took the place vacated in the Vishnugram subdivision. He opened negotiations with the leper Raja, who had driven his tentacles in and firmly clutched five hundred votes, all belonging to his tenants. These would go solid for him, but he was aware that he would get no others. So, since he had intended from the first that his candidature should be merely a financial transaction, he sold them to his new rival for a thousand rupees, and felt justly pleased. The Kestanadi estates had done well this year; he had already squeezed over a thousand rupees out of his tenants, and had now farmed their political convictions for another thousand. Since the firm belief that it was best for them, first, last, and all the time, to do what the Raja wanted comprised the whole of those political convictions, there was no injustice or impropriety in this. He bought a second-hand car from a seedy European of sorts; by this means the righteous gods, using diamond to cut diamond, got even with him in his prosperity. It jerked over rutted ways, noisily and capriciously, for less than a month, and then, tottering into a deep, sandy nulla, resigned absolutely and irrevocably. The gods reserved the seedy European for other doom. Flushed with bullion, he entered upon fulfilment of a lifelong ambition; three sodden months in Calcutta brought on a fever, which slew him just as the Rains were due.

We must return to Vishnugram. The carpet-bagger's anguish was terrible to witness. He cursed the fate that had surrounded him with woollen-headed friends and had made him woollen-headed himself, so that they had never realized what should have been plain from the beginning, that the Raja was simply sitting tight upon votes that he meant to exchange for cash before withdrawing. Saratchandra Sarkar never recovered self-confidence, and left Vishnugram a broken man. Nevertheless, he put up a game fight first. A brother-in-law of imposing appearance was summoned from Ranchi for the polling-day, and stood outside the main booth, attired in "European" costume —"hat, coat, pant" is the technical summary. In loud tones he announced that the office was closed, but would be open after four in the afternoon. Many were turned away by this impressive official from elsewhere, coming back at the time indicated, to find polling finished for this election. Another similarly attired gentleman haunted the principal outstation, where he buttonholed electors and asked them severely if they were supporters of "the Sarkar" (the Government). Fawningly they assured him that they were; they were told to prove it by their action inside the booth. There they would find the Sarkar down as a candidate for their suffrages, the second of two names that would be read out to them. Let them put a cross against its name, or it would be worse for them. This was the testing-time, when the Sarkar meant to find out who were its friends and who its foes; doubtless, the knowledge would pass into the keeping of the police, and be put to use later. Saratchandra Sarkar got a great many votes this way; and at the third most important station he got still more, thanks to the commendably impartial and sporting attitude of Alden, who was in charge. Alden, finding that most of the electors looked to him for instructions and knew nothing whatever of either candidate, exhorted them to leave the affair to Providence. It did not matter in the least, he assured them, who was elected; but he advised them, in order to be fair to both candidates, to shut their eyes and, twirling the pen, bring it down on the ballot paper. Let them put a cross against the name thus indicated. Many of the electors were nervous, and hit the lower edge of the paper; Mr. Sarkar, whose name came alphabetically second, got the benefit. In spite of all this, he never caught up those lost five hundred votes; and it was Mr. Ghosh who won by a couple of hundred suffrages of the free and independent electors of Vishnugram. He and the Commissioner's brother travelled amicably down to Calcutta, the chosen representatives of a great and intellectual people. Local variations of technique apart, perhaps they were elected not so very differently from the members of senates and parliaments elsewhere.

12

APRIL. The year's turning-point was at hand.

Before the heats of latter spring deepen into the intolerable fierceness of May, there is a brief interlude of storm—the season of Rudra, the Terrible God. Waiting for that cleansing outburst, the earth was tremulous with little gusts of wind, sudden panting tongues of sand. The *bhuts,* like mortals now thirsty at all hours, went to the water-sides from dawn to dusk; the coppersmith sent abroad his note of sombre rejoicing; kites hung motionless, as though strung on those quivering wires of blazing air which bound the sun to the world. Finished was the magnificence of *simul;* its red bowls were tumbled everywhere, and the ground was covered with the white cotton that wrapped the seeds. To Douglas, viewing all things according to their utility, the tree was an unmitigated nuisance; it "made the compound untidy." All its crimson grandeur—there was one tree in the College grounds which made a vast pool of brightness on the sky, a full hundred feet above the beholder's head, splashing and staining the azure into an incredible glory—was as nothing beside the trouble that it gave to sweep up the seeds. That other loveliness of Indian spring, the *palas,* was a similar curse; caterpillars ate its leaves into unsightliness, and then these strewed the floor. This year annoyance was intensified by a wonderful flowering; there seemed an indecency, almost, in the way the criminals flaunted their existence, and flashed and tossed their jewelled lanterns in his face. He loved tree-cutting; nothing so gave him the feeling that the college was progressing as the sight of ax-wielding coolies beside a row of logs. So it was easy for condemnation to pass to sentence, and he set to work to have felled the long line of *simul* and *palas* which made the western side of the great tank something that people turned aside to see. Once this offending beauty was out of the way, there would be room for another ugly hostel, so close to the water's edge that its inmates would have no distance to go to bathe or throw away garbage.

Alden, knowing that protests were a waste of breath, tried tactics, just in time to save the remaining fringe, one superb *simul* and two dwarf *palases*. It was a Mission belief that the only way to get Douglas to do a thing was by hotly advocating its opposite. So one day Alden, abetted by Hilda, expressed warm satisfaction that those beastly trees were going at last. It was perfectly vile, the way their litter cluttered up the paths.

Douglas frowned. "Oh, I don't know," he said. "I've sometimes wondered whether I'm doing right in clearing them out. It must have taken fifty years, at least, for that huge *simul* that I'm going to cut down this evening, to grow to its present size."

"Yes," said Hilda persuasively. "But that one makes the biggest mess of all. It must have had a couple of hundred blooms, if it had one; and they simply ruin the look of the place when they fall."

Douglas set his jaw doggedly. "It doesn't take more

than a couple of days to sweep it up. One *mali* can do it. And the cotton's worth a trifle to them, too; Heaven knows they're poor enough."

Hilda Mannering's eyes said: "You're a dear good fellow. But you're talking sentiment and not sense."

"I used to get an old boy to sweep it up simply for the sake of the cotton," Douglas said aggressively. "It's worth four annas a *seer* in the bazaar."

It was then that Alden put in his reserves, and bundled the enemy out of the position. "Findlay'll be glad to see what a clearance you've made," he said. "He must get sick of the sight of *simul,* out at Kanthala."

That settled it. Douglas was singularly without personal enmities, but for some undiscoverable reason Findlay roused a deeper opposition in him than anyone else. He in no way disliked Findlay; but for Findlay to support any proposal ensured his irreconcilable objection to it. Next morning, when Hilda took her early morning stroll, she saw that the *simul* was still standing, flanked by the two *palases.*

Though *simul* had finished, sal still flowered. The jungle tops had spun themselves into a filmy green cloud, from which the most elfin fragrance fell through the burning air; and *neem,* now that sal was fading, was taking its place with a sweetness hardly less adorable, the last gift of spring. Rain was due almost any day in the next three weeks—swift, savage showers, with a battle in the skies, stabbing of lightning, rolling crash of thunder, cataracts of jagged, heavy hail. The tempest would shatter the last of the sal nebulæ, like a sack of stones tumbled on a cobweb; the *neems* would pass suddenly into their garlic-scented berries, the showers would cease as suddenly as they came, the skies would harden. This was the season which Bengal's poet has celebrated as the visitation of Rudra:

O Dreadful One! O Terrible *Baisakh*!
With rough, brown, flying, matted locks, grey with
dust,
With hot body weary with the heat! Lift to thy lips
Thy shattering horn, and blow!
O Dreadful One! O Terrible *Baisakh*!

Everything was crumbling; the soil, the spring flowering, the very air, men's endurance.

Tasks that remained to be done were hastily rushed through. It was now that Major Henderson arrived, bringing a sergeant. The latter put the station through their shooting tests, the former asked a few perfunctory questions.

"If an enemy convoy were coming along that road," he demanded of Nixon, "what would you do?"

Nixon made a nobly British answer. "I should lie in ambush behind those cactuses, and mop them up."

The soldier smiled with superior intelligence. "That would simply drive them back," he suggested.

"Well, isn't that what you want to do?"

"No. You want to capture them. You should divide your force, and put some in front of the convoy and some behind. Then you catch it between two fires. You must aim at surprise always."

It was then that the Major noticed Hamar smile. Hamar was a nuisance—this civilian who had seen fighting, and thought he knew all about it, just as he thought he knew better than everyone else about everything. Henderson stammered out feebly a repetition of his last statement. "You must always aim at surprise."

Yes, thought Hamar—with some damned fool of a staff officer chattering about it for a month beforehand, on tennis-courts and at parties and dances. It was wonderful how much you could learn about the front, if you hung about in the right circles in Paris and Rouen and Cairo and Alex. Well, his mind asked irrelevantly, what man wouldn't tell Hilda Mannering anything she wanted to know?

Hilda and Mrs. Nixon had been watching the shooting tests. Even a master strategist can find the undisputed squiring of two pretty ladies delightful; and when the group decided that enough had been done for so hot a morning, the Major did not relinquish his pleasant duties. Hamar felt aggrieved to see how swiftly and readily Hilda Mannering had established a *camaraderie* with their visitor, whose manner, on meeting him again, had reminded him of what he was forgetting, that he was in disgrace with decent people. But what right had Hamar to be angry with Miss Mannering? Or with the Major? Naturally, a man wanted to chum up with a girl who could give every other woman points in any quality and beat her in all; and why should she be expected to be rude to Henderson? Because Henderson was rude to Hamar? She did not see that he was. And Hamar had Mrs. Nixon for companion. That lady's manner had been momentarily frigid, as she saw him instinctively go up to Hilda, with some shamefaced and foolish observation about nothing in particular. Hilda had not even heard it, she was so engrossed in what

the Major was saying. Mrs. Nixon had rallied, for-
given Hamar, and taken possession of him in her most
gracious way.

But Hilda hardly noticed his presence. Her face
was dimpled at some drawling jest of the Major's.
There was nothing to fit it, but Meredith's over-quoted
"rogue in porcelain"; but no porcelain was ever half
so dainty or delicately tinted. And Hamar, like a fool,
was listening without hearing, while Mrs. Nixon
favoured him with charming insipidities—he was
raging because Miss Mannering was giving her courtesy to a visitor. He tried to excuse himself to himself, to think her in the wrong. Well, but, his mind
told him, there has been nothing to make her suppose
that you care about her. You have hardly ever
exchanged a dozen sentences with her, you have found
no way to exchange any more. Why should such a
lady go to a man so much a fool that he cannot find
his way to her side?

Even so, he said doggedly, he had spoken more
than words. Had she not seen famine in his face, when
their eyes met by chance? Why, else, did she turn
away so quickly as she had done this morning?

The shooting-butts were at a distance from the
main road, with a wide buffer state of terraced fields
between, such as no car could traverse. Mrs. Nixon
left Hamar, for Alden and Douglas; then the whole
group gathered together, as they walked to the road.
The Major was in fine form over the absurdities of
the swarajists. Anglo-India was hugely pleased with a
recent case in which funds collected for patriotic purposes had been misappropriated by two leaders. The
Major drew the obvious moral.

H

"In fact," he said, "there isn't an honest man in the whole gang. We could buy Gandhi to-morrow with a couple of hundred rupees. Don't you think so, Miss Mannering?"

The Major knew a good many ladies, some of them very charming, who would have agreed at once; he felt he had assessed the Mahatmaji's price generously. Piqued at Hilda's silence, he appealed to Mrs. Nixon, who accepted his estimate unhesitatingly.

"Come, Miss Mannering. If ladies like you turn pro-native, no wonder we have fools in our own ranks whose heads get screwed the wrong way."

The Major, with a well-bred Englishman's tradition against making conversation serious and with a satirical bent of his own, habitually talked a good deal of light nonsense. Some of this, especially when it concerned the people of India, he accepted—more or less—because it was the settled view of the United English Nation. Even so, his head must have been dizzied that morning, by something fiercer than the heat. When Hamar knew him better, he realized how great the impression that Hilda's loveliness—there was no longer any question with him of whether she was pretty—had made on Henderson, to betray him into such rubbish as he now talked. Hamar was surprised at himself, too, for bothering to refute it. Even Alden did not think it called for comment.

"It's queer, then," said Hamar, "that Gandhi ever gave up his practice. Everyone knows he was making ten thousand rupees a month at the bar, in Natal twenty years ago."

Henderson flared up. Hamar again, vilifying his own people and sticking up for these rotters! "As long as we've traitors among ourselves who'll always believe their own country in the wrong, these skunks will be encouraged to spread bolshevism through India," he said. "And when murderers are brought red-handed before our courts, they'll be let off."

He could have bitten his tongue off as soon as he had spoken. He knew that his speech was unpardonable; it might have passed in a club, but not anywhere where gentlemen congregated, "themselves by themselves" (as Plato would say) and without a liberal sprinkling of brainless cads. Hilda Mannering, suddenly enlightened, understood. She looked quickly at Hamar.

"Mr. Hamar," she said, "do you mind my walking with you to the car? I have been wanting to ask you about those old records in your office—you know, those that date back to the days of John Company, and Clive."

Henderson was scarlet. But he redeemed himself at once.

"Shake hands, Hamar," he said. "Miss Mannering's right. What I've just said was inexcusable. I don't understand how I did it. I'm sorry, really."

His regret was genuine. He had no intention of hedging or qualifying in his apology, searched for no excuse or justification. "I'm going to invite myself to breakfast with you, Hamar," he said. "Mrs. Nixon will forgive me this once, since I've got to go on to-night, soon after dinner. Like Miss Mannering, I want to ask you about things that go back to John Company's time. I'm not going to quarrel with a chap who can tell me all *you* can."

He had his reward from Miss Mannering's eyes; and the whole party chatted gaily as they went to their cars.

13

HILDA'S mother had died while her two children were young, and their father, a Somerset doctor with a scattered practice, had let them run wild on Exmoor. That morning when Mrs. Nixon's huge dark charger leapt from the scarred underworld of nulla and black volcanic outcrop—as though Persephone, to revisit Enna, had taken one of Pluto's chariot steeds—the air had blurred for Hilda. Thought became a confusion of gallops on misty hills, where flint and iron made a clattering music, and of soft plashy rides through coombs where the fern was bronzing beside the path and the steep banks shone with purple of heath and the darker blue of fruiting bilberry. In the mind's many-patterned mosaic the grey jungle swelled into a hill-top that was one gorgeous flood of colour, the low gorse golden in the ling; and an August sun distilled from the heather, whose separate spikes are so scentless, that faint fragrance of the whole, which is like a floating honey in the air.

Their mother had left them money enough to save them from anxiety for a livelihood. The girl knew her life had been exceptionally fortunate; and (though she did not know this) her exemption from the battle had given her that aloof beauty which haunted imagination and held men's eyes. She had been mistress of her own ways and thoughts; and, had some celestial scientist analyzed her loveliness, as men examine and docket each segment that goes to make the indivisible glory of the rose, he would have found some of it a glamour caught from the wildness with which she had lived.

14

AWAY from the squalor of the crowded hovels which twenty-five thousand people infested, old Vishnugram lay in the sleep of death. Its nucleus, the fort, was crumbling, but there remained mighty earthworks, a stone-built gateway with iron doors, and a hundred yards of stagnant moat, a tangle of water-weeds. The fort's interior was now a thorn-jungle, a home of poisonous beauty, of dhatura trumpet and sleek, glimmering snake-coils. Lal Madan, the long eighteenth-century cannon, was tumbled into a thicket of pink-flowering tiger's claws, the plant with taloned seeds; in winter, when the cruel growths had shed their weapons and the *karaits* had slunk into their holes, it was a favourite playground of children. Once there had been two guns; but in 1743, when the Marathas swept to the gates of Vishnugram, the local god had saved his people, confronting the onrush with a cannon under each arm, from which miraculous floods of celestial missiles poured into the foe. The other cannon now lay buried in the mud of the Red Tank— so people believed.

Tanks and embankments were scattered over twenty miles of jungle. The Red Tank alone still covered, dying in its net of flowers and reeds, a vast tract, whose shores were temple-studded. It was beautiful with lotuses and a species of blue lily that seemed to grow nowhere else, and a colony of water-hyacinth had rooted itself in the one corner where deep water still remained and was rapidly clogging it. Formerly crocodiles had inhabited it, and local faith held they were here yet, especially where a huge pipy jungle of lush, snake-crawling weeds ran up into the paddy-fields. Thickets neighboured it to the northward, where the beach was steep and sudden, and a slim track led through impenetrable thorn to a tiny building shut in with trees so thick and lofty that the sunlight never pierced to its stones, never lit its deep well. This had been the retreat of the kings of Vishnugram when enemies pressed them hard. Westward of this and of the lake was the Mahasati, "the Great Place of Sati," a sandy foreland. Here, when women were chaste, before this evil age had corrupted the pure minds of India and the foreign Raj had put down the good customs, women had burned, serving their lords. The ridge immediately above the Mahasati was clustered with *chattris,* platforms surmounted with a stone canopy, under which was an upright plinth, embossed on its four sides with sculptures of his wives ministering to the dead chieftain—one fanning him, another offering food, a third walking before his horse with umbrella to shade her master from the sun, a fourth with his head in her lap as they burned together. The *chattris* were interspersed with lines of stones on the ground; the big one in the centre was the king's, the smaller ones at each side represented the satis who had died with his corpse. Hilda, horrified to find that one of these rows counted up to sixty, had questioned Alden; for reply, he had handed her Sewell's *Forgotten Empire,* where she read of how thousands of women used to perish when a King of

Vijayanagar was burned. Thereafter this sombre, awful place of dying overshadowed thought; she found herself wandering here, and, lying on the rough grass at the edge of bluffs that overlooked it, she dreamed of the past and gazed across to the forsaken temples and mango groves and palm clusters. Old Vishnugram was not a place where the past could be forgotten. Desolate, it kept its record, in ruins and stone-cut pictures, and in the sati-stones strewn through its brakes. These thrust up everywhere, memorials of some sati too lowly to perish in the Place of the Great Faithfulness, wife of cultivator or merchant, who had died imitating her betters. They carried the sculpture of a woman's foot or vermilioned hand, to tell that once a wife passed through her fiery ordeal on this spot.

Hilda's presence at the shooting-butts that morning had been the more victorious for its rarity. Latterly, she had been a slack attendant at station functions, she had increasingly spent the brief twilights in the old city. Mrs. Alden, nervous and long ago tamed from the freedom of her girlhood, hinted at snakes, wild beasts, wilder men. But Alden made light of her fears.

"No snakes except in the Rains. And Hilda won't go wandering then, it'll all be flooded and filthy. She may just as well see something of the country, the short time she's here. Men will be all right—more afraid of her than she of them."

"What about wild beasts?" asked Hilda, hopefully.

"Beasts? Jackals. We get a leopard now and then. No bears," he added sorrowfully, "none nearer than Sonakanchi. Yes, yes,"—impatiently, as Mrs. Alden

challenged his statement about the absence of snakes
—"she'll see a few snakes. But they'll be harmless,
long *dhamans* or *haldis* or———"

"Or cobras—or *karaits*," said his wife. "Or Russell's vipers."

Alden considered the possibilities soberly; he knew
the jungles pretty well. *"Karaits,* of course. She'll see
Russell's vipers, if she goes clambering over the rocks.
But not on the flat. Cobras? One whiles, swaying out
of the hole of an ant-hill. But you'll be careful, Hilda
dear, won't you? You won't see a dozen snakes a year,
barring in the Rains."

So she had wandered in the dead city; and had
seen nothing but a few hares and partridges, and a
great many jackals. Her wanderings had been mostly
in the evenings, for even in March the days grew
swiftly sultry; the rapid swirl of dawn lights faded,
the brief wind dropped, glare settled on the land. But
evening would find her on some great heath sprinkled
with zizyphs, a sandy track winding through it to
oleander-bordered pools. Here she could sit and
dream of that past when men and women endured and
thought and did things inexplicable to us; and she
would see nothing but what had happened age after
age unchangingly—the dust smoking behind a bullock-
cart, a wood-cutter gathering fuel. For the jungle is
lonely and silent. Europeans invade it for their
shooting-parties, town-dwelling Indians not at all.
Though the latter write a great deal of poetry about
the charms of nature and of solitude—especially since
the work of Mr. William Wordsworth became a tradition in the land—they respect both far too much to

meddle with them. Never a stray babu came this way, visitors would be none but genuine villagers, although this was famous ground and a city of many thousands was not three miles away from its heart. Children would come, and watch the English lady toying with the wisps of withered grass, and would ask her questions that she did not understand. No one else.

She could never explain the peace these deserts gave her. She knew they were not beautiful, by any canon that her own people accepted. There were few stately trees, no pastures of bright flowers; only the dry, motionless thorns, the sals and the mangoes. There were few brilliant birds, or quick, vivacious lives in the undergrowth—she had seen more snakes on a Cornish moor. There were only the flashing circles of a green bee-eater in flight, an occasional strutting hoopoe, or a flock of parrots in an incredible hurry overhead. Lizards would lift suspicious eyes, and puff out the loose folds of their necks; or, very, very occasionally, the thorn would rustle with the shuffle of a long, ropy *dhaman*-snake. Dimness would gather, and a wonderful whiteness in the west, an astounding calm of crystal clearness. The sun would deepen suddenly to a glowing, orange ball, hanging above the mist made by the cart that had passed twenty minutes ago; the dust would be transfigured, while the silence grew to a more perfect stillness, as though the jungle paused to watch. The burning globe sank, and far off could be heard the cries of children at play; their shouts died down, a curtain dropped on the world, the jackals began to slink past. Another day had joined the vanished centuries. Thus it had happened, age after age.

15

THE Aldens were expecting a baby in August, and Alden was anxious for his wife to get away to Darjiling. She refused to go before the end of April, when the Agricultural Exhibition would be over, and they could spend a few days of holiday together. It was arranged that Hilda should go at the same time, and remain until her sister came down again in the autumn.

Alden was worried because his wife would not go earlier. But for himself he cursed the prospect of going at all. "Darjiling!" he said to Mrs. Nixon, as they walked back from the butts. "It's just a long street on a hill-side. You can go *up* the hill—or you can go *down* the hill. But you can't do anything else."

Mrs. Nixon was out of temper that morning, and did not trouble to be polite. "There's the Club there," she replied. "I get sick of this hole, and long to meet some people."

"Damn the Club!" growled Nixon. "I agree with Alden. I never met a man who didn't detest the hills."

Mrs. Nixon turned her fine eyes indignantly on him. "Percy Fowke told me he loved them. So did Freddy Furnevaux."

"They're not men, they're just dancing-partners."

Hilda Mannering had not played tennis for a fortnight. She overheard this conversation; and the men's impious words made her more determined than ever to get as much as she could of India's greatest gift, solitude, before she was sent to the compulsory sociability of the United English Nation. Fortune abetted her. That breakfast, Alden read out a letter from an engineer friend who was supervising a branch line in Bihar.

"Wintersgill writes that he's ordered to Travancore, to advise about a line there. 'I'll be away the whole of April,' he writes, 'and I'm dumping Akbar on you. He's a topping little beast, and there's no one here I dare leave him with. It's only a short trip down to you.' " Alden looked up.

"Who or what is Akbar?" asked Hilda. "A dog?"

"A polo pony, apparently. What am I to do? *I* can't look after him, with all these jobs tumbling in. And I want you two to get away."

"Don't you *dare* refuse!" cried Hilda.

"I *can't* refuse. He's on the way now, and will be here to-morrow."

"*I'll* take charge of him. Only get me a *sais* and grass-cutter."

"He's sending his own *sais*. Says he remembers the trouble I used to have, and he won't trust our local folk. He knows how rottenly they do shoeing; they pare a horse's feet to the quick, and send him lame. But what about a saddle?" He looked at her doubtfully. "Mine's lost its stuffing. Horses have clean gone out in small stations like this—the only person who rides here is Mrs. Nixon."

"You could get a man's saddle of sorts from the police lines," said his wife.

"No," said Hilda, "I've seen those saddles. I'll ride the way I'm accustomed. There are second-hand saddles advertised every day. I'll catch the noon train to Calcutta, and be back on the midnight express."

"My dear Hilda! In this weather! There isn't a

man who would do it, unless he jolly well had to!
You've no idea how that train drags!"

"Well, *I* jolly well have to! I'd go through a week
in torment to get a gallop again!"

At dawn next morning, in a station siding she
caught a glimpse of Akbar, who had arrived a couple
of hours earlier. Largess worked, and he reached
the bungalow by eight o'clock. He was a bay, whose
shapely head and slender limbs showed mainly Arab
blood; technically he was out of the "pony" class, since
he certainly touched fourteen and a half hands. Her
eyes appraised his quality—the quick, fastidious step-
ping, the energy compact and ready—and imagination
skimmed the gulf between appraisal and proof. How
easy it would be to gather him for the sudden ditch
that interposed! She *felt* the thrilling, instantaneous
tension of his body curving at the check! Her foot
tapped the ground in her impatience.

"Better leave him till the evening," Alden advised.
"Let him forget the jolts and bangings of the train."
But he hardly expected to persuade; even as he remon-
strated, he handed bridle and saddle to the *sais*. The
latter took them uncertainly; Alden questioned him,
then interpreted. "He says the horse has never had a
lady's saddle. We don't know if he'll take one."

"I'll answer that he will," said Hilda, who had confidence in her powers. "If I choose to ride a horse,
he'll take me in the saddle I prefer."

The horse did; and within half an hour of his
arrival she rode him out of the compound.

The day was clouded and comparatively cool, and
Alden, with a last appeal for prudence, warned her
that a storm was likely. She would not listen, but

laughed as the pony sidled past the pillars and into the road.

There was no destination in her mind. She would try Akbar's paces, have a scamper, and return. It was ecstasy to feel beneath her not a dead, mechanic thing, a car or cycle, but life and intelligence and the will to understand and respond. Hamar, passing from his office to Nixon's, watched her out of sight. Her face was shining, her eyes were proud and happy. The electric knowledge of her gladness, the spur of fresh surroundings, were exciting her mount; as she nodded to Hamar, her whole body, to the inexpressibly lovely tilt of her chin, stated decision. This was the woman he had assured himself was not pretty!

There are many to whom riding is only a social business, a "keeping the old equestrian game alive." They are ignorant of the glory of a lonely ride at leisure through wild country, of the sense of choice and skilful mastery, of comradeship between rider and horse. Hilda did not see Hamar's gaze, she had forgotten everything but Akbar and herself. The old experience was in her hands, she had given herself up to the joy of swaying the strength that fretted against even such firm, accustomed government. Her pony's ears were tense, she was aware of eyes glancing back to catch every glimpse of his mistress. She knew there was risk in this ride over rutted, unknown country, on a horse whose ways and training were yet to find; Hamar knew it still more surely. It was clear that a side-saddle was strange to Akbar, and his initiation as a lady's hack might be stormy. He flung away from her habit, and nearly tossed her against cactus spines.

She settled down to be mistress from the outset

and to make it plain that pace and direction were in her sole control. Taking a sandy track, she yielded so far as to let him trot; but the track was narrow, he shied and flinched annoyingly. Lizards rustled in the hedge, her shadow was a goblin at his feet. When he swerved to the left, the grey background of his vision blurred with her skirt. His attention jumped to every leaf and tremor—it must be focussed elsewhere, she resolved. The girl's slight figure stiffened as the will to rule took possession, and her grip tightened on reins and riding-wand. But she checked him now, till they should reach open country.

Open country came, and a grassy pad beside a lake, an edge soft from the excessive rains of last year. He continued nervous, and his rider's mind was made up that there was nothing for his funk and spirits but the indulgence of speed. As a snake whipped into a pool, he started, doubtful whether to shy; she took decision from him, into her own hands, and switched him smartly, into a gallop as hard as he could go. An Arab, she knew, was safe when flying, however he might appear to stumble when fidgeting at a walk; Akbar picked up his feet with swift, clean action. Once, where an egret rose from a plat of reeds, he arched his neck to look; implacably she hurried him on. An ancient ditch whose rims had crumbled apart yawned in a widish gap; she saw no reason for hesitation, and allowed none. Once for all this nonsense, of supposing it his business to watch for dangers by the way, or to study anything but her mood and pleasure, must be swept aside! His limbs, cooped through a day in that truck, were tingling for exertion—the **vast, strange wilderness and these unaccustomed** glimpses of his rider made him skittish with fear. But the pace shook his terrors from him; and the sense of newness vanished, in the ease and imperious sureness of her handling. The teasing world of shadows, and of sudden movements leaping out of silence, was forgotten.

"Not tired, old boy? After that long day and night in the train!"

Her tones were a caress, as she soothed and praised him, checking him where the lake curved in their front. He accepted her; this dimly silhouetted burden thrust him at the water, and without hesitation he obeyed. He splashed across the shallow bay, and climbed the steep further bank, to a dusty track through forest. They cantered along it till the trees spread apart above cliff; she reined him in by a solitary *neem*, and broke off a branch to pin to her dress. Startled by the sound of snapping wood and the menace of the nodding bough, he would have set off again. She comforted him, and wheeled him back to shade.

By leaving the metalled road for the first soft by-way, they had missed the Red Tank. But it was here, the ground abutting grandly on it, and she could see the memorials of the dead queens. She sat there like the Spirit of Freedom looking on a world in servitude. Woman the slave, the faithful drudge and foil and martyr, was meant for other and nobler use; for these radiant eyes were a woman's. Those other women, many of them beautiful and spirited and young, had died for men; here was a woman for whose whim men might be glad to die. Gazing on those stones of suffering, her eyes dimmed. She saw the past in vivid procession, she heard the beating of drums on the still air, the blowing of shells and cries of acclamation. The ground suddenly became flames spiring upward, and she saw faces that had not been shown on earth this hundred years and more; they were agonized, miserable, or exalted and fanatical. Some seemed mutely appealing to her, to woman the petted and worshipped, to come down and share the lot of woman wronged and enslaved. Not here alone, not here—those fires of sacrifice were quenched for ever—but everywhere, wherever weakness is trodden into the dust and made miserable! The joy of riding passed from her, she was wretched. A sati-stone—that appealing hand (still, after the rains of a century, faintly vermilioned) thrust up to intensify its witness —stood in shadow of her tree. She slid from the saddle, and rested on it.

And it seemed to her that nothing of good that could come to the world now could compensate for the uncounted wrong that had gone. The ages had passed, with their wars and their persecutions, their slayings and serfdoms. The weak had been crushed, women had been killed with torment because they were old and poor and ugly, or—as in this place where she sat —because they were women. Nothing that happened now could matter. There could be no Mind in a world where good has always come so slowly and so late.

She thought of her own life, and how aimless and careless it had been. She had been happy, she had loved beauty, she had enjoyed action and conversation. She had been given brains, without any necessity for using them. She realized that she had always had her own way, and that any resentment she felt for what

women had suffered must be vicarious, for everyone
had been good to her. But bitterness came with the
reflection that kindness follows the waning physical
loveliness, and goes when that goes. She would grow
old, and men, who have the strength which rules the
world, would leave her; with all her intellect and
power, she was a plaything. No! Not unless she
allowed herself to be! She would keep the friendship
of men like her brother-in-law and John Findlay. But
how? Only if she remained in India, for they were
here; only if she had some purpose in life, as they had.
She knew that daily their lives were striking deeper
roots in this arid land, were drawing enrichment, in
knowledge, interest, emotion. Already, in her stay
of less than six months in India, she had seen how men
and women, husbands and wives, fall out of sympathy
with each other when the work is a man's work, and
a woman merely exists by his side.

Yet how could she remain in India? So far, she
had not been greatly attracted by the people. It had
dawned on her that there must be "more to it" than
the surface appearance, since both Alden and Findlay
had more than affection, had genuine respect for those
they served. She had never known Robin so angry
as when a young missionary guest had condemned the
people he had known for less than a year. "You get
to see with their eyes," he told her afterwards. "I
know how vexing they are, in ways enough. But *we*
never shake free from our herd-morality, any more
than they do; and we go on judging them because
they're not first-rate Englishmen in dark skins. I suppose it's a question of different ethics. They *hate*
many of the virtues that we praise; and we hate many

I

that *they* are keen on. We seem to them incredibly rough and rasping; and they seem to us worms. We're both right—by our own standards." He had told her of the patience and courage of the villagers who starved if rain failed and were ruined if it came in excess— of their uncomplaining heroism under disaster. She had seen something of this, in her twilight vigils in the jungle; the peasant and his beasts had become a symbol of the Indian age-long trudge along dusty ways. That faded majesty of Vishnugram, with its solitary wooden chair for visitors, its dripping roof and mouldering walls, stirred her pity. She dimly saw how galling must be this alien domination, to Indians of any pride. Even in the Christian community, she had learnt, a sensitive nationalism was awake; Alden and Findlay had done nothing to discourage it, Douglas also thought it a good thing. Even if there were only a hundred Indians who were free from all servility and sycophancy, then there were a hundred who suffered shame and humiliation inexpressible. And were there a hundred of her own countrymen who saw India's past with eyes of understanding and sympathy, or a hundred who knew how their presence in the land and their overwhelming prestige with the outside world, even in matters relating directly to India, affected the noblest Indians? Hamar suddenly crossed her mind; Alden said he had done a brave and upright thing in that Lambertgarh case. She had caught a glimpse yesterday of how his own nation punished him for it. But evidently it betokened no real understanding or friendly feeling; the man was a boor to the Indians at Vishnugram, and outside his duties he was merely the ordinary official, anxious for relaxation and to forget the country he served.

Hamar went out of her thought, and she was back with her own problem. Like all intellectual women, she wanted friendship with men; even the dullest man seemed to have *some* touch with life somewhere. She had not realized this so strongly till she came to India. But men's friendship never seemed free from some dominion of the senses. As long as she was young and beautiful, men would throng to talk with her; but their friendship was not the thing it seemed. Men had given her the best of comradeship, and then had wanted to possess her. A year ago she had been engaged. There had been no doubt of her lover's pride in her and in his relation to her. But she had not loved him; and she had ceased to believe in his love for her. She had been frightened; better be sure of safety than risk the years that were coming to rob her of youth and loveliness, with a man who had never cared to look past her outward person. She had come to India to escape from herself and from that memory.

A warm head rubbed against her shoulder, the pony reminding her that he was forgotten. Relief was instantaneous; she was recalled to action, which was easier than thought. Springing up, she fondled him—ungrateful, not to have remembered how swiftly and obediently he had carried her! She was loth to return —this desolation was so friendly. Clouds had masked the sun, and it did not seem an April morning far advanced. But her pony's shoulders proved that there was heat abroad. Thunder rumbled in the distance; the storms of early summer were coming soon, sooner than their wont. Alden's warning came back to her. "If it comes, it'll come as a bolt from the blue."

She looked at the sky, then at Akbar, remorseful for having kept him out so late. It seemed sacrilege to use the sati-stone as a mounting-block; there was nothing else, though. She could not have let the stirrup down; he would never have stood for her to tighten it again. Something was so exciting him that she began to think he would never let her spring to saddle. But she succeeded—hardly reaching his back, for the moment he felt her weight he was moving. They swung down a nulla fissuring the cliffs, to a path beside the water. They had struck Mrs. Nixon's favourite ride; hoofs had marked this bordering sand. A wind, a slight but gathering ground-swell, blew in spurts, and the sky had changed to black. Even so had Thor threatened Olaf, and his challenge had been flung back in his teeth and grim beard. Hilda accepted it now, shaking her whip in defiance; storm or no storm, she would race to the temple where she had seen the horses emerge that morning. She touched Akbar, but the hint was superfluous; to his dread of coming tempest her emotion added fire, transmitted by every contact of her limbs and quivering hands. Over the level he flew; up the ravine at the end, where a stumble might mean lameness to him or death to her, she could scarcely restrain him. At the top she swerved him aside and lifted her eyes to the temple terrace where she had stood before. Then she saw that Hamar was standing by her. He was trembling.

Startled, she said: "I thought I passed you on your way home, Mr. Hamar."

"I was not going home," he said, "and I could not

have gone home after seeing you. I love you. Don't you know that I love you? I had to tell you."

In his face was a humility that she had never seen in a man's eyes before. She had thought little about this man—she had known, of course, that his looks followed her, and that he admired her. But men, she had known for a long while, always did that. He was just an official, a chance acquaintance, a man whom —yet, as she saw that desperate hunger, her self-control strangely wavered. For one moment, her woman's instinct urged her to give herself to this man who wanted her so badly, who wanted her more than any man had wanted her yet. He saw her hesitate, and renewed his pleading.

"Hilda, Hilda, I want you more than everything else in the world. I have been watching you this half-hour. I came out to this tree because I thought you would pass here; and from that temple I saw you ride out to where you dismounted. You are not a woman, you are a goddess! No man could ever love you as much as I do!"

Quickly she took possession of herself, and quelled the woman surging up for mastery. Her brain began to work with rapidity and coolness, as a man's does when he has to decide swiftly for life or death. This man had been watching her, all his thought and imagination had been riveted on her far-seen figure fleeting by shores of vanished history. She did not know how women appeared to men; but she did know that no man could give himself up to the undivided watching of her for so long as Hamar had done, and remain in his normal mood. He now saw her glowing with exercise and the warm morning; she knew that her hat and habit sufficed; there was no fault in the horse. Five minutes ago, this man had been nothing to her. Nothing? She frowned, as for the first time a doubt crossed her mind. She put the question by. Now, without a warning, a tide had swept up from a sea she did not know, and was swelling round her. She dared not trust herself to those waves. Once before they had seemed to encompass her, she had accepted them, it had all been a mistake; a second mistake would be one without extrication. So, holding herself coolly there, she took stock of the situation, guessed how desirable and adorable she must seem to a lonely man meeting her so; she gave the fullest discount due on account of the loneliness, of her quickened loveliness, of the romance that had clothed her as she sped across that desolate landscape. Out of pity for him and herself all this must go, for what she did now must meet the rigid arithmetic of daily life. Many a man on far less provocation than Hamar had imagined himself in love with her. At last she spoke.

"Mr. Hamar, I don't care for you—you must know that I don't care for you like that."

Yet—she marvelled at herself—why had she not rejected him in the very moment of his suit? And why did her voice sound now so hesitating and uncertain to herself?

He began to plead again; poured out his passion, his eagerness. She had been intolerably, ineffably, lovely in her silence there, as each thought in its turn touched her face to new delightfulness. Her eyes had softened at the thought of his vigil; they had quivered —as though some spirit of vision in them caught his breath—when she saw that skimming, headlong race

beside the water's mirrors. She had assessed herself
as picture there—the tree, the gnarled wilderness at
her back, the horse, her neat perfection; and her head
had lifted, in unconscious and quite impersonal pride
in the beauty she had created. But it would not do.
She checked him hurriedly.

"You have not known me. I have not known you.
I know what it means for a man to speak to a woman
as you have done. I thank you with all my heart. But
it is impossible."

It sounded queerly stilted. But what was one to
say?

He saw that he had failed. But she was worth a
whole life's service. He gathered together all that
had grown slack and casual, and he faced his chance.

"Is there anyone ahead of me?" he asked.

"Yes," she said involuntarily, thinking of Findlay.
Then hastily, "No. Not in that way."

As he asked his question, she saw what her answer
meant to him; and there was something which went
out to this courage, and cried out to her to trust in it.
She bowed her head, lest he see her face.

The fragrance of the branch she wore was shaken
towards him, as the pony stamped impatiently. The
animal threatened to grow unmanageable; in the fierce
tension gripping her she had held him, but her mood
was relaxing and with it his acquiescence. She was
seated on an energy that had reached explosion-point;
she gave him the rein, and he was galloping at once.
The rapid motion gave her mind, distressed and tossing, the relief it needed; the trees raced by, she sur-
rendered herself to the one sensation of speed.
Thought could wait. Hamar watched her figure as

it flashed and dipped between the groves. Grace, ease and poise of mastery, fearlessness—everything that can bow a man's spirit down in adoration—all this was passing from his sight. Like the memory of her presence, the scent of *neem* flowers hung in the air.

But she reminded herself that she was riding a horse that had been travelling all night. She tried to rein him to a walk; it was impossible. A winding path crossed their way, and after hesitation she took it, for the city, she could see, lay in the direction in which it led. Her mount was madly restive, he kept plunging to get forward. She thought: "My skirt and the saddle are bothering him again"; and she bit her lip in vexation that so beautiful a creature should be so stupid. But the crowding excitements of this morning would have communicated themselves to an animal less sensitive by far; she remembered this, and forgave him. Then she understood, as the sky opened its artillery. Lightning dazzled about her, hail pelted. She had not known that such hail fell any-where in the world. Great stones of ice struck the ground on all sides, they sang past her face, they spanked her pony's flanks. One jagged piece stung her cheek; she was glad of her helmet. Pieces fell thirty yards away, and whizzed through the air like the nose-cap of a shell. The pony leapt and strained with fright; she dared not let him go, in that mood and in a country whose twists and changes she did not know. She could hardly see the track, and more than once they had to retrace their steps, when he had jumped off it into some old paddy-field. Frenzied with terror at being turned back into the storm, as it seemed, he almost stood erect. He bounced down a gully, and refused the path; with desperate patience plying whip and voice and heel, she forced him to it. She was ashamed that any horse should be so hag-ridden by her. But, with safety not ten minutes away, she could not dally with the chances of death and blinding. She never knew how she kept her seat, nor understood how she managed to hold him in. Her arms ached with the effort.

They reached the region of roads, and she let the pace quicken to a trot, intermittently a hand-gallop. They had the road to themselves, and she knew the way now. Thankfully she entered the College com-pound. For some reason Douglas was on the veranda, and not Alden—she found out afterwards that he had gone out to meet her, and had followed the hoof-pads in the bypath by which she had left the main road. Douglas was shouting like a schoolboy. He seemed unaware of her peril, heedless of the lightning; he may not have noticed that she was riding. He bellowed gleefully.

"Look, Miss Mannering! Did you ever see, ever hear of, such hail? I've been measuring it, and I've some bits that are two inches—no, one is two and a half!—by one and three-quarters across!"

Two of Alden's servants were rushing out, and bringing in any piece that seemed extra large; their deaths would have seemed to Douglas a small sacrifice in the cause of science. Already an article in the *Statesman* was shaping in his mind.

Hilda sprang from her reeking pony, and handed him over to the *sais*. She was soaked to the skin. Adjusting her hair hastily, she came on to the veranda

and duly admired the size of the stones that had been
battering her helmet. Once in her room, she saw that
her face was bleeding.

16

APRIL ran its blazing course; the storms were a
forgotten episode, two or three days of ravage which
left a brief welcome coolness, quickly over. Neither
Hilda nor Akbar took any harm from their sopping;
and for at least a week the earth, which in India is
so hard on a horse's feet, was soft and delightful to
ride over.

Social amenities languished. The College folk
were busy with examinations, except Alden, who was
commonly away at Kendudi, organizing the exhibits
of that great agricultural centre. Only the Nixons,
with Neogyi often and Jacks sometimes, kept a pretence of tennis alive; often there was not a four, and
the game was abandoned. Hamar was immersed in
the business of cleaning up his office, a task which
gave him an excuse to stay at home.

He need not have sought excuse, for he would not
have met Hilda. Like him, she took no risks. The
sais, who complained that it took till midnight to cool
the pony down, suggested dawn as a better season for
riding; but that would have left her without a reason
for cutting tennis. The month lived in her memory
of after-life as a period of quiet, absorbed happiness.
Soon after five the air grew tolerable enough to walk
Akbar through shaded byways, till the woods began;
then she had the long evenings to herself and solitude.
India became a presence comforting and friendly.

These hamlets, lapped round by the ancient forest, into which they subsided as into arms that they trusted, by gradual encirclement of mango groves and tall, dark tamarind spinneys, watched for her coming. As the slender form, a shadow gliding through the last sunlight, cantered over the heath, the level shafts and rays on the quivering sal copse would be a lifted eye of welcome. Reaching some tiny village, she would draw rein and ride through it slowly. Its naked children stared as she guided Akbar past them, dipping her head to avoid the sweeping boughs of the tamarinds that shaded the narrow path between the cactus hedges. On the further side, the jungle wrapt its desolation about her again.

The intelligent creature who carried her learnt that no pace beyond a circumspect walk would be allowed where the earth was fretted with up-thrusting rock. But he understood also that where a softer stretch interposed, or a heath with even the short burnt grass—enough to take the jar off his limbs—he was expected to canter, and if the hour were late might show his speed. With a mistress as spirited as himself friendship was quick and comprehension complete. The Indian ground is cruel and unyielding, and can wreck perfect limbs in a moment for ever. She watched it jealously, and the sensitive life at her bridle's end never leapt out of control. The *sais,* who had hoped for a month of idleness, might look askance at dripping flanks; but it was April, when either twilight has the warmth of an English summer noon. Beneath a cold or timid rider Akbar would have fussed himself into a foam at once and, reined and chafing, have been ridden to exhaustion. For at first he knew

one duty only, the polo pony's, whose work is done at
top speed. But places where this was safe were few,
and his rider had other intentions than to be bucketed
across these at chukker pace. Six months previously
he had left the dealer's hands as a "made" polo pony,
trained to stick and ball; the test of his training had
been the exacting and enthusiastic games with which
a large camp of engineers and settlement officers—
whom chance had stationed contiguously—celebrated
the close of day. Speed and blood had endured the
strain when horses less endowed with either—horses
of every size and varying degrees of competence—
had been flawed in wind or limb. Now, in these forest
rides, there was no fierce thrill of rivalry or comradeship; but the hour was the same, the hand upon the
reins was easier and alive with an eagerness more
subtly exciting than his master's, his load was light
and firm to the saddle. Yet in a surprisingly few
days he was "made" afresh, and his rider had tamed
the impetuous fire in brain and sinew to wait on her
convenience. To her it was occupation enough, the
most enthralling that human hands can have.

Yet there remained one place, the wide bed of a
dried-up river, that Akbar always insisted on passing
at his wildest gallop. One would have thought it
heavy going, over its sands, and dangerous, with its
frequent holes where the village women had dug for
water. But he had decided that a rush here was "his
stunt," and that his mistress would acquiesce if he
proved that he could bear her safely across. In this
he was right; and as they approached the bank and
he began to pluck at the rein, Hilda, laughing, would
tighten her chin-strap and sit back to revel in the mad

wind of their gallop. They had a ritual about this business; once up the further bank, she would call him by name, and he would turn his head towards the saddle to be rewarded. The rush had been his own idiosyncrasy; but the gracious fussing and fondling which conveyed his rider's pleasure and approval confirmed it into custom. That morning of sudden, savage tempest, when she had ridden out both the storm and his own intoxication of terror, had given him confidence for every step of all the ways that she took him.

In the village where the road climbed from the river, the English lady who rode like the wind became a legend. But had its people seen her in their jungle paths, they would have formed far other picture of her. The valkyr became a wood-queen pacing the solitudes; she disappeared into the dense spinneys of forest laurel, the evergreen wilderness closed round her figure. In some tiny glade far within, she listened to the dry-tongued whisper of the leaves. The noises which the generations raise seemed to be nothing—the struggles of insects flung into a sea which is drowning them. This rustle was the eternal voice of the sea itself, the sound which was before man and will be after man has perished. All was unreal, nothing mattered. The universe was but a dead frieze, a canvas painted with sunlight and green woodland; and here were figures thrown upon it, a horsewoman sculptured in shadow-stuff, in the dark marble of emptiness. That was but a tale that they told, of urgent, fiery suns and spinning, restless worlds, of ages and empires that passed away. See, this evening light was unmoving; the day lazily was standing still!

She tried to think of Hamar; but she was too happy to need anything outside herself. It was not in the waste, but when she was at home, that memory came back of his pleading, humble eyes.

As for Hamar, he caught but one glimpse of her; and that was not of the wood-goddess, but the efficient, athletic woman. One evening he left his files and he wandered, as he used to do at Suriganj. He reached the riverside in time to catch his breath as he saw her lightning passage of the sands. Surely she would be down, in that treacherous, deeply pitted surface! But her horse leapt the holes or lightly swerved by them. He was clambering up the bank, his nostrils quivering with excitement in his service of so gay and gallant a mistress. She was leaning forward, encouraging him up the steepness. Hamar's heart jumped; he felt he envied any creature that had the happiness of responding to her will. He caught her glowing eyes, and they smiled.

"I'm sorry to be so unceremonious, Mr. Hamar! Akbar isn't willing to stop, you see!"

She nodded, and was past him; the quick hoof-beats sounded on the metalled road. Then she was back again. She had seen, in that moment of leaving, anxiety in his face.

"I was in no danger, really. It was Akbar's choice; I don't usually let him go like that, I assure you!" Her laughing face bent low as she spoke. "But he was quite safe; and so was I. The sands are harder than they look from here. And I always give him his head. You've no intention of coming down with me, have you, old boy?"

He had this glimpse when April was drawing to its close. Two days later Hilda was in Darjiling with her sister. Mrs. Nixon, also, had gone to the hills. There were only men-folk left in Vishnugram.

17

FOR the plain-dwellers May held no events but its own monotony. Offices opened at six, and closed at ten-thirty, when the Europeans returned to their bungalows, for bath and breakfast. After that, servants shut the glass doors, salaamed, and retired to sleep. A wind, scorching as from an oven, swept the dry upland. Foiled, the fiery blast raged round the little forts where Douglas or Nixon or Alden struggled somnolently with files and correspondence.

The heat was the most tolerable of the ills that infested day. Eye-flies—coal-black demons the size of a large pin-head—swung into eyes and ears, with sudden maddening buzz, and settled on any sore part of the body that was exposed. When sated with mischief, they festooned strings and tapes, whence their victims would singe them off on to newspapers— the acrid stink of their burning went up like incense to the tortured spirit that snuffed it. Yet—since one can by itself make existence misery—enough always survived to ensure the continuance of torment.

Afternoon brought lethargies which sooner or later compelled sleep, out of which awakening came in a bath of sweat and with unrested frame. And night was windless and unstirred, a wretchedness that longed for dawn to come, with the mockery of *kokils'* laughter. As sleepless night followed night, Findlay, watching his child fretful and sickening, and his wife failing beneath a burden beyond her strength, sprang to the same resolve as hundreds of other husbands and fathers in India.

"You two are off to Darjiling by to-night's train," he announced, one breakfast.

They both protested. "Daddy, we were going to *explore,*" said Marjorie, "the head-waters of Siuli Brook."

They had their own maps, unsanctioned by any ordnance surveys, of the wilderness round Kanthala. Findlay, the Great Lone Voyageur, brought tales of the unkenned wastes beyond, of Wolf Heath and Palas Running. But the other two were steadily enlarging their range. The preceding winter had seen them pass from One Tree Heath and Wild Date Spinney to where a tiny brook came tumbling, through fifty yards of cascade and cataract, from a thicket of *siuli,* more fragrant, when the west wind blew from it, than any cinnamon-scented shores of fable. Beyond this was terra incognita, marked on their maps with "Here are BEARS" and "Leopards, wolves, sambur." That these creatures were not unknown there was indeed probable, since the woods harboured them everywhere, resident or visitant, and they came sporadically in Findlay's way from village to village. The "head-waters of Siuli Brook," he surmised, lay in a hollow scarcely a hundred yards upward from where it chattered out of its covert. A tank of ancient digging lay there, amid fields that the jungle had reclaimed centuries since. A wise chieftain, he kept his guesses to himself, and Marjorie looked forward excitedly to a day when they would all together push the borders of knowledge a little further.

"We'll do that when autumn comes," he told her. "Now I want you both to explore Darjiling, and bring back cheeks of a different colour."

As he looked at her, his heart suffered. She was peaked and wasted, her eyes dry and sunken, her face sallow and old. Her whole life had been one of anxiety for them. Its first year had been one of constant sickness, a bad start from which she had never recovered. He knew that after his next furlough he must return alone; this knowledge made the last year of their comradeship a time over which he would have lingered, losing no minute of it. But there was no question that wife and child must escape now, from the desolation that was wasting men's lives.

Next morning, between trains, he enjoyed a few hours in Darjiling. Fate was kind, and Kanchenjanga shone out intermittently, like an Emperor granting *darshan*[1]—Kanchenjanga, that day and night "glitters like the eternal laughter of the Great God."[2] He cleansed his eyes with the dazzle that had brought happiness to the ancient poet—those vast up-thrusting snows and enormous ice-fields purified more than the outward vision. Then he returned, and settled down to face rigours tolerable to the man who is alone and who gets out often and at all hours.

As May drew to its burning close, one dawn he journeyed to Khamadhi, a village a dozen miles from his bungalow, to see an "inquirer." The inquiry turned

[1] Sight. Rulers in India used to show themselves on balconies to their subjects; the sight was considered auspicious.
[2] A quotation from Kalidasa.

K

out to be what he expected, one whether the Mission would provide bullocks, as rumour said, for any agriculturist who turned Christian. Findlay very forcibly and explicitly said that it would not, whereat the awakened conscience relapsed into contented heathenism. Findlay, scanning the throbbing earth and the sky that leapt and strained with its heat, wondered if he could cycle the twelve miles between him and home before day became a vaulted furnace. He decided that he could not, and had better drowse away the awful hours in shade of a banyan; he would return in the afternoon. It was then that he saw the would-be correspondent of the United English Nation, leaning against a wall and watching him with good-natured amusement. Findlay laughed back, for he was amused at himself—and not very ruefully, either, for no labour which entailed a journey through his beloved wildernesses was wasted labour in his eyes. He had started before the sun rose; and even in May there had been a dewy semblance on the leaves. And dawn had been a sudden spouting up of incredible gold, like a heavenly firework which blazed and vanished.

"Saheb," said the man, "these people care for nothing but their bellies. I could have told thee this yesterday, when I was in Kanthala. But it would not have availed. Thou"—he used the *tu* of brotherhood, not of ignorance or of contempt—"art the servant of the Name; and when thou art called thou must answer, though knowing it but a fool's errand."

Here, on his native heath, he talked Bengali. He seemed gentle and happy, his mind, at any rate temporarily, rested from brooding over the United English Nation's recalcitrance as a debtor. Findlay, finding that his name was Nilkamal Ghosh, was pleased, for it recalled that most charming of Bengali novels,[1] where another Nilkamal—standing, in absurd green garb, with long tail, before the audience of a play—explains that he is not the monkey-god Hanuman in reality, but just Nilkamal, bullied into taking this ignoble part. Nilkamal flits through the story thereafter, chased across Bengal by small boys crying "Bacha Hanuman" ("Child Hanuman"). Findlay, with difficulty refraining from calling this new Nilkamal "Bacha Hanuman," asked him where the Sadhu Jayananda lived.

Nilkamal jerked his finger westward, over a line of unpolled jungle.

"We are going there now," he said. "Come. The Sadhu would see thee."

"How far?" asked Findlay, casting a wary glance upward.

"A *krosh*, maybe."

"But what kind of a *krosh*, brother? A broken-branch *krosh*?"

Now a *krosh* is two statutory miles, "there or thereabouts." But in the wilds there is a custom of breaking a branch from the wayside; when it wilts, it is considered that a *krosh* has been travelled. Findlay had horrid memory of a sweltering, dragging day with Alden; their goal had been "two *krosh*" away when they started at dawn, and continued to keep its distance with every inquiry, till nightfall found them still "two *krosh*" short. The "broken-branch *krosh*" is a measure greatly variable, according to the season

[1] *Swarnalata*, by Taraknath Ganguli.

of year when the estimate is made, the tree that provides the branch, the bearer's standard of wilting or habit of sauntering, walking steadily, or running. As Alden had said despairingly, if a branch were broken in January, a *krosh* might mean a week's hard tramp. He believed that the surveyor who set the standard for their toil that day had been a murderer fleeing towards the forests of Orissa.

Nilkamal laughed gleefully, and conceded a slightly longer distance.

"It may be a *krosh* and a half. No, saheb, not more. It was at this season of the year that I broke the branch."

Accordingly the United English Nation and its petitioner set out together to find the abode of the Bliss of Victory. The village where they were was a tiny one, and a short stretch of cracked paddy-fields and ridges brought them beyond its purlieus and plunged them into deep jungle. The wild laurels rustled drily in the heat, as though the wood-gods were whispering tiredly together; the sun splashed the forest beside the path with the unbelievable brightness of a dream—the trees were painted and varnished and then painted again. And then the jungle opened on a clearing of about an acre, studded with the pollarded *arjuna*-trees on which the tusser silk-worm feeds, and with tall-towered feathergrass that indicated the presence of water not too far below the surface. There were remnants of a few vegetables, there was a patch where stumps of last year's sugarcane still lay. Squirrels were frisking in half a dozen mangoes. Nilkamal paused, and gazed with satisfaction.

"There has always been a Sannyasi here," he informed Findlay, "since the time of Ramachandra, King of Ayodhya. The last one lived five hundred years and five. Behold his *samadhi.*" He pointed to a mound, one of several. "The Sadhu," he laughed, "grows sugarcane and maize and *brinjals.* He grows them, and the squirrels and wild deer and pigs devour them. But the Sadhu has the sight of their green leaves growing—till the beasts eat them."

"But where is the Sadhuji himself?"

"There!"

He pointed to a banyan, under whose roof spiry bushes of hibiscus starred the blackness with crimson. Against this background Findlay saw as satisfactory a Sannyasi as any globe-trotter could have desired to see—sitting upright on a mat of tiger-skin, his naked body gleaming silverly with its smear of ashes. Findlay knew that Jayananda must be forty-five, at least; but there was mark of neither age nor youth upon him, he was impersonal and timeless. Beside him was Kamalakanta Neogyi, lying on the ground. Nilkamal led Findlay up, and disappeared. The Sannyasi, staring expressionlessly at Findlay, spoke.

"Sit down, Findlay," he said; his thought, rather than any discernible gesture of body or movement of his eyes, indicated a chair so rickety that Findlay wondered if it had been lent by the Rani of Vishnugram. He declined to be ridiculous; following Neogyi's example, he sprawled on the turf. Neogyi rose to go; but Jayananda, with a gesture surprisingly vigorous for a yogi, waved to him to be seated.

Findlay was bewildered. He was not usually greeted as "Findlay" by an Indian met for the first time—and that Indian a naked, ashen-hued ascetic, with elf-locks as matted and as earthy as the dangling roots of the banyan above him. And what was Neogyi doing in this galley?

The Sadhu read his mind—not a very occult feat, under the circumstances—and vouchsafed part of the explanation.

"Kamala Babu," he began.

Findlay noticed that, like most Indians who associate with Europeans on equal terms, he was readier to drop affixes of courtesy with them than with his own countrymen. He remembered, once in the up-country, calling at an Anglican Brotherhood, to ask after an old school-friend. "Churchill?" the Indian *padre* had said. "Churchill? You want to see Churchill? Mr. Mukherji, do you know where Churchill is?" And the information had been given: "I think Churchill must be with Montagu-Curzon, Mr. Ghoshal. Or else with Baldwin." Better all of us keep to our own ethos, Findlay's mind noted in passing; they have a decent one of their own, but this hybrid mess that they pick up, thinking it is ours!— It was natural for them to be conventional and stiff. He had often been amused, when watching College football matches, to hear the players' cries at the very tensest moments: "Pass, Bijay Babu! Make a goal, Anil Babu! Oh, well shoot, Jatin Babu!" And this from the same students who talked bigly among themselves of "Douglas" and "Alden" and "Jacks."

"Kamala Babu," said the Sadhu, "is fed up. Fed up with everybody—with his own countrymen, with your friend Alden, with the rest of your people. His mind has gone altogether bad" (this in Bengali). "So he has come here to talk sedition with me. Yes, I know your Anglo-Indian papers are very cross when we Indians criticize the Government. But what *we* say is nothing to what *they* say when they get their bally rag really out."

(The Sannyasi, Findlay's subconscious mind noted, pondering amusedly amid its bewilderment, now passing off, was a trifle more idiomatic and slangy than an Englishman would have been.)

"You see, Findlay, we must all have our grouse sometimes, or else go mad. And Kamala Babu has been talking the most mutinous and blasphemous stuff to me."

Findlay saw a clear course before him. In any case, he never played any cards but those of utter frankness. He knew, too, that straightforwardness would rout, as by sheer surprise, the cunningest adversary in India, whereas any and every form of subtlety would be foreseen and countered. Again, he knew that there were Indians who were Aryans indeed, noble (as the word signifies) with a simplicity and clarity beyond anything that the West has yet believed or understood. The Sannyasi's record made it unlikely that he was one of these. But—since he was evidently taking the line of utter frankness—well, if *that* was the bowling, Findlay knew how to play it.

"What's Alden done wrong?" he asked.

Neogyi flushed. "Why did you and he laugh at me when I held that meeting for the Exhibition?"

Findlay was remorseful. "I know. I'm sorry. So's Alden. It was my fault, not his."

Neogyi did not understand. "How could it be your fault?" he shrilled. "It was Alden who laughed out loudly when I was speaking. What did I say that was funny? I suppose you thought it funny that an Indian should be magistrate at all! And Alden pretends to be a friend of Indians—is proud of his reputation as the only Englishman who understands Indians!" In his anger Neogyi was sneering.

"Look here, Neogyi, I apologize, honestly. It wasn't Alden's fault, it was mine. *I* made him laugh, not you."

"*You* made him laugh! In a meeting where I am trying to get these wretched people of mine to work together for their own good! Your Government sets me here to administer the affairs of a million people, in the poorest and most ignorant district in Bengal! My God! what a job! My own people call me a traitor and work against me. And you Englishmen sneer and are jealous, and laugh at me! And"—his voice rose almost to a shout—"for Commissioner you set over me the damnedest, vilest, oiliest, basest rascal that even India under British rule ever produced!"

"Oh, damn!" Findlay involuntarily swore. "Am I *always* to be the United English Nation? Have I got to be held responsible for Deogharia?"

Jayananda interposed. "Kamala, this tree, in the thousands of years during which men have sat beneath its boughs in meditation, has never heard a shout before. Or swearing," he added. "And Findlay is here as our guest."

Neogyi's anger evaporated as quickly as it came. "I'm sorry," he said. "I apologize, Findlay."

Jayananda continued. He enjoyed his rare exercises in the English tongue, and he now spoke as if he were presiding over a Swadeshi meeting, in the spacious if intolerably noisy days of the Partition.

"In Neogyi's last words I fancy we got at his real grievance—and, fortunately, it is one that offers us all a basis for cordial agreement. Mr. Findlay, your nation pride themselves on going by concrete instances, instead of being discursive vapourers"—he was pleased with the phrase, paused, and repeated it, rolling his lips round it as if it were a cigar of very rich flavour—"discursive vapourers like ourselves. Let me follow your excellent example. Your papers and politicians often point out that you have generously given us a lot of self-government. What you mean is, you have given us many Indian officials. But what does this boon amount to, seen at close quarters in detail? Deogharia as Commissioner, ruling a country as big as half England, and with absolutely unlimited opportunities for graft! Jaychand Bhattacharyya in Chandbasa! Ghosh——"

"Oh, don't, don't, don't! cried Findlay, stopping his ears. "I know, I know. We've evolved a method of selecting you which picks out all your swabs and sets them over you."

"We thank you for seeing our grievance," said the Sadhu gravely; "the more so, since we were both of us honoured by your Government with selection by that same method! I was once a magistrate, as Neogyi here. And—who knows?—I might now have been Commissioner in Deogharia's place!"

All three men laughed delightedly. "Why don't you bring that grievance forward?" asked Findlay. "My countrymen would understand at once. But, anyway, Neogyi, I'd like you to know that we all think *you* are all right."

"How *can* you think me all right"—Neogyi's annoy-

ance was kindling again—"when you laugh at me, and
make a fool of me before my own people?"

"Tell me what happened," said the Sadhu. "Kamala's side I know—he was full of it when you came."

Findlay explained, shamefacedly. "The whole
thing was silly. Only Khaliara turned up in that boy's
blue football jersey that he always wears with his
slashed doublet and hose. So I suggested to Alden
that he was Sindbad the Sailor. Don't let him know
this—I wouldn't have the old boy's feelings hurt, for
worlds."

"I see." The Sadhu's voice was slow and sardonic.
"And I dare say you'd be still more sorry if he gave
up wearing the jersey. It's all right, Kamala. My
countrymen"—to Findlay—"will never understand
yours. Kamala, listen! When our minds go bad, we
commit suicide or take up politics. When the Englishman's mind goes bad, he drinks hard, or he takes to
religion, or he saves himself from insanity by playing
the fool and laughing at himself. Now, Findlay has
been cooped up with his Christians—and we know the
sort of folk they are—all right, all right, Findlay,
we're slandering them and you're going to stick up for
them! I'll drop them, and will illustrate by the
case of Alden. He's had six months of incessant
strikes——"

"Six months!" said Findlay. "Six years—ever since
Gandhi bit all you folk!"

"Six months of incessant strikes by those silly children under his supervision who are learning books by
heart for Calcutta University examinations. He's had
to put up with uninterrupted lying and slander and
babyish imbecility." The Sannyasi's voice hardened

with contempt. "Then one day he comes to a solemn public meeting. And instantly sees the whole universe as the jest it is! It was a moment of illumination, Kamala—the mystic's sudden laughter leaping out to join the mirth of the Creator! Alden wasn't laughing at *you*."

"You quite sure of that?" Neogyi was smiling.

"Oh, well, perhaps he was—a bit. You know, Kamala, you *are* a richly comic character, in your way. Now don't get offended! So am I, sitting on this tiger-skin and talking faultless English, when I haven't washed for years. So is Findlay, cycling twelve miles in this weather, to see a man who was hoping to get a pair of bullocks out of him. Only, Findlay knows he is, and has the sense to laugh at himself—that's where the English have the bally bulge on us!"

"You beggar!" Findlay had to laugh out loud. "How do you know what fetched me here?"

The Sadhu chuckled. "The whole village knows. They had a meeting on this great bullock question, three days ago. How a good yoke of bullocks at Stamford Fair, Master Shallow? It's been a bad season for cattle. Now, Findlay, if you had a thousand bullocks, you could use them to draw five hundred families into the Kingdom of Heaven?"

"That's not fair," said Findlay hotly. "It wasn't bullocks that brought——" He stopped, discreetly. After all, why should he discuss his converts with these two scoffers?

"No," Jayananda conceded. "It's *not* fair. But it has as much truth in it as most calumnies. Anyway, we knew yesterday that we should have the honour of your presence, and I borrowed for you this chair which you are too proud to use. All yesterday I had it standing in the sun. So that, even if it were a saheb's 'babu's chair,' you need not fear it."

Findlay blushed. He himself had no visitors but Indians and he kept no "babu's chair." But the hoary jest seemed like a breach of hospitality on his people's part; he felt that he, and not the Sannyasi, was sitting naked. What knowledge would Jayananda next betray?

"I keep no 'babu's chair,'" he said abruptly; and Jayananda was apologizing.

"I'm sorry, Findlay. I beg your pardon. No one ever supposed you did. Though it isn't the keeping of one, but the bragging about it that makes the offence. Many who talk about one don't keep one."

"But *why* have I got to be *always* the United English Nation?"

"Don't your people always make Kamala—or myself—the United Indian Nation? If he vexes you by anything he does, don't you say: 'That's just like an Indian'?"

Findlay reflected. "Yes," he admitted, "I did—once. But I don't think I do now. Not so much, anyway. And if I do," he added, with a sudden welling of friendliness as he looked across at Neogyi, "doesn't the United Indian Nation gain? Haven't I learnt to think better of Indians, largely because of Neogyi's decency?"

"I'm sorry you got that out first," said Neogyi. "I wanted to say that the United English Nation has taken no harm by your being its representative here during seven years."

Nilkamal reappeared, bringing mangoes and sweetmeats, with a large bundle of parched rice. He went again, returning with brass tumblers of milk and *bel* sherbet. He sat down beside the others.

"*Apani khaben*" ("Your Honour will eat"), he said to Findlay.

Findlay shook his head. The Sannyasi broke in.

"It is noon overhead! You have cycled twelve miles! You have had no breakfast! Come, missionary. Thou shalt not tempt the Lord thy God! You see, the Devil can quote Scripture, as well as have it quoted at him!"

"I've left some grub with my bike."

"Two miles away! You are hungry?"

Findlay laughed. "Desperately. But how can I eat when you fellows aren't doing it?"

"Set your mind at rest," said Neogyi. "*I'm* going to have something, if the Sadhu isn't."

"I'll take something gladly," said Findlay, "if Nil-kamal Babu will let me have it a little apart from the rest of you, so that he and the Sadhu won't mind eating as well."

"We shan't mind as it is," said the Sadhu. "I haven't touched anything but *muri* and water since I took my vows. But, Findlay, I'll break my rule a little to-day."

Findlay knew that very few educated Hindus, even in his jungly parts, would scruple to eat with him if alone and unseen; and Neogyi, as a Brahmo, could have no logical objection, though Brahmos, like other people, can be illogical. The Sadhu, of course, had in his day dined freely with Europeans. But Findlay was a little surprised that he should be ready to do it now, with Nilkamal and Neogyi witnessing. However, he had learnt to accept whatever happened; he had no generalizations left where Indians were concerned.

He was hungry; he and Neogyi and Nilkamal fed heartily and well. The Sannyasi satisfied himself with a handful of parched rice and one sweetmeat—"for your sake, saheb." But Findlay felt he had never been the guest of a host more festive. The rays of the meridian sun were sending glittering shafts through the leaves. The alternation of sunlight with the polished emerald of banyan or the browner green of tamarind, while the coppersmith beat his maddening gong without ceasing, made the woodland an accomplice in the incongruous scene—a kind of "white-eyed musical Kaffir" lying on its side and watching them. Findlay felt that he understood the Sitwell view of the world. Pan and Sylvan had vanished, and the sweet freshness of leaf and flower; instead, Harlequin and Columbine were chasing rocs and unicorns under the shadow of Popocatapetl and Chimborazo. He wanted to laugh, to turn head over heels, he had an almost irresistible desire to scrag this absurd Sannyasi. If he once started a rugger scrum, the forest would join in. That stooping mango, with the huge brown knee-cap, was just waiting for a chance to tackle the banyan low. He caught the Sadhu's eyes, and they twinkled.

"Laugh, Findlay," he said. "Eat, drink, and be merry, for to-morrow all will be a dream. Look! it is all *maya;* nothing but illusion. You think you see me, I think I see you. But to-night all will be a blur in the brain. This sunlight will be a dried pigment, one with a million faded tints on memory's wall; and death will come to whitewash every smudge and smear. Shall you and I, shadows and less than shadows, quarrel and argue? There was a Sannyasi here, two and a half milleniums ago, and Buddha sent a missionary to try to convert him. They are dust, the winds that carried their words have been stilled these thousands of years. When they met, Time had a millenium to run before Mahomet was born; it was fifteen hundred years after them that William the Norman conquered England. Thou and I, O missionary, are both flitting images in Another's dream; even before the Sleeper wakes, we shall vanish into crannies of his mind where none will ever find us again."

"A bleak creed, *Gurudeb*," said Neogyi, cramming a ball of sugared rice into his mouth and reaching for another. "Almost thou persuadest me to be a Christian. I'm glad I'm a Brahmo, even though to-day we none of us believe a thing. Findlay, if you—knowing what modern thought teaches, as you do, of course—honestly believe a tithe of what your religion teaches, and are not simply the zealous philanthropist that everyone knows you are, you are the luckiest man of us all."

Findlay's hands were clasped behind his back, and he was watching a star of sunlight, silvery in their matted roof. "I'm not going to argue with you fellows to-day," he said, "when the whole world seems to have got a sunstroke. My brain is upside down. If we are merely flickers in some Sleeper's dream, then all I can say is, it is a good dream that brings us four into fellowship, and the Sleeper must himself be good."

Said the Sadhu: "Findlay is wise. He knows that these banyans are in league with the ancient gods of the land, and he puts up a flag of neutrality."

"Yes," said Findlay. "I remember something that happened last Rains. I saw some coolies teasing a small black cobra. I thought they were snake-charmers; but they suddenly stopped, and let it go down-bank and into the jungle. I was indignant, and asked them why they hadn't killed it. 'Ah,' they said, 'who is going to fight with Death in the eventide?' *'Sandhyabela kaler sahit ke larbe'?* I seemed to be looking back into some primeval terror, to race-memories of battle with dragon and swamp-eft as darkness fell. The ooze sucked at my feet," he continued dreamily, "and a wind came creeping through the reeds that overshadowed me. I had only a stone-hatchet; and I was fighting with Death in the eventide, with all things unfriendly and terrible. Well?" He looked about him defiantly. "I am not going to fight now with Brahma in his dream-wilderness, with you fellows and myself all drugged and narcotized by the branches and sunbeams passing hands over us."

"I like that yarn," said the Sadhu. "And I like Findlay's exposition of it. But when did it happen? I'm going to bring the scientific mind to bear on it."

Findlay thought a moment. "Just before the Manasa-*puja*. I remember now, because I came home with my mind full of cobras, and was vexed to find that some of our Christians, who used to be snake-charmers, had got cobras in their house and were charging for making them dance."

"You thought, no doubt, that it was snake-worship back among your Christians?"

"I did," said Findlay. "I killed the snakes." He did not add that he had compensated their masters.

"He did right," said Neogyi, almost to the Sannyasi.

"We won't discuss ethics here," said the latter. "But I'm afraid Findlay's picturesque interpretation of what those coolies said was mistaken. All they meant was, next week is the Snake-Queen's *puja,* this is the very eve of her power—who is going to be such an ass as to provoke her now, by harming one of her chief subjects? There was no primeval memory, Findlay Saheb. What! are you also one of those who would make every Indian peasant out a subtle mystic? But you have reminded me. *We* have fed; now for our *devata's* share."

He signed to Nilkamal, who rose and poured from a brass pot some milk into an earthenware saucer at Findlay's side. Nilkamal drew a flute out of his clothes, and began to play. Findlay, absorbed in watching him, received a sign from the Sannyasi to look to his left. He did so, and saw a magnificent cobra; its neck was puffed and distended, as it swayed to the music. Findlay could not help starting; but he knew that his wisdom was to remain still, and he trusted the Sadhu. Slowly, gradually, the bamboo reed's thin tune quavered down into silence; the cobra suppressed its hood, lowered its head to the saucer, and drank. Then it moved away, and was lost—a sluggish glimmer stirring in the central roots of the banyan, a slow lustre that gradually subsided and withdrew.

"Something for your next furlough's missionary meetings," the Sadhu gloated. "You can allegorize it. What'll it be? The false heathen philosophy playing its seductive flute, and inviting the demons of the wilderness to share its wicked feast?"

"Saving your sannyasiship," said Findlay delightedly, "thou art a scoffer and a knave, a consorter with serpents and goblins. Many, having heard thy words

L

this day, would call thee no true sadhu, but atheist and sorcerer."

"And by this token, O Findlay Saheb, all men know that thou hast found God—that thou canst both take and give a jest, even under the shadow of the Name. For it is the son that plays where the servant dare not enter. I have known missionaries, not Christian ones only, who would have gone in anger, because we made sport of their office and purpose. God is not with that man who thinks: 'I am I, this great and wise and serious one, and men must honour and regard me.' "

The noon heats were pressing down—down—like heavy hands shutting the brain and soaking it with weariness unendurable. Even the coppersmith flagged, and at last was silent. Neogyi rose, and excused himself; he had a bed spread in shadow of a mango, and was going to sleep. Nilkamal had already gone. Findlay was left alone with the Sannyasi. He looked at the keen, emaciated face. It had changed, suddenly and utterly. The momentary fire of eagerness had died down, only serenity shone there.

Findlay remembered Headley's words, when he was visiting Vishnugram and they had met at lunch. "You out in those Orissa marches? You've got that Jayananda fellow your way. Sannyasi? So I'm told! Not unless you can quench a furnace with a thimbleful of water. The very Satan of all the restlessness that there has ever been in the world was in that chap when I knew him. He's not the knave he's supposed to be. But no Sannyasi!" But there was no devil of restlessness here now. Unless a face can lie in every line and lineament, this man's spirit was a great calm.

"Vairagi," said Findlay, lying now at full length,

and lifting his face to the Sannyasi, "you have been in the world, and you know that its waves are restless always. On all sides there is misery and sickness and poverty and anxiety and bitterness and cruelty. Tell me—for you are still a young man—how can your mind be at peace? For you have imagination, to bring its echoes even here."

"Desire is dead in me. There is nothing within me by which these things can catch fire. That is what Jesus said—the prince of this world cometh and findeth nothing in me. Nothing. For all longing is ended, all striving is finished."

"For yourself, perhaps, yes. But does not the world call you through others? I've talked to Headley about you——"

He paused, scanning the Sannyasi's face. That remained impassive and incurious.

"Headley? Oh, yes. The Chief Secretary, is he not? I hear these things, and some of them remain in memory, others drift away. Yes, I knew him once."

"He says that you were always a decent enough district officer. A bit fussy—you don't mind, Vairagi? After all, these things have nothing to do with you now."

"Nothing at all. Go on. I *was* fussy. I had no peace. A demon of doing possessed me. I think you English had bitten me."

"A bit fussy, but *keen* on your people—distressed by their poverty, heart-broken when floods or famine caught them. Now a man doesn't change his character utterly. How can you be happy in this forest peace, when you remember your own people, when you think how——"

Findlay stopped abruptly, reminding himself that what seemed to him most pitiable in the condition of the Sannyasi's countrymen might not seem so to the Sannyasi himself.

"You are remembering that I was their political leader?"

"Yes. They say you went through this nation like fire through dry thorn."

"I was blinded by ignorance. I thought of myself as *I*; and these aliens in my land were pressing, it seemed, upon that self which I thought the most precious thing in the three worlds. I did not consider that this life was but a wave flung up from the quiescent Life, and that the English were but other waves; and that even in the moment of our uprising our sinking had begun, and we were all alike falling back into the one sea. We were clamouring against each other with voices that were already dying into the great spaces, were being robbed of their momentary being by the eternal Silence. At last my eyes were opened, and I saw that all was passing, and that the English would be gone from the face of the land, and forgotten as Akbar and Allah-ud-din are forgotten, who also were great names in their day."

"Yet—while these things are here—or seem to be here—the English, if you like to trace all India's misery to them—I know you don't, but still—well, aren't these things, these conditions, bringing evils which would cease if they were once gone? Vairagi, how *can* you find peace in yourself, while your people are weak and ignorant and wretched?"

"My peace can be theirs. When the Pindaris swept through the land, and thousands of homes were desolated, there were men who were not impoverished, for they had kept their jewel where none could seize it. There are no evils except the things that make us say *I am*, and desire to clothe this strutting self that to-morrow will be gone from its place for ever. I have conquered desire. It is not. Once I was a magistrate, and I ruled over a million people, as Neogyi does now. I had a wife, I had a child— they are gone. I had money, I had honour—both are finished. I had furniture, carpets, clothes, books, horses. When I lost all this, I was bitter, and I hated the English who, I thought, had taken it from me. Then I gained power afresh, in other ways—and greater power than before. It is known that one of your viceroys said to his ministers: 'It would have been better if we had made that damned Ramsaran Lieutenant-Governor of Bengal, instead of having driven him into making such a nuisance of himself!' They thought that it was envy that was urging me on against them. Well, perhaps they were right. But all that is over. That Viceroy himself, who was great in his day and held durbars and was bowed to by rajas and maharajas, is gone. There is no villager in all this land who fears his name. He is one with Sikander, and Prithviraj, and Hastin Saheb"—the Sannyasi used vernacular names, a ceremonious acknowledgment of his guest's awareness of Indian thought. "All is finished, and my mind is at rest. I have found the truth that brings release."

"Yet," said Findlay, persistent, "what of these others—blinded and poor and starving? Who is to help them? Did not Buddha himself, when he had attained enlightenment, draw back on the very shores of peace and refuse to enter it, that he might show others the Noble Fourfold Path?"

Findlay was leaning forward, the fanaticism of his compassion burned in his face. The Indian was moved.

"Findlay," he said gently, "it is you—and the few who are like you—who have corrupted my people. You have made it impossible for us to hate the English, and to rise resolved to sweep them out of our land, though we died in our millions to do it. There is not a swarajist in this district who does not, when envisaging the future, take it for granted that we shall somehow still have Alden at the College, and you here for famines and floods."

Findlay's heart ached to receive this praise, which Indians gave him so constantly. "That's not what either of us is here for, as you know," he said. "Isn't it rather like rubbing it in that we have failed—that we've just been useful, good-natured sorts, instead of men who made you feel that our religion was a burning, living thing?"

"Ah, we manage to fool you, as the Giants fooled Thor. Do you remember how he tried to kill that sleeping fellow, and all that happened was, the sleeper muttered: 'Was that a leaf that fell?' He struck three times with his hammer, and that was all. But when they dismisssed him from their land, the Giants showed him three valleys split asunder by his blows. They had blinded his vision with their enchantments. We've done the same with you. If I were an orthodox Hindu, I should wish that you might never guess the damage you've done."

"You know that I've baptized no one but jungly

folk, in seven years. You know that no student who leaves the College ever becomes a Christian."

"I know that no student who leaves it is anything else! We've no orthodox Hindus left in the district— as they used to count orthodoxy. But why are you still worrying about baptisms? Do you think that Jesus Christ worries about them? Do you think he has that egotism to trouble whether his name is acknowledged or not, if his spirit is accepted and if life and thought are changed? We've had a great activity here by the Ramkrishna Mission. Are they Hindus? Ask Alden and he says: 'Yes—the most troublesome kind.' But ask an orthodox Brahmin from the Mysore, and hear him curse them for half-Christians. Wherever there's an old student of the College, there's a household that's showing kindness and decency to the poor and even to the outcastes. When you came here, every Durga-*puja* there were thousands of goats and buffa- loes killed—hundreds in Kanthala alone. They are offering flowers and sugar-cane now."

"That's the general movement of the age."

"Oh, yes. Yes, of course. But the general move- ment of the age happened to reach us incarnate in an Englishman. Vishnu has had many avatars—but some of us are expecting his next one to be as a football- playing, famine-relief-organizing person in shorts, with a hockey stick for discus and a bicycle for *vahan*. That's the way you have corrupted our good old Hinduism. And we've made a difference to you, too. Confess, missionary. You're half a Vedantist. *Tat tvam asi*—isn't *that* where you're finding the Kingdom of Heaven? Do you remember preaching at the

Lektesvar *mela,* and the Sannyasi who entangled you into the most dreadful heresy?"

Findlay started. "That was you! I wondered where I had heard that voice before. You threw me off my guard when you struck right in with *Findlay*."

But the lethargies of afternoon were claiming Findlay. The Sannyasi's voice was merging with a multitude of dreams that were floating round him, seeking to enwrap him. He threw out incoherent words, but his head sank on the ground. He slept. When he awoke, with a jerk lifting his head from the earth, he found it was evening. There was a pillow beneath his cheek; it was saturated with perspiration, his whole body was dripping. The Sannyasi was still seated on his tiger-mat.

Nilkamal mysteriously appeared with a *lota* of tea and some sweetmeats. Presently Neogyi came, and offered him a lift back in his car. Findlay, knowing it was out of his way, declined.

"I'd rather cycle, really. But thanks, awfully. I'll go along and get hold of my bike now."

"It is under that tree, saheb," said Nilkamal, who had brought it from the village where Findlay had left it.

18

MAY became June; June drew to a rainless close. The monsoon this year crossed the Arabian seas in fitful squalls. That sight in which Indian poets rejoice —of the clouds surging northward, like endless sky-caravans of wild fowl seeking the sacred lakes that lie in the snowy loops of the mighty hills—was refused. Heaven and horizon were a glimmering deception, a fire-mirage, the cruel dance of the rain-dragons in their swamp-mists. Clouds gathered in meagre groups and parcels, making the air dense and insupportable, magnifying the fury of the hidden furnace of the sun; and in and out of them the adders of lightning darted. Eve by eve they lit the world's edges, but rain did not come.

Yet once, by the most heartless jest of all, it seemed to come. There was a day in the last week of June, when the lands were wretched. The ryots, their stores finished, were beginning to break into their borrowed seed-rice. And suddenly, at last, it seemed as if the monsoon had arrived. All day the air was close and gloomy. A tiny fitful breeze whimpered and nosed to and fro, like a dog trapped in a strange garden. Shortly after mid-day, the west darkened; the breeze escaped, the air fell dead. And a solitary wind came running, courier-wise, steadfast and with girt loins, its face set one way. In its wake followed a mightier blast, sweeping before it vast walls of red dust, their front a towering cobra-head of hooded mischief. Alden, peering from his veranda, saw a jackal slinking to cover, his head half averted towards this anger at his heels; birds were scuttling to shelter, the highways were emptying, all the monotonous noises of an Indian summer were stilled, as though their makers dreaded to betray their presence. Men crept out of sight. The glass doors of the Europeans' bungalows were hurriedly shut, and their iron bars drawn. Then the swift, searching lances of the rain fled by. The sky artillery crashed, lightning flooded the air with sheets of vivid flame and rocked through the houses. The roar of thunder deepened. The rain thickened, till an endless mountain of solid water rushed past, so dense that nothing was visible at a furlong's distance.

But this was all. In an hour, the storm had gone. Night fell, noisy with rejoicing clamour, the chorus of frogs whose long Ramadan was over. The white ants swarmed, their battalions came flying into men's homes, where they shed their wings and covered table and floor, fluttered into soup and wines and water, extinguished lamps and candles. The wall-lizards gorged, till they were distended and could eat no more. Every discomfort of the Rains arrived. But none of their benefits.

Day again followed day, torridly, unwinkingly; and day after day the lightning-festival continued, as if the Great God and his goblins were holding celestial revel. But rain was withheld; and the rice sown in the mud of that first shower perished.

19

FINDLAY had been disquieted by his wife's letters during May and June. Marjorie was no better; her mother was breaking under a strain continued beyond her strength. She fretted for her husband's strong assurance and companionship.

He did not dare to look into the recesses of his own thought, and see how much of his happiness had no existence apart from his wife and child; but from time to time a stab of terror, piercing in upon his crowded days, told him. He managed to run up to the hills for a few days, and was frightened to see Marjorie so pale. But she seemed to pick up in the short space that he was there, his wife also was cheered, and he returned feeling a little reassured. After all, they had been pulled very low, and could not be expected to recover immediately; rest must first do its work. Hilda Mannering, who was giving them whatever time she could spare from her sister, promised to let him know if there were any cause for real anxiety; meanwhile they would all do their best together.

He returned to a growing wretchedness that soon drove out every thought but that of itself. The roads were beginning to be lined with living skeletons, wandering processions drifting aimlessly, anywhere, they did not know where. People were migrating to the towns and larger villages; but these held no food. They were like so much human chaff, at the mercy of rumours that fanned them hither, thither. The first day of his return Findlay went into Vishnugram, to consult Douglas and Alden; he ran into Hamar, who told him how, the previous day, when cycling to his court he had had his passage barred by a crowd across the road. When he alighted, very respectfully they informed him that they had had no rain. Would His Honour see to it? His Honour, with no clear idea of what he was to do, said he would "see about it," and with that formula was allowed to proceed. At tennis that day, the sahebs were worried and listless, and hardly bothered to play. Nixon wanted advice, which no one could give. Discontent was increasing and spreading, and unscrupulous forces were exploiting it. The Revolutionary movement had been more active for some time past; arms were being smuggled up the Hugli and the myriad creeks and backwaters of the Sunderbunds; the usual anonymous letters threatening assassination were being received. Various philanthropic bodies, with excellent professions and inadequate means, were distributing relief. Nixon trusted none of them. He became more and more harassed.

Government proclaimed a famine. But before this had been done, Douglas had taken action. The College and Findlay divided up the country between Kanthala and Vishnugram. Douglas outlined the campaign, Alden undertook the begging. With the skill born of practice, the latter indicated the situation in letters to the principal papers, with just the right admixture of details and hard fact with sentiment and art to enlist the practical sympathy of both Europeans and Indians. The response was poor; and it depressed him that so little came from his own community. Ten years ago such need would have brought in generous gifts from great business houses all over India. But the bitterness of the Dyer controversy and of the Non-co-operation troubles smouldered. Indians thought they could run themselves, did they? Well, they should run their own famines. They should find that they were not the only people who could "non-co-operate." A big firm of Scots merchants, who had spent lavishly in the dreadful famine of 1915, even with all the War claims to meet, sent twenty rupees, and a snarling, irrelevant letter. Alden replied temperately, and a further fifty rupees followed, with a semi-apologetic note. But really, the writers asked, why didn't "Mahatma" Gandhi use his great power to make these "fat babus" "cough up"?

However, the College opened relief stations, and

sent its students round the villages, collecting information as to each hut, the number of its inhabitants and
their ability to earn. This distress was going to be
long-continued, and not a pice could be spent whose
spending could be avoided. Alden, at his station Sunday by Sunday doling out each week's wretched supply
of food—hardly what would keep a good horse for
one day—again and again hesitated when a woman
with a baby at her breast came up or an old man
emaciated by years of semi-starvation before ever this
last cruelty befell. "She can work, sir," his student
helper would assure him, answering the question in his
look. And Alden, steeling himself to be pitiless, would
dole out the half-allowance which was all that could
be spared to the quasi-able-bodied. For work had
been started for them, road-making and well-digging.
The College seized the famine as a chance to tap the
underground waters kept by the laterite from good
seasons; and you can see to-day, if you visit the villages to the south-east of Vishnugram, large tanks
whose main ghats are entered past the inscription:
"Dug out of funds collected by the students of Vishnugram Christian College, in the great famine of
1925–26."

Findlay, whose territory marched with the southern confines of the hundred square miles that the
College had taken over, had no such outside resources
as Alden touched through old students. But he took
charge of the Government road-making. He spent
the blazing days cycling from one relief station to
another, examining the piles of broken stones and
testing if they could pass through a two-inch ring,
before the tally cowries were exchanged for the daily

three or four annas that had been earned. As the
famine ran its iron course, some money came in,
chiefly from sympathizers in England, and he was able
to open grain-distributing centres for those incapable
of any work.

Meanwhile the Europeans at Vishnugram were
encouraged by a most unexpected and unseasonable
visitor. The Bishop of Burra Sappur, returning to
Khassoorie from a brief business trip to Calcutta,
remembered—or was reminded—that they had been
without outside spiritual consolation for six years. He
broke his journey for them. Hamar, ungrateful, to
the equally ungrateful Nixon spoke of the loathsome
parades that occurred during the War, whenever an
episcopal descent levied a huge compulsory conformity,
fishes of every shade of belief and of none wriggling
in the meshes of stringent orders from head-quarters.
"Yet was not the net broken." Alden curtly declined
to attend—he had his Sunday work already, with the
famine daily crescent and terrifying. Douglas, too,
was unable to come. So the Bishop preached to Jacks
as the Mission representative, and to Nixon and
Hamar. He took as his subject "Christian Hope,"
and the one memory left by a feeble twitter of plati-
tudes, most of them doubtfully true, was his reiterated
assurance—as he mopped his brows in the cruel heat
of morning—that "the Church in India-h is growing
. . . and-er *growing* . . . and . . . *GROWING.*"
The audience seemed less comforted than they should
have been; Jacks shook his head as the dense blackness
of the heathen mind gloomed before his vision. At the
open doors of the church throughout the service stood
a gaunt, spectral mob, their hands insistently patting

their shrunken bellies. It was hard to preach through
that moan of "Saheb, saheb."

The Bishop meant them well, and we are told that
the spiritual world, unlike the natural, allows no seed
of goodness to be wasted. But he had the feeling, as
he continued his journey, that he had been cultivating
rocky ground. He was a dapper little man and felt the
heat.

20

THE Bishop's visit made Hamar more restless than
ever. Every deed of man was futile, and his own
were the worst mockery of all. He looked about for
some escape from himself, and suddenly Findlay came
into his mind. He had wanted to get to know Findlay; he would like to help him now.

After Hilda's rejection of him, knowledge of her
presence in Vishnugram made his days a wretchedness.
His excuse for cutting every social function was the
necessity of bringing order into a chaotic office; and,
since the line of least resistance was to fling himself
into hard work, he had done this, and had made that
haunt of ancient peace, the judge's court and its
purlieus, a humming disquiet. The white-bearded
seristadar began to wonder whether this saheb were
not madder than others, and in far more vexing
fashion.

Hamar was not a jealous man. But the sight of
even ordinary courtesies between Hilda and other
men—and how dazzling and beautifully friendly were
even her commonest acts of acknowledgment!—made
him miserable. He knew now that his whole life was
staked upon winning her; but he knew, too, in the new

great humility that had come to him, how very much other men possessed that he had not, to draw a woman's admiration and love. Not here, perhaps, in Vishnugram; but the world was wide, even the Indian English world, and this brightness could not be confined for ever to a poky place in the mofussil. She would go to Darjiling, to Calcutta, to Simla, to Kashmir. It was unthinkable that men should not turn to so radiant a loveliness. Well, here she was in Vishnugram; and those to whom she could never be more than the charming comrade of an hour were meeting her in easy, unembarrassed intercourse. He could not; he could not be in her presence without his eyes watching her only, and hers being unhappy with knowledge of this.

So long as he avoided sight of her, his heart-ache was endurable. But the little semblance of peace that he had rested upon a crust so thin that the tiniest sights, and, still more, the most momentary of sounds broke through it. Behind that outward self which was all that he controlled—and how imperfectly!— was an unsleeping, terrible self that was watching and listening—having seen and heard, he would be awake for ever! Especially, the tap of hoofs on the road, even though his ears at once detected the spiritless shuffle of a garron and the drag of lumbering wheels, made his blood leap with vision again of that riverbank and the eager steed goddess-burdened. He saw her body swaying in perfect rhythm and reply to the surging wave of tingling life that carried her, like a flash from some glory seen in a dream of spring-tide, into men's vision and again, in a moment, beyond it. Her eyes were stars trembling on a sea of movement;

her actions were spirit guiding and ruling this world
of matter, yet disentangled, and unclogged by its companion. Even as Akbar begged and fretted for release,
with the soft, wide sands before him, Hamar had
noticed that she could free a hand to brush back a
straying tress. He reflected that the fairest sight our
modern world possesses is one the Greeks never knew
—a beautiful woman riding like a Valkyr—if a Valkyr
could have stooped to the neatness of a habit and the
poise of a side-saddle. But his fears and his ecstasies
were alike imagination. He would not have met her,
even had he mixed with the rest of the station; and
she did not overtake him on any road, except in that
dusk by Gandeswari. And then, one day, he knew
that she had gone—knew what, it seemed to him,
everything knew, the trees and the creatures and the
silent face of the sky, for all had changed. He could
breathe an air which stifled him no longer, and could
move released from tension of eye and ear. But he
felt that his mind, though no longer wildly, fiercely
aching, was scarred and dead.

Neogyi was organizing Government relief measures in the northern parts of the district; and the
College had no lack of helpers both keen and efficient.
Every Bengali is a born nurse, and compassion comes
naturally to the race; and Douglas and Alden could
pick from hundreds of students, and infuse their own
energy and vigilance. So Hamar motored out to
Kanthala, and offered to give Findlay the latter half
of each week. Office work was slight at this time of
the year, and the *seristadar* and his congeners might
let the place go hang, if they chose. Findlay gratefully
accepted the offer.

M

The colleagueship was good for both men. Findlay found Hamar the least of an official of all his tribe that he had ever met; Sannaiyat trenches had knocked a lot of that nonsense out of him. He had a number of annoying tags, the second-hand creed of his service; but he was willing to see another side—anyone's side, in fact—and he did not repeat a fallacy once corrected by experience. And the man *did* work! and seemed quite free from the Englishman's besetting devil in the East, bad temper. He did not blame Indians for circumstances, or consider that they were responsible for their climate or their pests. Findlay thankfully commented on this one evening. Hamar laughed, and added: "Well, if we do curse them for their climate, they sort of ask for it. Aren't they always bragging about their country? Last cold weather my babus gave me a musical entertainment, when I was leaving Suriganj. There was a song that went on interminably, and the whole upshot of every stanza seemed to be a question, 'Searching where will you find such a land?' I asked my file babu the same question a week ago, and he saw it was quite a good joke. I *will* say this for the blighters—they do see a jest, even if it's against themselves."

"That depends on their mood. When patriotism gets to their heads, they see nothing. *Then*—if an angel from heaven came and buttered them up for five hours on end, they wouldn't be grateful but would all rag him for having observed in parenthesis that Madeira has a better climate. An 'insultation to our Mother,' as one of Alden's students remarked, when Rob said the Ganges was a somewhat muddy stream."

And Hamar liked Findlay better with each meet-

ing. He found him shy of generalizations, except in
moods of jesting exaggeration, and he never seemed to
expect to find any barrier of essential difference between East and West. He was sometimes silent, with
his anxious mind elsewhere. But often it was the dry,
parching land itself that absorbed him out of all power
of speech. Hamar most of all enjoyed the walks
across country, when they came to paths impassable
by car. Here his companion's double consciousness
fascinated him. There was the quick surface appreciation of every flitting bird or shaking leaf—Findlay
was almost as aware as the jungle folk of what wild
things had crossed their path before dawn. "See!" the
forest people with them would say, pointing to tracks
barely visible in the grey earth, *"Hural!"* ("wolf") ;
Findlay would nod eagerly and comprehendingly, as
though he had seen it as soon as they, and read its
meaning. Or they would indicate an ant-heap recently
ravaged, the upturned soil showing black, not yet
bleached by the sun. *"Bhalook!"* ("Bear"), Findlay
would interpret their silent look.

All this was new country to Hamar. Higher than
Vishnugram, it lifted itself by passes of a few hundred
feet into companionship with the tiny mountains of the
Orissa border. Yet even these few hundred feet made
a difference, in richer and more luxuriant jungles, after
the polled and stunted sals of Vishnugram. The deeper
nooks were studded with fern clumps, the height of a
man, and feathery pink-tipped plumes of mimosa
walled the ways. "Eminently baghiferous country,"
Findlay assured Hamar; "and we saw this morning
that it is bhalookiferous also." Those *pugs* in the loose
soil furnished abundant proof that he was right; it

was good to feel in the wild at last. The Sonthals, cunningest of the world's bowmen, devastated the jungle populations, and in their big annual shoot, which Findlay always attended, devastation became local massacre of all that flew or crept or climbed. Even so, these jungles could not be utterly desolated, for they were the highway between the forests of Midnapur and those of Orissa. The wild elephants still used it, and tigers sometimes; while leopards lay up in every steep nulla or mango coppice. Jungle-fowl crowed, hares and partridges ran across the track; the good-natured, black, stupid, thick-lipped faces that they met shone out beneath dark, matted hair that peacock feathers crowned.

But all Findlay's delighted awareness of what was passing in the sun-dazzled world without seemed to rest upon another consciousness, an ecstatic absorption too deep to be called thought, a sea too peaceful and profound to throw up many waves of utterance. Hamar had never been with a man who said so little while remaining always companionable. Neither taciturn nor garrulous, he said freely what the mood or moment needed, and then withdrew into some fastness of eternity. His happiness was so steadfast that it attracted his comrade within its scope; and Hamar's mind began to lose some of its disquiet. Though Findlay knew times of racking anxiety for his wife and child, away from him and unwell, the will of God encompassed him with peace, in the desperate need of these others.

Slowly feeling revived, as Hamar faced this elemental misery, a people famishing and a land cracking and gaping in waterless wretchedness. He felt that he and Findlay and the Europeans at Vishnugram had taken up the challenge of Fate itself, and had sworn that no life should perish. Sworn——and, though mind and body broke, their oath should be performed. But their resources were pitifully insufficient. Only by rigid cruelty, by cutting relief down to the least possible allowance, could they save every possible life. A pound of rice given away over and above the amount necessary to keep the recipient barely alive; and another life was lost, by a pound below its required minimum. And all things induced to despair and abandonment of the struggle; the bitter, mocking heats and shrivelled land and air, the expectation of the folk they served. These last, accustomed to Nature's ruthlessness, were inclined to accept it as something to be endured and probably died under, but never to be fought. Alden was luckier; he had some students who came from happier districts, with no long record of defeat to grind them down.

The comradeship between Findlay and Hamar became a deepening friendship. The former, though respecting and liking officials, never took any *rapprochement* very seriously; like most unofficial Englishmen, he had learnt how rigidly the herd ethos rules that hard-working and conscientious class, the I. C. S. In a small station and in a larger centre——such as Calcutta or Shillong (or even a provincial capital like Ranchi)——the covenanted ruler of millions is two different persons. When floods have islanded tiger and sambur and pig on some lessening stretch of silt, the forest lord is tolerant or even courteous. Even so, in a small mofussil town the I. C. S. man is glad to tennis and dine and shoot with missionary or educationist or policeman or coolie-catcher. But his preference is for flocks of his own kind; and when these are at hand, self-respecting outside acquaintances leave him to them.

But Findlay soon realized that Hamar's mind had been loosened from tribal taboos and ritual. He was in the condition of the intelligent heathen who has seen the missionary walk under the Sacred Tree unstruck by lightning, and whose faith has been unsettled to the point that he is ripe for conversion. Rags of his old righteousness still fluttered on his person, and Findlay sometimes had cause to wonder at a bad-tempered smartness picked up in a club or a stock evasion of some problem that called for lonely thinking. But Hamar was shedding these impedimenta.

The last time he dodged a problem by using a cliché was one day when Alden turned up with a letter from his sister-in-law.

"Hilda has written," said Alden. "She's worrying about these folk here. Says she'd never have gone away if she'd known this famine was coming. That's all rot, of course; she's gone, not simply for her own sake, but because my wife wants her. But she's fussing to come back. You see—before she went away she used to get about the villages a lot, and the people sort of got hold of her. They do, you know; you can't curse them if you know them at first hand. What do you think, Findlay? There isn't much that she could do. And one wouldn't like any woman to have to face this vile weather."

Hamar interrupted. "You mustn't let her come. It would kill her. She'd insist on slaving all day, in this furnace, and she'd break down. This is drayhorse work, not thoroughbred's. For God's sake, Alden, don't let her do it!"

Findlay had been, to his own great surprise, wondering. Was it wise that our better-class women should be so scrupulously sheltered from rigours that Indian women endured year after year? Women with children, yes. He knew that there were plenty of women, wives of minor officials with poor salaries or of missionaries, who spent the summers on the plains. But the women who make such "society" as India can manage to produce, and whose idle shallow opinions presently drift into the corresponding stratum of thought in England? He wondered how much of the poisoning of the world's thinking comes from the idleness and ease of sheltered women, especially young women.

But at Hamar's impetuous words he shelved these blasphemies hurriedly. "Hamar's right," he said. "She mustn't come."

"I think so, too," said Alden, more doubtfully. "But you know the sort she is. No one has ever managed to stop her from doing anything she wanted, unless he could prove to her that it hurt someone else."

"What! let her kill herself for a lot of black people!" cried Hamar. "And there isn't one of them who knows what gratitude is! You can slave and slave—and they just go on cursing you!"

It was the first time since his return to India that Hamar had used such a term as "black people." His companions exchanged looks, Findlay of surprise, Alden of indignation. The latter spoke.

"We seem hipped on the subject of the gratitude we ought to get from India. There's Headley, who

ought to know better—who generally does know better
—last St. Andrew's Day almost sobbing about the lack
of reward that good work gets here. Hang it all! He's
K.C.I.E., isn't he? and will be K.C.S.I. And has a
bigger salary than the Prime Minister of Great Britain
gets, and will retire on a pension of what?—£2000 a
year? And in addition"—Alden flung up his hands in
disgust—"he wants to have a whole nation grovelling
before him, and intoning: 'We humbly thank Your
Honour for condescending to come and have so distinguished a career among us.' " Alden's imitation
of the Bishop of Burra Sappur was excellent.

"Well, but look what we've done for them!"

Alden interrupted him. "Yes, do look! Only look
with your own eyes, and not with the spectacles that
have been handed down from one generation of Anglo-
Indians to another. Do a course of history—*honest*
history, if you can find it anywhere, and not the nause-
ating tripe that our people grind out. Oh, shut up,
John! I'm angry, and I'm going to get my say said."
He waved away Findlay's attempt to check his fiery
comminations. "And then do another of Indian
thought, damnably dull though it is. You'll be
ashamed then, to say what every jutewalla says. Good
Lord! after Headley's speech there wasn't a single
Dundee-Dumdum merchant who got up to speak, who
wasn't weeping with whisky and self-pity—all because
Indians were giving him so little *gratitude* for choosing
to be a millionaire at *their* expense, instead of some
other people's. And then, next day, our beastly papers
publish the spectacle for a whole province to see!
And, lest they miss it, write fatuous leaders on it!"

Hamar said doggedly: "All the same, no Indian knows what gratitude is."

It was a truism in his service, that Indians were a constitutionally thankless race.

Alden looked at him resentfully; it was the first time that Hamar had seen him out of temper. "Cut it out, Hamar; and continue being a decent chap, and not just an official. Indians know *exactly* how much an Englishman's worth; the recording angel's books aren't kept more punctiliously. You get a sight more gratitude here than you do in England. I'd like to run across Lloyd George or Ramsay MacDonald or Baldwin or——"

"Any old political bloke," laughed Findlay. "Rob, Rob, my boy, you'll have a stroke if you get so excited in this weather. Let me fan you."

But Alden had not finished. "——In their after-dinner moods; and hear them sob and sigh and break down weeping, because of the little gratitude their unselfish labours have called forth. Ah! let's hope they've most of them got more sense. I'm sick of the word gratitude. The world pays us while we are alive, and some part of it subscribes for a tombstone to cover us decently out of sight when we're dead. What more do you want? All right, Findlay, I'll tell Hilda *you* say, and *I* say, that we won't have her here at any price."

Findlay drew Alden aside. "You mustn't think that Hamar really feels that way."

"Well, why the deuce does he talk that way, then? I thought better of him. If a man goes on talking nonsense, he jolly soon *thinks* nonsense."

"Don't they all talk that way? But *he* doesn't,

anyway. I can't find words for what I think of him.
He's first-rate—in *every* way. I mean it, Rob. There's
been no trouble too great for him to take for these
folk."

"Oh, I can believe *that*," Alden grumblingly conceded. "It isn't in their *actions* that our folk come
down. You can rely on the average saheb to do his
job till he drops. He doesn't blather about his high
ideals—he leaves that to our official propagandists at
home. And to our own newspapers out here. Madness doesn't take the Englishman that way. *But he
carries his ideals out!* They call me anti-British. If
my countrymen knew what I think of them—I could
worship the ordinary saheb for his decency and genuineness! Only, only, only"—his long arms shot up in
despair, a gesture not lost on Hamar, watching and
unhappy—"when our *actions* are so decent and so
honourable, why—why—*why*—do we always talk as
if we were half cad, half imbecile?"

"Hamar doesn't. He's never talked like this before
—not once. No man could be more patient, more
good-tempered, more courteous, than he has been—
with *everyone*."

"Oh, all right, all right! But don't let him get a
touch of sun again."

And Alden strode over to Hamar.

"Good-bye, Hamar. I must be getting back now."

"I say, Alden. You mustn't misunderstand what I
said about Indians not showing gratitude."

"That's quite all right. Findlay has explained to
me that you were pulling my leg."

As Alden cycled off, Hamar turned to Findlay.

"What *did* you tell him?"

Findlay told him.

Hamar went very red. "I'd hate it to get back to Mrs. Alden, through Miss Mannering, that I said what Alden thinks I said."

"Don't worry. Rob isn't that sort. Once a breeze is over, he finds every sort of excuse for the other man, and blames himself for a hasty idiot."

"What I meant—and what I feel—is"—Hamar spoke slowly and defiantly—"if a hair of Miss Mannering's head suffered because of anything she did—for anybody—no amount of gratitude could be adequate."

"That," said Findlay, laughing as he looked curiously at him, "is a more understandable statement than the one you did make, and you've made it with commendable clearness. And you would not find many men who knew Hilda Mannering quarrel with it."

21

MEANWHILE proof accumulated that discontent was fishing in the troubled waters of famine. The community was thrilling with excitement, winds of some mysterious terror were making men's minds a shaking grove. The End of the Age was at hand, and Hara Deva the Destroyer was about to appear. Nixon, scanning his reports and seeking for some focus to all this wide-winging rumour, some place to search for a definite foe to strike at, settled on Trisunia.

This was a hill that outcropped from the thickest of the wilderness on the Orissa borders, and humped itself to a height of a thousand feet above the surrounding plain. It was a good fifteen miles from

Findlay's bungalow, and a favourite haunt of his whenever his wanderings brought him near it. However
weary his limbs or however late the hour, he found
his way to its summit, and rested there.

It was a characteristic enough hill, one of many
thousands, of every height from twenty feet up to
several thousand, that are scattered over India. You
may see them from the train, as you go through Central India or the jungles of Chota Nagpur or Orissa.
They stud the Mysore plateau, they sprinkle the
Madras plain; they rise everywhere from the thorn-
pampas of Rajputana. When the volcanoes were
lighting vast sheets of shallow ocean or the huge
rivers were silting those sheets up with soil filched from
Himalayan peaks and gullies, these rocks were there,
blazing and smouldering. The geologist finds no fos-
sils in them. The temples of post-Aryan India seem
alien, an annoying excrescence of yesterday.

Round Trisunia's base ran a forest belt, for each
of these hills must have its terai, even as its mighty
kindred of Himalaya. The way upward through this
belt was by stony watercourses, a stair thrust through
overcanopying greenness. Half a mile from the summit, the forest ceased suddenly, giving way to a tiny
prairie of prickly, insidious grass, a torment to the
flesh and certain to insert itself into any boot or sock.
The "road" skirted this prairie till the top was reached,
a level place where trees reappeared, noble groves of
wild mango and teak. Here was a fountain, some
dozen yards below the actual highest point, a flow of
perennial water tumbling through the lips of a stone
lion, and then running underground to the hill-foot.
Facing this lion, which was a recent embellishment,

stood another stone figure, aged and mossy, a crude
lion with paws folded under its chin, upright and facing
the fountain. Its predecessors, idols that had had
their day and had fallen, lay in the tangles of the
neighbouring thicks.

There was always, even in the hottest day, a cool
inner core to the airs that blew on Trisunia's summit;
and its silence and majesty were the peacefullest thing
in the world. The fountain's water was pure and
considered sacred; mothers brought their children
here, to bathe them on the great day of Holi festival,
when the whole sunrise-fronting slope of the mountain
was a fire of *palas* blossom. But during the rest of
the year the place was deserted; and that grim animis-
tic idol—its head, crowned always with faded marigolds, slumbering upon its stone paws—seemed to say:
"Before Siva and Vishnu were, I am." Man's spirit,
facing the wilderness, with its lurking death and mystery of life ever renewing itself, had fashioned this
expression for the Power that was there.

Findlay, hearing the rumours flying from this hill
as their centre, wondered whether some haunt of mischief might not shelter there. He knew its caves and
copses. Most of all, he knew its fountain. Often,
tired in the dusk of a hopeless day of toil, he had sat
by that falling coolness till its music had cleansed his
spirit, and the soughing branches of the forest had
shaken down their own peacefulness. He remembered
one evening when he had passed through the village of
Hatna, at the hill's base, at an hour when a Vaishnava
singing-party were engaged in a "twenty-four hours";
a superstitious Government clerk, who had retired
from service and settled here, had employed them to

heap up merit for him, by an all-night and all-day clash of cymbals and imbecile skipping and calling of the names of Radha Govinda. Findlay the Christian caught the gaze of an Indian Vedantist whom he knew; unconsciously they exchanged the scorn both felt for the hired ecstasies of unthinking religion. He had gone his way up the hill, and sat down by the fountain. Dusk was about him, and the first stars and fireflies were shining. The noise of the worshippers came faintly from far away, as he climbed the track, and then the distance blotted it out, except for occasional gusts of exceptional fervour. He remembered how pagan his thoughts had been, and yet how comforting. That absurd idol! Here persisted a worship whose roots were twined with the very rocks of this ancient land, a worship that had been before the praise of Krishna and his Mistress, before the cults of Kali and her Consort, a worship that still raised its head above them, a towering paramount. He called to mind the wood-worships of his own ancestors—he thought of Easter the spring-queen, whose offering, the egg that is the symbol of all life, is still brought year by year, in the supreme festival of the religion that has supplanted hers. Once it was given to the goddess of opening leaves and lives, now it is offered to little children—an innocent happiness surviving down the ages! So, one day, the faith of the carpenter's apprentice who loved the uplands and oak coppices of Galilee and the winds that were caresses from the Love that abides with the heart that trusts it, even until death, though that death be the death of the cross—that faith, Findlay dreamed, would sanctify this tumbling water, the joyful crowds, the yearly festival. Yes, even the marigolds could be kept; they should garland children. And no one should lift an ax against these trees. He would be sorry to see even the stone idol vanish. Must it go? It was a carven symbol of the Power that roamed the forest and from out the spongy breast of the mountain flung this gift of sweet, pure water——

    Gaunt simulacrum—ghost forlorn——
    Grey exile!

Findlay could almost imagine the divine Carpenter Himself resting beside the image, and looking down on the plains where they winked, as if dazzled by the great heats—looking on the homes where men, His brethren, lived out their swift-flickering lives. Or would He have sternly thrust it to the ground? "Every plant which My heavenly Father hath not planted shall be rooted up." Well, but the heavenly Father *had* planted this; it was man's earliest expression of his sense that the woodland had a *numen,* it represented knowledge that must have burst upon his childish spirit, bowing it with awe and humility. There was nothing here of the unclean ecstasies of Vaishnava worship, where men swayed in meaningless excitement and danced through days and nights till they fell in swoon. Findlay had been through the Sonthals' all-night worship of the Power of the Harvest, and had seen how its comparative innocence was bespattered and fouled by an intruding Hindu world; here had been the full moon, glorious in the soft sky of autumn, and beneath its rays the jungle women, their tresses bright with leafy branches and peacock feathers, dancing in crescent—and there was a Hindu ascetic with blood-ghastly face, leering drunk and drugged, with a knife through his out-thrust tongue. He shuddered at the remembrance, and glanced at the stone lion. No obscenities clustered round this form; the superb Indian moons, shining on its tranquil head, dappled a wilderness deserted of men. The blood-stained cults of Hinduism had not annexed it. At the hill's foot was the grove of the demon-queen Padalsini, almost as old as this grim king; she was now a minor manifestation of Kali and was worshipped with blood of goats. The village Brahmins had flung their crimson skirt of adoption over the jungle waif, and made her part of their cruel pantheon. But the lion statue of Trisunia remained what it had always been, a childish toy, the central pillar in the vast woodland nursery where these simple folk revelled and played amid the fragrances and splendours of their flitting springtide.

22

IF YOU crossed Trisunia's summit, and began the northern descent, you reached a rocky surface pitted with caves and cracks. This was a great haunt of bears aforetime; but one Ooeelkins Saheb (Wilkins Saheb), a Vishnugram police superintendent of twenty years ago, had killed them off. Now only an occasional pair took up temporary residence, to be shot by some prowling European, when the next spring festival published news of their presence.

One of the caves went deep into the hill. No one had ever been interested or hardy enough to explore it. Its mouth was matted with creepers and the dark-spotted pink flowers of the tiger's claws, the dwarf shrub with sharp, gripping talons. The rocks at its entrance harboured Russell's vipers—you were watching a mottled piece of rock and soil, and suddenly it would develop sluggish, sullen movement. It was from the unknown heart of this cave that Hara Deva the Destroyer was now roaring. Terrified crowds had heard him, at the spring festival; but the rumour had died away, only to be revived tenfold as the miseries of famine grew to their height. Far over the plains his voice boomed. Nor was this all. At night the wings of impending destruction whirred through vast tracts of sky, where fires flashed.

Hamar had almost persuaded himself that his educated Indian friends were free from "superstition." He did not take the rumours seriously; there were so many rumours. But one morning Nixon dropped in at his office.

"About this roaring stuff," he said. "You know, the whole community's gone dotty. I wish you'd get hold of Alden or Douglas, and find out what they think. Could you bring Alden round this evening? We've got to find out something about it."

Hamar called up his chief clerk; from force of habit and curiosity to know what sahebs were discussing, the *seristadar* rolled up with him. Hamar questioned them. They looked at each other, an essential preliminary before any reply could be vouchsafed.

No, the chief clerk had not heard the roaring himself. Neither had the *seristadar*. But both knew people who had—yes, lots of people. "Oh, sir, he is roaring like a bull of Bashan," the chief clerk twittered. The *seristadar* shook his head gravely. A good Mussulman, yet he knew, as his co-religionists knew, that

N

these demons of the heathen had their power. The Mohammedanism of Bengal is half Hinduism.

Alden and Hamar were at Nixon's that evening.

"What do your police think?" Alden asked.

"They? Why, the Great God Siva is kicking up a shindy, of course. The affair holds no sort of problem to their minds. They've even found a satisfactory reason for his playing the fool now."

"What's that?"

"The usual kind. Finance. He's peevish because his pension was stopped. A century ago, when John Company sent regular tribute to Juggernaut and Saugur Island, a bullock-load of trash used to be sent to this Trisunia place, and fifty dibs as well. The place was more important then; and a lot of these Saivite priests made out a claim for its being a shrine of their own particular chap."

"Don't you think the roaring is all just imagination?" asked Hamar, vaguely feeling back to psychological theories, he did not know what theories. "One or two cute lads start a yarn, and frighten the others with it, till every fool imagines he has heard the bellowing? One has heard, and all the deaf will hear."

"No, I don't. It's not imagination. Something *is* bellowing, especially at night. I'll tell you another thing that's happened, that worries me. A fortnight ago, my police report, some *bhadralog* whom no one in the village knew brought a dead body and burned it at Hatna. They were youngsters, not much older than Alden's students. The man they burned had died of snake-bite, they reported. My sub-inspector thinks they were camping somewhere on the hill, and got caught there."

"You don't think the snake-bite was a yarn?" Alden asked, remembering how many cases of manslaughter and murder that explanation covers, in a land where post-mortems are few and the dead are soon ashes.

"My people don't think so. They saw the body, and it had been bitten right enough. But it was jolly bold, to fetch the corpse in like that."

"Ye-es. But how could they help it? A pyre on Trisunia, at this time of year, would set the whole hill ablaze."

"I'm going to raid those damned caves. But I'd like to have some theory first of what's happening."

"A few hefty chaps revelling under the midnight stars," Alden suggested light-heartedly.

"Don't be funny. Besides, it's not that sort of noise. It's pukka roaring. And please don't suggest that a tame tiger is employed to do it. I'm too worried to take it kindly."

"That tiger reminds me," said Alden, who wanted time to think. "I met a saheb at Burdwan the other day who said he and some pals had *khubber* of bears at Trisunia—he got the name wrong, but that was the place he meant—and were going to get out there and shoot them if we once got a spot of rain and some coolish weather."

"Bears?"

"Oh, the people who started the roaring stunt have set this yarn going also, to frighten off investigators. I saw Findlay last week, and he knows nothing about it. It's a silly trick; these chaps always make some sort of bloomer. It's just the yarn to fetch a whole mob of sahebs down on them, all armed and with tiffin baskets. As you know, everybody's got a gun nowadays; and every youngster comes out to India with the notion that it's packed stiff with shootable things, whereas there's nixes in the jungles, bar jackals. Why, last Easter, after a driver reported that he had heard a partridge calling when his train was at Nabekganj, next Sunday there wasn't a saheb under eighty left in Calcutta. They had to cancel the church services, because the clergy and other non-combatants were needed to run the dozen special trains that they put on."

Nixon looked at Alden with justifiable disgust. Then he picked out the sound nugget of sense that underlay the rubble of extravagance. "I suppose *khubber* of bears *will* mean a lot of fellows up from Calcutta."

"Bound to. Now or later. Remember how the tiger fetched them last year?"

"Why can't these shopwallas stick where they are?" asked Nixon resentfully. "They've no call to come shooting *our* bears. However"—with a sigh—"this isn't getting us any forrarder with the roaring question."

Alden thought hard. Then he said: "I read something some time ago, about what seditionists had been doing in the Philippines. It seems they had a cave of sorts there also; and they fixed it up with a whopping megaphone. It was a place with magnificent echoes."

Nixon regarded him with admiration and gratitude. "Alden, when you chuck trying to be funny, you're as useful a man as any I know." Alden bowed his acknowledgments. "I believe you've got it. I'll have the blasted thing out. I'll get an elephant, and

send one of my constables down the bazaar, bleating
through the thing. These fellows are cute, though!
They're not above taking a hint from any part of the
world."

"March of science, march of science," said Alden.
"There was a missionary telling me last year how he
went to a jungly hamlet and offered them a magic-
lantern show, thinking he was bringing them a great
treat. They shook their heads, and said, 'Magic lantern no good. We want bioscope.'"

"But it isn't only bellowing that has made the folk
crazy." Hamar spoke at last. "What's all this about
fire in the sky, and whirring wings?"

"A slight expenditure on rockets?" Alden was
fatuous again.

"No," said Nixon. "Even in the jungliest parts
they've heard about rockets. And seen them, when
we've had a tamasha on at Vishnugram."

"Could they get hold of an aeroplane?" asked
Hamar.

Nixon stopped at the suggestion. "I don't see how
they could," he said slowly. "But they can manage most
kinds of devilry, if the notion takes them. But
where'd they find the folk to fly it?"

"Couldn't they send some of their fellows to Japan,
to pick up instruction there?"

"The Jap Government wouldn't allow it. But they
could do it in China—or Russia. That's what's happened," said Nixon, with conviction. "And that
explains a lot of things that have been puzzling people. You remember when those fellows were flying
round the world, a couple of months back? They were
heard one night, flying over a tract of country where

they weren't expected to come. There was a correspondence about it, and the papers decided it was a wonderful example of the clearness of the Indian atmosphere—you could hear a sound scores of miles away. But the flying chaps said they weren't in the air at the time, and never went anywhere near where the row was heard. The mystery was never cleared up."

"Anyway," asked Hamar, "what's at the bottom of the whole business?"

Nixon looked doubtfully at Alden, who looked back, for all the world as if they were the clerk and the *seristadar*. Alden spoke, hesitatingly. "As far as the noises go, foolery, I expect. I shouldn't think there's much to watch at Trisunia. It's like a conjurer and his assistants. They do you down because you keep your eyes on the wrong man, the one who's ostensibly doing the trick but who's really only a bit of living eye-wash. I don't think these bellowings and fires will go on much longer. They'll be afraid of Nixon dropping on them suddenly, and their whole show being given away. They've already attained their purpose, in setting the whole district on the seethe."

"Alden's right," said Nixon. "If I'm to catch them, I've got to raid that cave sharp."

"And if you raid it, you're no nearer the real trouble."

"What's that?"

"Has that aeroplane been heard lately?"

"No. Why?"

"You won't hear it again. Remember what these

people have been saying. Hara Deva is going to end the Age by raining destruction from the sky."

"You don't think——" Nixon stopped short. The suggestion was too terrible to entertain.

"It was merely a possibility that crossed my mind. I wouldn't take it too seriously. But you can't rule it out altogether; there are some of these folk who wouldn't stick at anything or at any expenditure of life. And—*if* there's an aeroplane—of course, it's only a guess that there is—then you *can* have bombs rained down from the sky. That would be the destruction foretold."

"My God!" said Nixon.

"But why isn't the plane going to be heard any more?" asked Hamar.

"Because they're not going to risk its being caught by a Government plane, once we spot what it is."

"Then where is it now?"

"Lying in some clearing in the wildest jungle of Orissa—or Chota Nagpur. Or Central India. Covered with green canvas," Alden suggested.

Nixon's eyes shone. "If I could only catch the beggars! If I knew the lingo as you and Findlay do! Alden, can't you pretend to be going to the hills, and then slip away in babu kit and find out what people are saying? It's the chance of a lifetime!"

Alden laughed. "There isn't an Englishman in India who could do it. Probably never has been. It's only in our lady novelists' imagination that these things get done."

But Hamar was not willing, any more than Nixon,

to part with an old favourite legend of his people. "What about that Mutiny chap?" he asked. "The one who disguised himself and slipped out of Lucknow?"

"He wasn't a pure-blood saheb. Besides, Nixon, it's not a job I could take on. I'm out to stop blood-shed and violence, and I'll do anything I decently can. But you can't ask me to spy on these people."

But where that aeroplane was—or if it were an aeroplane—was never discovered. As Alden pre-dicted, the "manifestations" ceased suddenly. Nixon and his police raided the cave on a day of unspeakable heat and misery, and found nothing for their pains. They spent the morning hacking away the herbage at the entrance, only to discover when once inside that there was an easy way to an unsuspected opening else-where. They killed a dozen *karaits* and Russell's vipers, and had as many more scares and narrow escapes; and twice stones that hurt uncommonly tum-bled on Nixon's back. In neither case did he believe the dislodgment was accidental; and he heard—or fancied he heard—laughter in the dense jungle near by. He was badly bruised, both in body and temper.

They entered the cave at last, cautiously and with loaded revolvers. It rose abruptly into an inner chamber with a lofty roof. A shaft had been pierced from the hill-summit above, for ventilation; and, as I have said, there was an easy way out to an opening in an unpathed tract of the forest. There had been cooking and sleeping and habitation in the cave. This they discovered, beyond a peradventure; but the rest was guess-work. The real discovery was made unex-pectedly, and in an unexpected place.

23

LATE in August Alden was summoned to Darjiling, just as the unsatisfactory weather at last showed signs of breaking. A *badal* swept rapidly up the Bay, and a spate and incredible fury of rain overwhelmed the land. For three days and nights it poured without slackening. On the fourth morning Hamar, looking from his veranda as dawn was spreading, clear at length, saw Nixon in gum-boots wading through a river that splashed and squelched round his feet. Nixon came nearer, and explained that he was "out for a squirm across the marshes." He had been cooped indoors by this infernal weather, and felt he *must* get out. He invited Hamar to join him.

It was rather fun, guessing at one's footing and staggering through swamps. Hamar was reminded of Tigris banks after the winter rains had slaked the bitumen into a gummy slush. He told Nixon of an evening when it had taken him twenty minutes to do a hundred yards of embankment, a progress embarrassed by several full-length falls. "You must have been pretty thoroughly blotto," said Nixon. It was not a brilliant joke, but they both laughed heartily. It was jolly to be out again, even with this mess underfoot.

Once the jungle was reached, the land lifted slightly and was already draining. They pushed ahead faster, and soon came to the first of the broken temples. This was a mango-hidden enclosure, with steep mounds to its north-east; at the foot of these mounds, and in the courtyard, stood a stone chariot containing effigies of Radha and Krishna. As they came to it, to their surprise the chariot, supposedly a fixture through centuries, had been shifted aside; beneath it a flight of steps ran down into the earth. The water was pouring down this, and half a dozen Bengalis were toiling on it, removing boxes. At sight of the police saheb panic seized them, and they bolted. The Englishmen rushed forward.

"Well, I'm damned!" said Nixon. "Those were *bhadralog*. What the devil were *they* doing coolie work for? Some of Alden's precious lambs, I'll take my oath."

It was Nixon's fixed belief, if he came across any action, word, or even look that he did not like in an Indian, that the offender, whatever his age or appearance, was one of the College students.

He was excitedly examining the boxes when a movement in the bushes caught his attention. He jumped from his stooping position, a moment before a revolver bullet struck the ground. A fraction of a second earlier it would have pierced his brain. He leapt behind the chariot, dragging Hamar with him.

"Ass that I am!" he said, "to go out in these days without a gun of any sort! They'll just perforate us through this nice stone trellis. We're trapped. Better run for it, Hamar."

"Right-oh. But let me make a diversion first."

An old self, purely animal and trained to sharp, instinctive senses, awoke in Hamar. As to Hobbs or Jessop it is one unthinking action to gather and to return the ball, so once upon a time, when he had skulked in scars and ditches of the earth, his brain had been quicker, untroubled by any of the complex nonsense of civilized life. He now stooped swiftly and picked up a shattered nubble of chariot, that must have weighed several pounds. He tossed it from their shelter, lobbing it like a Mills bomb. His hand had not forgotten its war cunning, and the missile dropped close enough to the revolver's owner, or to some companion of his, to cause an exclamation.

Then the Englishmen ran for it. Both were reasonably athletic men; their action was unexpected and had this additional advantage, that their pursuers were anxious not to expose themselves to any chance of recognition. They would have shot the sahebs down cheerfully, if it would cover the evidence of their activities. But unnecessary murder would not help their plans.

"They won't bother about us now," said Nixon. He had guided Hamar away from the cover that his reviving war-self would have sought, into the open. They raced, as far as gum-boots permitted, towards the road.

"Still, hadn't we better keep moving?" asked Hamar. "From all that I have gathered, the grand old Hindu doctrine of *ahimsa* hasn't a very firm grip of revolutionary Bengal."

"Yes, we'll hustle. But if they want they can easily run us down in these beastly things. They are barefoot, as you saw."

"What's our next move?"

"*Yours* is to sit tight. You didn't recognize any of them? No more did I. One babu's exactly like another, especially when they're young. Well, you'll have to try the case when we catch these fellows; and the Swadeshi press will make the usual outcry about the judge being prejudiced, if you've been back with me when I raid the place. You're compromised enough as it is, by what you've seen this morning." Nixon chuckled. "My hat, but they'll be sweating removing whatever stuff they have there! They haven't any time to waste on the pleasures of the chase. They know I'll be back in an hour."

He was back in less; and he and his police raided the place very thoroughly. It took the best part of two days to clear out what they found in the flooded chambers beneath the temple. A good deal had already gone when they arrived; but what remained was the largest store of small arms ever confiscated from the revolutionary party. Nixon reported results to Hamar, the first evening.

"There must be thousands and thousands of pounds' worth of revolvers and ammunition. They've got stands of rifles, too, though not so many rifles as revolvers. There's at least a couple of hundred live bombs and hand grenades, all fully detonated, and thousands of springs and bomb parts. There must have been an aeroplane somewhere in the offing, as part of the scheme. It was the ammunition and bombs that those chaps were busy removing this morning. A lot has gone west, waterlogged. They had it mostly on shelves and stands, too; hard luck for them, this sudden Mississippi weltering down the stairs. And to think that the whole thing was being done under our very noses! While I've been watching the desolate wastes and putting a tooth-comb through bushes where there was nothing but a lizard or two, they've had the time of their lives, watching *me*! And all that cave-bellowing was just their fun, and a red herring for me!"

Nixon thought a minute; then a new light burst upon his view of the Indian situation.

"I've got to smash these chaps, of course; and they're devils out for bloodshed. But you know, you can't wonder that any kid with any spunk prefers this game to being a tame clerk and saying, '*Achchha,* saheb' for the rest of his days. It takes some pluck to handle all those things we found to-day. And think of it, Hamar! Imagine yourself a young Indian! And you know every inch of this land, and you feel you can fool these sahebs and tie them up in its jungles, and have them in a fog all the time, because they *don't* know things, don't know what the folk think or feel, don't know *anything*! You'd want to take a hand in the movement!"

Yes, Hamar thought; and he felt the pulse of wild excitement and hatred, the excitement greater than the hatred, but both great, that was knitting the educated classes together. No doubt Hindu and Mussulman had their quarrels; and, whenever a communal riot broke out, and they slew one another, the British press, in India and in England, gloatingly pointed the moral— they *could* not work in unity, they were still far from self-government. And every Anglo-Indian colonel and every ex-Bombay-merchant now in the House of Commons would repeat the stale old yarn of what Pertab Singh had said—or had not said—that within twenty-four hours of our abdicating power there would not be a cowrie or a virgin in Bengal or Bombay or—anywhere except the Sikh country and Rajputana. But to man it is the voice of the present that is loud, the future only whispers. Hindus and Mussulmans would

quarrel after we were gone, and they quarrelled now.
But what did we know of systems in whose interaction
we bore no part? Nothing. Nothing whatever. The
people of the land understood them. Once before, in
the Mutiny, hatred had built a bridge above their
differences. Could that *never* happen again? Officially,
and loudly, our papers said no. But were we so sure
of this, privately?

He imagined himself, young and an Indian, sensitive
to that point which to us seems sheerly maudlin,
touched to hot tears by any song which spoke of the
land as "Mother"; and he was wandering in the wildly
beautiful desolation which Hilda Mannering had made
eternally lovely for him. Here might an Indian have
seen—or imagined that he saw—some lady of his own
land, slender and exquisite, standing framed in the
greenwood of sal and *siris* and drooping tamarind.
Here might he have visualized the *Bana-Lakshmi,* the
"Forest-Queen," riding through her paradise, as
Indian queens had done aforetime—the Rani of
Jhansi whom our bullets slew in battle, or that Moslem
lady who for seven years ruled and led her armies.

And, if an Indian once were caught in the wide web
of intrigue and left for ever the shallow, dishonest
folly that we called education and the bitter struggle
for the tiny prizes of official service, and if he came
to some waste place as the sun was setting—or in the
glory of the passionate dawn—how could he help feeling that the landscape was a living creature, appealing
to her sons for liberation? Aliens were "civilizing" her
beauty, they had brought in mills and factories and
heavy, squat, white buildings; they had no homes here,

they merely ruled and criticized and had their pleasure and went away. They did not care to understand, they did not love or praise or feel happiness.

24

IT WAS some time before any arrests were made. But from the first it was clear that the plot was widespread. The Anglo-Indian press was sure that Moscow had financed and run the whole show. The Indian extremist press favoured the theory of a got-up affair; Government had hidden the weapons, and then sent two Europeans to make the alleged "discovery." Otherwise, why were no Indian officials present on the occasion?

Both sides were equally indignant, when it was known that Hamar was going to try the case, after the preliminary inquiry before the district magistrate was over. The Europeans went so far as to send home a formal protest. The Indians had meetings in Calcutta squares and on the Maidan. The magnitude of the preparations unmasked awed and delighted the nationalist subconscious soul. "Hero," a word generously used in the recent literature of the province—though perhaps not more so than in any other centre of perfervid patriotism, from China to Peru—tumbled through pages of happy and excited journalism.

Headley set his jaw against both agitations. He ran up to Vishnugram "on other business," and saw both Hamar and Nixon.

"I see the *Britisher* suggests that you're bound to let these anarchists off, as you did on a former deplorable occasion," he told Hamar, with a grin. "I've sent the editor a chit, with my compliments, warning him that he's sailing very near the wind for contempt of court. The same notion had already struck our friends of the opposition. The *Subrita* had a leader, the same day as the Secretariat chit was delivered, asking why a Government paper—for so the editor is pleased, facetiously, to refer to the *Chowringhee Wobbler*—is allowed to take it for granted that innocent victims of a police plot are guilty, when the trial hasn't even begun. So what's to do, Hamar, my boy? The enemy object to your being judge because you saw some of the stuff actually there. Well? It's not disputed that it *was* there. And it won't hold water that you and Nixon manhandled some lorry-loads of heavy explosive, packed it, and then suborned certain base fellows of the lewder sort to start heaving it out again, and in filthy weather. I'm not going to be bounced, either by the enemy or our own silly rags."

"Quite right," said Nixon. "It's Hamar's pigeon."

"Precisely. And we know he'll pluck it honestly and intelligently, though it's a beastly bird. Providence has been good to you, Hamar; it's given you your chance back. You'll be straight, I know. The only thing"—Headley looked at him musingly—"you are the sort of chap whose danger is to be *too* straight. Don't be too afraid of seeming to do the obvious thing."

"And what's that?"

"Jail some of these fellows. *Some*one's guilty, this time!"

Hamar frowned. He knew that nice questions of ethics were not much in Headley's line. Headley was an administrator pure and simple; he shone in summary justice. He had been a wonderful prefect at his public school; and he would have been an ornament of the services in Henry the Eighth's time or—to take India—in Akbar's. Unfortunately, his day was passing. It might still be all right in your own compound, where you could turn a corner unexpectedly and catch your *gowalla* with his clarty fingers *inside* the milk-pot that he was carrying. You clouted his head before he had time to duck. Or you found your *sais* in the very act of pinching the horse-feed, and you booted him. That was justice, and it was over in a second. All this weighing of evidence—of one lie against another lie, rather—this jury and assessor business, Headley maintained, was just rot. It wasn't suited to the East. But you had to go by it, since it was the law of the damned country now. What fools we had been ever to introduce it! Or the "so-called Reforms" and all these Legislative Assemblies! Headly had gone in "at the deep end" when dyarchy was established.

Hamar felt unhappy. He loved Headley, as everyone did, and yet he knew that truth—or doing one's job—was a greater friend than Plato. He said morosely: "Ye-es. But I've got to be sure that it's the fellows who are alleged to have been caught."

"Oh, of course," said Headley. "That was what I meant."

"Either way," mused Hamar, "I'm going to get it in the neck. If I find any of the accused guilty, it'll be because the uproar about that wretched Lambertgarh business has put the wind up me. If I acquit them, it's because I'm an anti-British rotter and a humbug, the friend of every set but my own."

o

25

H ILDA at Darjiling wondered if there were any country where it was so useless and ineffective to be a woman—at any rate, an English woman. She found Alden's letters to his wife of absorbing, tormenting interest. The men she knew were busy all day, and every day, in work that was steadily, inexorably, building their minds away from hers; these letters recorded a life they would not let her share. And then came the head-lines in the paper, "Gigantic Revolutionary Conspiracy in Mofussil." She was out of doors when she read them, sitting beside her sister as she sewed, and she startled Frances with her sudden shout. She remembered that temple, that tumbled stone chariot. She had passed them a score of times; pausing in the heats of late afternoon, she had been glad of the shelter of those mangoes. There was always some sort of breeze blowing up from the Red Tank, in the hollow a mile to the west.

She read excitedly of the vast subterranean anger and murderous hatred upon whose signs two Englishmen had come that morning. She saw Hamar's eyes looking fixedly at the scene as he and Nixon ran down the mound towards it; he had a strangely attractive way of opening them very wide, when action stirred him. He looked "bull-fashion," like Socrates; even so he had faced the United English Nation when he had "done his job" at Lambertgarh, and they had brought him to bay. And, like Socrates on another occasion, he had stalked off the field unmolested. What would he do now, she asked herself, when it became clear that the case was going to come to his court? The United

English Nation was gathering at his heels again. The clubs—this club, the clubs everywhere—were echoing the newspaper talk. Her countrymen, patient, in the main fair and anxious to be fair, were bewildered and exasperated through many years by a stirring that they could not understand. Revolutionary plotting, the collecting of bombs and revolvers—this, at any rate, ought to be stopped, and someone ought to be taught a lesson. They had no confidence in that blighter Hamar. "When a man's once made a mess like the one *he* made—and when he's known to be one of these crazy pro-native folk—Government ought never to let him get where he can do it again."

She must get away from her constant surroundings of so many weeks. That evening she hired a pony and rode out to Senchal. Oak woods, bearded deep with the lichens of a century, canopied the road; a parasitic shrub with scarlet flowers shone in the upper branches, and orchids gleamed, stars in the subdued field of her thinking. The way-side begonias were varnished like the buttercups of a Thames meadow in May. She was overtaken by a subaltern she knew; but his joy in his good luck was dashed by the decision with which she refused any escort. She was firm, and plainly uninterested. He misinterpreted her abstraction; Miss Mannering, riding alone, had evidently had a tiff, he thought he knew with whom. He went on, saddened but enlightened. She loitered up the hill, crossed its summit, and disappeared in a tiny glen hidden from the buildings of the crest. She spread her raincoat out, and lay on the turf, the morning's paper open before her.

What a squalid business was this of living—untidy,

disordered, sprawling! It was worse, it was unjust and unclean. You began with enthusiasms, and dreams, with faith and hope and boundless joy and fathomless despair. And then—you were gripped for a coldly impersonal end, you became a reed through which the biological purpose passed, draining as it went the pith and sweetness away. A few swift years saw the finish, and you were tossed to the dust-heap, glad that it was over. But at least *men* got something from it, some fun and action that seemed to have value in themselves and not to be merely a sordid contribution to the next futile jostle of automata and instruments that imagined themselves alive and of importance. She remembered her sister's girlhood, her activity and happiness, a happiness scarcely less than her own. But Frances was now simply waiting for a baby to be born—all that eagerness of mind and body had come to just this. And she, her sister, had no better or nobler occupation or use than to wait beside her, planning nothing, doing nothing. Oh, yes; they sewed, they took short walks to the first bench on the hill-side path, and there one could read while the other made clothes. Once upon a time they had read the latest book, they had studied the newest theories, Frances had written half a novel. They had held decided opinions about everything, and those opinions had been heard with the flattering respect that is never withheld when a young woman who is both charming and intelligent talks. A frown clouded her face, as a doubt recurred. *Had* their opinions been as valuable as they had always believed them? Would a man, saying the same things, have been listened to so? She had wondered since coming to India, noting the different tone that men insensibly

took when they talked to each other—when Nixon
listened to her brother-in-law as one anxious to learn,
even in matters that were his own province, and Alden,
having spoken, was eager to catch the experience and
thought that were Nixon's. She plucked the tiny, taste-
less wild strawberries, flung them away down the slope,
and bit fiercely at a dry stalk of grass. It was action
of a sort, and not much more futile than other action.

Gradually it came to her that England has evolved
a man's civilization, as surely as America seems to be
evolving a woman's. She had read a column in a Calcutta paper in which an observer, detached and
shrewder than his fellows, had explained this, in its
bearing on India. He had compared the Indian situation to a ship, sparely and just sufficiently staffed, every
man having his work and no time over. If you went
into the engine-room, you found each stripped and
toiling; there was no leisure for art or scholarship or
any sort of intellectual interest. Everyone had to get
on with his job, knowing its necessity to that complex
vessel of India's destiny and that it must remain
undone if he fell aside. It was true; and it had built up
the most astounding level of efficiency the world has
seen. As Alden maintained, every one of his countrymen was an able man at his job; the slackers or the
bunglers in the Civil Service, or the police, or any
other service, could almost be counted on one hand.
But intellectually the community was third-rate, and its
mind was fed on starch and sawdust. That was why
those who were great when in India, sometimes incredibly great and influential, rulers of provinces and heads
of huge departments, when they retired to England

became stagnant pastures of fat contentment or volcanoes of spouting impotence. Old friends of youth
marvelled that so-and-so, after his creditable school
and varsity record of thirty-five years ago, now
emerged as such a mouth and pen of folly and prejudice; marvelled, too, how he had ever risen to govern
a nation, and—so men said—to govern it well. So
India sank in England's estimation, envisaged as the
paradise and playground of the second-rate. But this
was unfair. Take these men away from this uneasy,
new environment of the West, where men thought and
where they were contradicted by their peers, and not
eternally deferred to and employed in action only, and
they would be giants again. The man who now butted
into all manner of intricate social controversies, with
bad-tempered wordy letters to *The Times* asking why
this or that obdurate problem could not be settled
summarily, by "common sense," would once more be
seen at his better level, administering the affairs of
myriads evenly and firmly—administering them with
an utter lack of perception of what was in the minds of
a subject populace and with an unshakable conviction
that he was in the place of God and could not err—
if you like, doing his magnificent work like a damned
fool—but has the world ever seen such glorious
damned fools? Has it ever seen such stupidity yoked
with such patience, watchfulness, courage, boundless
capacity for work, indifference to pain and discomfort?
Oh, not in officials only; in the men who controlled
vast businesses, in the missionaries who ran colleges,
leper asylums, Christian villages and communities.
There might be groups who only loafed and played;

but these were passengers in the ship, they were no part of the engine-room staff that we have set on board the Empire we found derelict and adrift.

And it was not fair to call this efficiency stupid; for at least half of intellect resides in action, and the brain is starved and despicable that never fulfils its thought in energy outside all cerebration. If mankind had to choose between these who worked so ably and those who appraised and criticized only, it would be right to push aside the latter as the shallower fools of the two, for all their pert accuracy of judgment. But the world has seen, both in Greece and in England, men who combined thought and action; and it is dissatisfied with the men of thought alone, and dissatisfied even with the men of efficient action, dissatisfied more and more. Hilda paused in her bitter thinking, and listened for an audible sound; that vague dissatisfaction which she had felt about her since she came to India seemed to become something that could be heard and touched —from every quarter of the globe seemed to be rolling up a storm of rebellion against this just and efficient masterdom. But there was no sound except the wind whistling quietly to itself in a bamboo copse near by. She laughed at herself detected in an absurdity. All the same, it was not mere fancy; a ghost *had* walked by her, though eluding vision and felt in quaking thought alone. Else, why had she started?

But what of the women in this civilization that men have made? She was frowning now, and that gathering storm of rebellion raised its flag within her own soul, the soul of a woman of this efficient tribe. Oh, yes, the women had their place—social, domestic, orna-

mental. But in the thought and action of the race—
where? The women of the middle classes—once the
flower of physical charm had dimmed, how dried and
desiccated they became, in their concepts, their beliefs,
their speech! There were other women, whose pictures
and deeds filled our society papers, who, outwardly
at least, were far from dried and desiccated. They
were wonderful—a strike or a war, and they flew to
manly actions, to driving cars and organizing canteen
work, and they photographed splendidly while engaged
in these occasional bouts of excited work. But, except
when their ease was threatened, they returned exigu-
ously little to the community whose incessant labour
kept them in such pleasure and health and comfort.
Well, the community was still content that they should
exist and be fêted and delighted, was content because
of their undeniable ornamental qualities. They had
found their jolly pinnacle in this man-built civilization,
by growing into manlike character. The softer texture
of their sex had been eaten away by the acid of man's
expectation, and only bone and muscle left. They were
superbly limbed and built, women of easy, swinging
walk and carriage, superb in the saddle or when they
drew their evening wraps about their firm, lovely
shoulders. They were efficient; and Nature's eyes
agreed with Man's, as they rested on them. It did not
quiet Hilda to suspect that her own place was with
these.

Then her mind wandered to her sister, who a few
years earlier had been one of these efficient, charming
girls. Right or wrong, that life had finished; and
Hilda, lying on the Himalayan turf, with Alden as her

imaginary colloquist, as when they had talked together before she came to the hills, quoted the old poem:

> Robin, that warld is all awa',
> And quiht brocht til an end.

"And a good thing, too, Robin," she said aloud. "But *what* have you done with Frances?" For, she went on to explain to him, to this unseeing member of an unseeing sex, at Vishnugram there were plenty of servants of a sort, but the day was frittered and fretted away in trivial and teasing detail. What did Frances do? Nothing whatever, so far as Hilda could see. But the days were busy. A dinner to a couple of guests was matter for as much consideration and plotting as Shakspere put into *Hamlet* or Conrad into *Lord Jim*.

An elder woman had told her that it wasn't the mere coming of a baby that fettered. That was nothing; a few months of careful idleness, a few times of sudden, terrible fear in the night, alone and facing the approaching darkness, mornings of sickness and lassitude, then an hour or two of increasing pain, with a last hour of sharper agony. If that were all, it were well, and the incidence of bearing children is a trouble that sentimentalists have exaggerated. Men might be justified in placing it against their liability to death or maiming in war, an exceptional danger against another exceptional one. But that was not all. For afterwards year followed year, with the mother tied to never-pausing care and drudgery and responsibility. The new life had to be given sleep, and food, and food and sleep, to be warmed, watched, cleansed, tended. There would be illnesses, and periods of racking anxiety. The bloom and exquisite fire of womanhood would vanish.

It wasn't good enough. Why should people be interested in a man all his life, but in a woman only until she became a bride?

But was she fair? Did she not exaggerate the interest and variety of a man's life? Has not the Creator played the same scurvy joke on both? Was Alden's life the romantic, eager thing she imagined? Teaching Milton, and Shakspere's dullest plays—and how dull and poor some of these are, if we had any criticism other than a second-hand, dishonest enthusiasm about things accepted but never examined! —for Calcutta University, to boys who had come, most of them, from the most meagre of experience in village homes! The answering of circulars sent out from Government offices, the liquidation of the constant debt laid upon one's time by the stupidity or laziness or incompetence of other people! No, that was Douglas's work, Alden escaped the most of it. Well, then, this matter of feeding thousands of people, all alike now that the steamroller of famine had passed over them, and this correspondence of scores of letters a day, hundreds a week. And, if Frances became worn and fretful, didn't her husband have to carry that burden also? If her work often seemed nothing to him, to her his was a mere routine, something that made no demand on nervous energy or on spirit; it seemed only right that his wife should have his share of these to draw on, as well as her own! There was Mrs. Nixon, so charming to the outside world—Hilda had had one illuminating glimpse of a different Mrs. Nixon, who reserved all her potent poison for home consumption. How many women there are whose husbands and children and servants would be happy if they received one tenth as good a time as the casual male stranger within their gates!

All the same, it wasn't good enough. It was damnable.

She returned to Darjiling.

It was about this time that Hilda met an American lady who, after explaining Egypt and its problems, was setting India to rights. It is an old stale story, this of the people who race through India and write books on their experience. But it has more truth than most chestnuts. The mass of shallow, foolish Indian travel-books, written by American and European women, is beyond either jesting or exaggeration. This woman was pretty still, for all her thirty-five years, and her vivacity gave her a kittenish charm. She had had a good time, everywhere and throughout her life, and now in India. She had been the guest of Government House in Bombay, Simla, Calcutta, Delhi, and half a score of lesser places; aides and smart, courteous subalterns had been placed at her disposal, the Viceroy himself had submitted to her very frank questionnaire. Hilda, listening to her happy chatter, suddenly realized within herself the mentality of a man, and felt how maddened men must be, how dinned and stunned and sandbagged, by this steady, glittering, spate-like folly. The woman's mind seemed to confront her sight as a polished, blinding, empty plate of glass; she was losing vision as she faced its blankness of sheer, self-satisfied complacency. Are we all like this, she wondered—all of us that are pretty, that is? She forgave men at once for the insolence which ignored the mind and gazed only at the face and figure. There was nothing else to do—this, or be driven into insanity.

Anything to escape having to give the brain to attend on this dizzying silliness which was put forth as clever and illuminating thought! If she, Hilda, were the shallowest of subalterns, she would do anything to stop this woman from talking about any problem that really mattered—but you could not stop her, nothing on earth could stop her! Well, then, indemnify yourself for having to endure her opinions, by watching her face, which was so undeniably good to see, and save your reason by shutting off the listening side of the mind, and by murmuring: "Quite! quite! I entirely agree with you, Mrs. Róckerbilt. You put it wonderfully!"

This woman had seen things that hardly any Englishwoman could have seen, chances had been lavishly put in her way by officialdom everywhere. Why? And Hilda thought, Britain is restive about this Empire of hers, she does not care what her own people think, but she is anxious to conciliate—if necessary, to deceive —these spies who come from outside, especially if they come from that annoying, powerful, wealthy America that is so highly moral and meddling. So, instinctively as well as from deliberate policy, the administration had gone out of its way and had fed this woman with flattery as a prize cat is fed with cream. She was now purring and happy; she was going back to America, she told Hilda, to tell her people that "these natives" were "vurry unreasonable" and there was "more real good democracy" in the British Government of India than she had ever believed. And Hilda felt there had been a contempt in this also, that men had cajoled and fussed over a woman, when with a man they would have been straight and honest. She was chilled and unresponsive; her American friend dismissed her in conversation next day as wanting in pep and go. "They just get my goat, these dull, stuck-up, brainless British dolls!"

Frances saw that her sister was unhappy, and she tried to persuade her to leave her for longer and more frequent periods. A party was going from their hotel on a fortnight's trip into Sikhim; they were keen to take Hilda, but she refused. A way of better escape came, in the chance of helping Findlay. Marjorie's health broke down altogether, and she was miserable with illness, with sores and boils and fever. Every scratch and mosquito-bite turned septic. Her mother was despairing and resourceless. Hilda wondered if Findlay had ever realized the price that his enthusiasm and unselfishness exacted; his wife had so given herself to his spirit of radiant service that she had lost her own individuality and was useless away from him. Seeing the child's weakness and pain, Hilda felt a stirring in her of pity from depths that life had rarely touched. Thus early this baby was being flung into man's battle of energy and creating! Missionary work! It was Findlay's way, after all, of fulfilling himself and of getting things done. She wired to him, curtly and indignantly. He came by the first train, and then she was wretched to see how tired and worn he looked, and his distress for wife and child. Angry with herself and her own futility, she had taken it out of the man who deserved it least. And, however unwillingly, *she* had escaped this summer of blazing heat and unremitting toil, that had left its brand, as though it had run over him with red-hot fingers, on every line of this athletic Englishman's body.

This was in early September. It was not yet cool enough to be desirable to travel to Europe, but the doctor told him that the sea voyage offered the only chance of restoration. Douglas was acting as head of the Mission, the chief being on furlough, so Findlay ran into Vishnugram and saw him. He arranged passages immediately, and they sailed a week later.

Hilda went with them to Calcutta, resolved that she would not return to Darjiling. The Aldens' daughter had been born the day before Findlay came up, and her sister was well and in good hands. Hilda would waste time no longer, her thoughts were where a few sorely tried men were fighting the famine, still at its height; there had been no further rain since those three days that unmasked the Conspiracy. But Alden was anxious she should come back, since he had to return to his work. Findlay, by sacrificing his own family to the needs of those others who were so helpless, had paid a terrible price; and, though Alden seemed more worried than he need be, Hilda could not criticize him. He assured her that there was nothing she could do at Vishnugram or Kanthala— nothing; this seemed to be always true in India. She returned to her sister.

While at Darjiling, she had not entirely escaped— or wished to escape—its society. She had met Major— now Colonel—Henderson, and he had been quick to claim old acquaintance. She liked him for his honesty, his underlying fairness, and the range of his interests—these, in the manner of the English, he sought to conceal whenever, as often, they were in any way intellectual. She was the more eager to show him friendliness because of that morning when she had

championed Hamar. Not one man in a hundred would
have been so frank and courageous in acknowledging
himself in the wrong; no shadow or suspicion that it
was remembered should humiliate him when they met.
He managed to see a good deal of her, and she was
drawn into his activities. Then she became suddenly
and teasingly inaccessible. Liking him, she was in no
danger of loving him, but it was plain that he found
her companionship dizzying. Also, people were talking. She found excuses for refusing her society, and
longed for the time when Frances might return to
Vishnugram or she could leave her.

Early in September Hamar spent a week-end in
Calcutta. He met an old schoolfellow, now in the
Army and stationed at Jalapahar, from whom he
heard about the simple pleasures of the heights.
Hamar, studying his daily paper as the weeks dragged
by, had seen Hilda's name sometimes; she had been—
"Our Special Correspondent" used the phrase, fumb-
ling in her bag of tinsel clichés—"an acquisition,"
shining in gymkhana and paper-chase and—once—
amateur theatricals. He asked his friend if he had met
a Miss Mannering; and received an enthusiastic reply
which told him that his fears had come true.

"She's engaged to Colonel Henderson, of the Norsets. Practically, that is. Everyone knows it'll come
off."

They talked of matters indifferent for a few minutes. A political question of the day was mentioned,
and Hamar swore with a ferocity that amazed the
soldier. He looked at his friend, and saw the ravage
the weeks had made. The lines and ridges of his life,

hard, mirthless, unhoping, stood up in the worn face and sick eyes.

"What's the matter, old chap? You're looking awfully rocky. You're not"—with a sudden access of generous intimacy and desire to help—"still fretting about that wretched Lambertgarh business. We've all forgotten that. Why don't you run up to the hills for a week or two? This famine *biznai must* be about over—and everyone's sick of hearing of it. Come up with me!"

"I've still got a bit of a head from a touch of fever yesterday," said Hamar, too tired even to lie efficiently. "Thanks awfully, but I can't get away, with this case coming on. Yes, I *will* have another peg. Thanks."

He caught the noon train back to Vishnugram, the train by which he had first gone there. September, most intolerable of months, was painting the scorched rocks and dazzling green leaves of the jungle—an uncomfortable, unhealthy splendour that afflicted him with a sense of squalor. It was as if the untidy Demiurge had spilled buckets of white varnish or sickly enamel. It was all drab, unbearably drab, colourless, hateful, a dead world steaming beneath a savourless, stagnant atmosphere.

He went straight out to Findlay that night; and he flung himself into the famine work with a demoniac's energy.

"The man's a wonder," Findlay told Alden, in a letter. "I never saw anyone who slaves as he does. He came back from Calcutta on that infernal day-train— in September—and he wouldn't even spend the night at Vishnugram. He must be fanatically keen on these people. He's been an inspiration to me all these months, and I shall never forget it. I don't know how I'd have carried on without him."

Alden enclosed the letter when he wrote to his wife.

26

SEPTEMBER'S third week. The cold weather seemed in imagination to be at the threshold of the exhausted year. Hamar, after his day's work in the office wandering aimlessly and wretchedly, one evening turned in at Neogyi's bungalow. Neogyi was a decent chap; Hamar wished he had cultivated his acquaintance better. He *must* talk to somebody, must escape from his own mind; his thought, like a caged tiger, was going round and round the bars of one theme.

Neogyi was glad to see him. "I'm feeling just the same," he told him, "fed up with everything. I want to curse; and I want someone to listen to me."

"Curse away," said Hamar, throwing himself back in a long chair. "Draw a deep breath, and then, placing the hands on the hips, at the word of command, ex-*plode*! That's what our old sergeant-major would have said, if you'd been training with me in the War. Poor old chap! He held that there was a solemn ritual for everything you did, and if the enemy jumped in before you had gone through all the preliminaries, and bayoneted you first, he felt there was some sort of umpire who would rule that it was a foul and that the bayoneting didn't count. There were heaps like him, commissioned as well as non-commissioned. No wonder we paid eight millions a day for a war that

P

would have been dear at two! Thanks, I'll accept a drink. Now, then!"

"I've just had the poor old Raja of Kestanadi to see me. Do you know him?"

"Isn't he the silly old boy that was sitting next to Khaliara at the Agricultural Exhibition opening? I just met him. He has a manner that suggests that he expects to be kicked."

"Well? What do you expect? He's really only a rather rich old peasant. And he isn't even that now; they say he's nearly bankrupt."

"What did he come about?"

"The Commissioner has signified his intention of visiting him for a shoot, towards the end of October."

"But what an honour! He's frightfully bucked, of course."

"He isn't. Says he's very hard up. All his land is mortgaged, and he's in debt all round. He'll be sold up before long, unless a miracle happens."

"Well, that's easy. All he's got to do is to decline the honour."

"Yes. That would be easy for you. But he isn't an Englishman. That brute of a Deogharia has sent his *hookum* through one of his jackals." Neogyi was trembling with indignation. "I saw the letter, so I know it's pukka. It's the coolest document that I ever knew even Deogharia sanction. Listen!" Neogyi took a paper out of his desk, and read. " 'His Honour the Commissioner proposes to visit your district on a tour of inspection, the last week of October. You will arrange to entertain him at a shikar-party, on the 26th of that month. He is bringing four friends, and there will be five *machans* for him and his party. These will be placed at the point where the beaters will drive out the game first. You have permission to erect another two *machans* for yourself and your own friends, but these must be placed after the *machans* reserved for His Honour's party. The necessary provisions will be provided by Messrs. Bellman, of Calcutta, and the bill will be sent to you in due course.' There! *That's* the document! I took a copy of it, it so struck me as the outside edge and limit. The poor chap wanted to know what he was to do. The last time Deogharia inflicted the distinction of his presence upon him, it cost a matter of over eight hundred dibs."

"Do?" shouted Hamar. "Why, return the dirty beast his letter, with a full exposition of the sort of cad and skunk he is! My sainted hat, Neogyi! What would happen if a saheb had the cheek to send a chit like that?"

"Oh, well, there's at least one saheb in the service who does do that kind of thing. I'll admit, not quite so impudently. But for any Indian who's lucky enough to serve the Raj this is part of his bed of thorns—he knows that the vilest bullies and tyrants are his own flesh and blood! I'd sometimes give anything to have been born a Roumanian or a Bulgar, or anyone rather than an Indian in these days. We get the worst of both worlds, our own and that one of yours in which we serve."

"I'm sorry, Neogyi. Anyway, Kestanadi's course is clear. He should take a ticket to Lurdawan, and boot Deogharia. The whole province would support the action. Of course you told him to shy the letter back."

"I told him he wasn't obliged to put up with the imposition unless he chose. I had to use diplomatic

language. Deogharia may be—is, as everyone knows—
a most utter swine, but he happens to be the Commissioner a benevolent Raj has given us, as a generous
instalment of self-government. He's got his knife into
me because I made his precious brother-in-law clear
out of this place as a candidate for the Council. Honestly, Hamar, I said as much as I could. And that
much was too much. Don't look at me as if I were a
worm! Why didn't the fellow go to one of these
missionaries, to Alden or Douglas?"

"Would they have done anything?"

"Probably not. But Douglas might. He's in a position to make himself unpleasant even to a Commissioner, and he's not lacking in courage. And this is
the sort of thing that once in a while makes Alden
go in off the deep end. He made a fool of himself last
time he took a case up, that coolie strike in the Sonthal
Parganas. But the facts are clear this time, and he
might have sent Deogharia a scorcher. Anyway, my
point is that Deogharia couldn't have done *him* any
harm. And either Alden or Douglas would have told
Kestanadi what I did, but in clearer language."

"It was better from you, an official. I prefer that
missionaries should stick to their jobs, and leave the
ruling of the country alone."

"Ye-es. That's the official view. It isn't the view that
Indians take, by the way. They regard missionaries
as sahebs, only sahebs who make big professions; and
they think they might be a jolly sight *less* neutral,
sometimes."

"But *you* don't think that?"

"I rather fancy I do. They've no right to come here
preaching a religion they insist is better than ours if

they're not willing to be as unpopular with their own people as Jesus Christ was. It's easy to be courageous slanging other folk. But how many dare stand up to their own crowd? And every Indian wants to know, why did so few missionaries *know* what we felt about the Punjab and Amritsar? Aren't they interested in what the people of this country feel, even if we're wrong in feeling it? There's too much talk about Christian statesmanship about."

"That's what Findlay says."

"Findlay? Yes. If Findlay carries on for another half-dozen years his leaders will be making allowances for him—a good-hearted, well-meaning man, but cranky—doesn't understand Christian statesmanship— the wisdom of always keeping in with your own Foreign Office and your Colonial Office and India Office, and helping to pretend that unpleasant things never happened—it'll all blow over if we say nothing, and just wait. But *we* know where Findlay stands— we may some day murder him, in some riot where we're just mad for foreign blood. But we shall know the minute after, as we know now, that the man's a saint and a hero. He'll be a legend a century hence. Ah, you'd forgotten that I'm an Indian! I often forget it myself."

"Shall we get back to Kestanadi?"

"He'll never dare to do what I told him. The visit will go far towards being the last straw that ruins him, but he won't say a word. He wanted *me* to write to Deogharia. It wasn't my job. It shan't be my job. If my countrymen can't learn to stand on their own feet, they deserve to be kicked, and I don't care *who* kicks them, whether Englishmen or their own flesh and blood. If Deogharia is a brute, Kestanadi is a worm. He'll be all salaams when Deogharia brings his gang of fat in-laws and they all wipe their boots on him. And he'll curry favour by telling how I advised rebellion."

Neogyi was depressed to the point of cynicism. The conversation contained no gleam of encouragement for Hamar, except that it is human nature to be cheered by the reminder that other folk have their troubles as well as ourselves. Hamar dismally remembered one of Alden's ecclesiastical jests—a chestnut— of the Methodist minister who tried to cheer an old lady of his church, when the year's returns showed a bad decrease of membership. She is alleged to have answered with quiet satisfaction: "Yes, but thank God, I 'ears as 'ow the Baptists 'ave done worse."

27

IT WAS perhaps unfortunate that Deogharia chose next day to motor over to Vishnugram, with a very exalted visitor from England. Sir Spencer Tomlinson, summering at Simla and revising at leisure the manuscript of his book, *The Problem of the Orient,* was recalled by unexpected warning of a general election in November. He hurried down to Calcutta, to find that his boat's sailing had been delayed for a week. Meeting Deogharia, he was persuaded to run up to Vishnugram and see the ruins.

Deogharia, having flattered and received flattery in return, was intoxicatedly happy. The ex-Secretary of State, reclining under a canopy in the shade of a thick-tressed *neem,* became intimate. A local raja had provided an excellent lunch—in Deogharia's name.

"You know, Deogharia"—Deogharia bridled and squirmed with pleasure at the condescension which now dispensed with ceremony—"my party have been slow to believe that Indians were—well, *quite* ready to run their own show. But what I've seen of one or two fellows like you has convinced me that the *right* Indian—mind you, he's rare; I've only met about one besides yourself—is not only almost as good as the right saheb, but in some ways better, for he understands his own people and he realizes what British rule and British justice have done for them."

"Quite, quite," Deogharia purred. "They have saved us from ourselves, and given us standards and principles we never dreamt of before. It would be a most retrograde step if you were to leave us now."

"Anyway, we've started the Indianizing business, and we've done it, I must say, uncommonly well on the whole. We may have been slow to start, but we've been generous when we did begin. I am told that ten years ago not a single Indian had been Commissioner."

"Two had *acted*. But none had been pukka."

"Quite. And now we have four in this province alone, four out of a total of five, isn't it?"

"Six."

"Well, you know, *that* strikes me as a pretty generous instalment of self-government. What on earth do the swarajists think they have to kick about?"

"You'll never satisfy them."

"No. They're like our own working classes, the more you give them the more they want. Look at that last miners' strike! All the same"—Sir Spencer Tomlinson stirred himself to a superbly magnanimous mood, worthy of the great tradition which he represented—

"we're not going to let their envy and cantankerousness make us shrink from the noble task that we have undertaken."

It was hard for the famous statesman to realize that he was not addressing a public meeting, and that no applause was forthcoming. He paused automatically; Deogharia's sympathetic murmur atoned for the apathy of the imaginary audience. The speaker continued.

"We've started well in keeping with the high traditions of British freedom and British generosity. And we seem to have begun with the right men. We must see to it that we go on with the right men. Sinha didn't do badly in Bihar, as the first Indian Governor of a province. When my party comes back into power—at the next election, all the signs are—*between ourselves* I'm going to take India on. I'm very interested in India, and I'm going to see if I can't build up her future on really sound, really *British* lines. A lot of this self-determination nonsense must be cut out or side-tracked. I'm looking for men who can be trusted to work with me and to carry out my ideals. And I think I know where we are to find our *second* Indian Governor." The great man laughed in a very friendly and infectious way.

After lunch the *entente* deepened. Before they reached the ruins Sir Spencer Tomlinson assured Deogharia of a knighthood in the first New Year's Honours after his party resumed the reins of State. But would the knighthood be worth picking up, with this new glorified creature in prospect, Lord Deogharia of Lardawan, Governor of a province? Like other members of the House of Lords, he would be the ancestor of quite undistinguished descendants born with a hereditary right of rule over the long-suffering United British Nation. Truly, the East was beginning to have its revenge, slowly and by instalment but with ironic and bitter quality, for the long oppression of the West.

That evening Neogyi as Collector entertained the station at dinner, to meet Sir Spencer Tomlinson. Deogharia was in exultant mood, happy and gracious. And then, suddenly, Hamar was shown in.

Hamar had just exchanged greetings with the guest of the evening, when Deogharia strolled up. "Hello, Hamar, old boy," he said expansively, "what sort of nights are you having now? Troubled with dreams of Lambertgarh, and of these jollee new revolutionaries who are awaiting your trial?"

He held out his hand. The devil entered into Hamar, and the flame of yesterday's anger shot up in his heart. He flung his own hand behind his back. Hamar, you fool!

"If you don't mind," he said, almost choking with indignation, "I'll keep my hand clean."

Sir Spencer Tomlinson's eyes jumped with amazement. He was actually witnessing one of those acts of intolerable rudeness which he had always held to be an invention of "the extremist press" and of Labour politicians. "And this, mark you,"—as he used to say when retailing the extraordinary incident—"to the whitest Indian that ever lived—the one man among them who's every bit a saheb."

As for Deogharia, this was the occasion when his self-command failed him. He went a jaundice colour and stuttered. Hamar found speech first.

"You propose to plant yourself and a gang of fellow swine on the Raja of Kestanadi, and you send him the letter which, of all the letters ever written, takes the cake for sheer impertinence and cold-blooded cheek! No decent man would touch you except with the end of a boot!"

It was now Neogyi's turn to go green. Deogharia found his tongue.

"If I were invited by an English squire to shoot over his grounds," he said lamely, "I should expect him to entertain me."

"You weren't invited, and you damn well know it. You planted yourself on this poor devil, because you knew he daren't refuse. If there's one thing that ought to keep us in this country, it's the necessity to protect Indians from blood-suckers of their own race such as you. And no English squire would let such a tick blacken his walls; and well you know it! I'm sorry, Neogyi. You *are* a saheb, and we all realize it. I'm behaving like a cad on your premises, and I'm wretchedly sorry for it. I'm off." And Hamar was off the veranda, and down the steps, gone to his own bungalow.

He left the others to a dismal evening. Sir Spencer Tomlinson alone had anything to say. He expressed his astonishment and indignation; but the response was listless and disappointing. "I could see what it was," he said afterwards; "they were simply crushed by the bounder's behaviour. As for poor Deogharia, I never saw a chap who suffered so. You simply couldn't get him to talk about it. Anyone else would have brought a libel action pretty sharp; he wouldn't hear of it. The man's a white man through and through. Talk of magnanimity!"

Deogharia's thoughts were a complex swarm, all stinging. He was wretched with the conviction that

that fool of a raja had parted with the letter to Hamar. Whatever happened, he could not risk any public exposure. He would find other ways of getting even with his enemies. Neogyi? Had Neogyi had anything to do with the affair? He would find out. In any case, he should pay for having witnessed his humiliation; it had happened in his house, too. As for the Kestanadi rat that had dared to betray the lion, he would crush him before the year was out. This he managed; all the debts that had been hanging over that thriftlessly run zemindari were called in and crashed down upon it. The Raja was adjudged bankrupt, and sold up. The College missionaries had also been present, secretly exulting in the downfall of the Indian they hated for being over them all. He would find ways to annoy them, too. So a vexatious law-suit was brought against the College, a claim from the man who had sold the compound fifteen years ago and who now alleged that he had not been paid for the land *under* the large tank whose pride of flowering *simul* Douglas had shorn away. The College won its case; but the accident that its rulers witnessed Hamar's explosion cost it a matter of fifteen thousand rupees.

Hamar? Deogharia and the ex-Secretary of State discussed him pretty thoroughly. The latter was for breaking him. "We'll have him out of the service. It's men like that who make revolutionaries in this country."

Deogharia sighed heavily. "Yes," he said. "You've seen how he treats me, the Commissioner. If the story gets about, think of my position! But I don't mind that—*I* can look after myself. You can guess how he behaves to my helpless countrymen. Shocking stories reach me of the way he treats his office, but I can't do anything, though I know the harm he's doing. He's on the judicial side, so not under me."

He became his magnanimous self again. "Tomlinson, I *refuse* to be annoyed into taking this seriously. After all, he can't do *me* any harm. And the poor fellow's not himself. He's had a bad time ever since he let off those scoundrels in the Lambertgarh case."

Sir Spencer was suddenly enlightened. "I remember that case now. It happened when I was in the Cabinet. Is he the Hamar who made that awful mess?"

"Yes. He started being very pro-Indian, you know. It's the easiest way to popularity with our extremists." Deogharia got the correct emphasis on "extremists," the stress which indicates that we have now reached "an end to controversy" and everything bad is explained by the magic wand of a word. "You can't be popular *and* do your duty."

"He's one of *that* sort? *I*—understand. Well, we've got our eye on him from now on. He'll find that sort of thing may pay when you've got a backboneless House of Commons and a Government that truckles to every sort of sedition. What we need is the Mussolini touch, and we're going to get it. You'll see, we'll soon have a Government that *does* govern. And you'll find it won't forget Mr. Vincent Hamar, or you, or the topping way you have taken his abominable and caddish conduct."

Sir Spencer Tomlinson was very sensible that Deogharia had done all that could be done to ensure his physical comfort in this terrible September weather; and gratitude was deepened by admiration of a white-souled martyr, a man who had no thought for self or for dignity. The British Empire had justified its existence by producing even one such man. There was nothing "Oriental" about Deogharia but his pleasantly light colour. The parting of the two friends was marked by the warmest expressions of esteem on both sides.

28

ALDEN'S letter to his wife contained a full account of the deplorable incident. He had the scholar's gusto in vigorous language, and Hamar's billingsgate lost little of its raciness, in concession to the fact that ladies were to read it. He added: "We're all worried about Hamar, though. No one was sorry to see Deogharia touched up; but Hamar's outburst was unpardonable. Nobody knows why on earth he went off like that, unless Neogyi does; and Neogyi's not saying anything. But Hamar has been going about for weeks like a man sentenced to be hanged. The chap's face is wretched beyond words. He's suffering about something, and John thinks his brain is going to snap. I can't say I've quite taken to him, but John says no praise is good enough for what he's been doing at Kanthala. He's an enigma. He'll do anything for these folk, yet he can't keep his temper."

Mrs. Alden, looking up as she finished reading the letter, saw Hilda's face a vivid crimson. Misunderstanding the look, she said: "It does make you feel mad when an Englishman treats an Indian in that way."

"It doesn't seem to have made Rob mad," said Hilda. "It's only puzzled him. I'd give a year out of my life to know why Mr. Hamar said what he did."

"Well, there's no way of finding out," said her sister.

29

THREE ineffably wretched days had dragged one
after another. Hamar, rising, like that other wildly
happy sage, Thomas Carlyle, with the thought that
here had been dawning "another *blue* day," found in
the pile of office letters on his table an envelope
addressed in a lady's hand:

Cliffville
Darjiling
21st. September.

Dear Mr. Hamar:

It's dull for my sister, being unable to get about. And I have
been keeping constantly with her, except for very short rambles
along the hill-side near my hotel.

We're taking up botany to amuse ourselves! I wonder, could
you spare that Roxburgh I know is on your shelves? You won't
have many temptations to botanize yourself in the dreadful
furnace where you are suffering! And from what I have heard,
Mr. Vincent Hamar is spending precious little time on himself!
Rob says that John can find no words of praise too high for
what you have done.

Mr. Hamar! Rob has told us that you gave Mr. Deogharia
an inkling of the way decent people feel about him, the other
day. It is more than I have a right to say—you don't mind?—
but I think it is splendid that there should be *some* Englishmen
who don't mind even being indiscreet—even what other people
call by harder names?—when they come up against a scoundrel!
Forgive me for saying this! Of course I do not know what the
rights of the matter were, *but I am quite sure they were not
with Mr. Deogharia!*

Yours very sincerely,
Hilda M. Mannering.

P. S. (I suppose a lady never writes a letter without adding
a postscript!) If you are too busy, do not trouble to post the
Roxburgh. Rob is coming up next week, and would bring it
with him.

Hamar's mind expanded to a wonder it dared not entertain. Hilda Mannering had written to him! For the Roxburgh? She knew as well as he did that Roxburgh was out of date and nearly useless. But they had been slanging him for that scene in Neogyi's drawing-room, and this was her reply, to tell him that she knew that he was neither cad nor boor, though he had seemed both.

He did not use the post. Hilda Mannering deserved a special messenger, such as carries the correspondence of royalty. Next day, at noon, a peon of his court presented her at Darjiling with Roxburgh and a parcel of better, newer books besides. She did not know that Hamar had gone into Calcutta with the messenger, and in the two hours between trains had ransacked the shops. With the books was a letter giving succinctly the genesis of the Deogharia affair. He did not excuse himself, he knew that he had lost his temper, had behaved like a fool and let himself down. There was no justification, and he did not try to find any. Then . . . last of all . . . if Miss Mannering would forgive his touching on a deeply personal matter . . . he did not know how far it was official knowledge, but he had heard it in such a way that he felt it was true . . . might he congratulate her on her engagement, and hope that her life would be very happy, as he knew that the man whom she had honoured must be radiantly proud and happy? She knew his feelings— that he realized that there never had been a man who was good enough to deserve her. Still, this man was worthy, so far as any man might be worthy.

For himself, he added, he wished he had been fortunate enough to do her service, for he knew of nothing that so filled him with happiness. Even now, if there were ever anything that he could do, would she make him in her debt by telling him what it was? If there was nothing, then . . . and he quoted Stevenson's lines:

> Here, lady, lo, that servant stands
> You picked from passing men;
> And should you need nor heart nor hands,
> He bows and goes again.

Her acknowledgment was guarded:

Dear Mr. Hamar:

Two ladies feel that you have been a cavalier beyond their deserts or hopes. Frances says you were "a peach" to send those books, and to send them in so charming a way—and so quickly! Thank you!

And thank you for your letter—for everything in it—*every-thing*. No man should write so—or think so—about *any* woman. No woman deserves it. But I thank you, with all my heart.

And thank you for telling me about *l'affaire Deogharia*. Yes, people will say it was "indiscreet," was "unpardonable rudeness." But no friend will misjudge it. It was like you to lose your temper not for yourself, but because a poor, silly cultivator—I understand that is really all the "Raja" is!—was shamefully bullied.

But what is all this about "congratulations"?!!! No, I am not engaged, and in no danger of being—so far as I know! Don't you know Darjiling? Everyone here is "engaged"—and often to half a dozen different persons. Some day you shall tell me who is the man our local gossip has honoured me by joining my name with! (That's a dreadful sentence!)

With warmest thanks and best wishes,
Yours sincerely,
Hilda M. Mannering.

30

THE Red Sea glittered, windless and stagnant. Day was setting on the African hills; those gaunt walls were a sink down which the almost visible spirits of evening were recklessly pouring away all the useless colours that in happier regions tint the innumerable leaf and flower and bird. Here was neither cloud nor tree, on which to lavish glory. Let it go, then. And swiftly over the granite wilderness fled river after river of rioting splendour, floods which tossed high and wide their waves of pearl and crimson and opal and emerald and amethyst, splashing the sands and the sky silences.

Marjorie Findlay's fever had been continuous since the vessel dropped down the Hugli. Blood-poisoning had set in, and her life was ebbing with the day. Her mother sat by her, in the calm which precedes the last breaking of the mind. Nights and days of unsleeping suffering had worn the body out; the light of the body was a flickering candle, round which the winds were raging.

Suddenly the doctor waiting beside the dying child looked up. He evaded the question in the mother's eyes, but he knew that she knew. He postponed the misery of disclosure; there was that in the wretched face before him which made him dread to be alone with her when the truth had to be told.

"I'll ask Mrs. Wilson to come, Mrs. Findlay," he said. "I'll be back in a moment. She'll take over for you—for Marjorie," he added. "Let her sleep now." And he drew the sheet over the girl's shoulders; her face was muffled from her mother's sight.

Q

As he went out, the mother lifted her dead child's face; and in that gust of anguish the light went out. Misery took possession of the darkness, and drove her on to the only escape from itself, and from herself.

The cabin was empty when the doctor returned. They stopped the engines and sent out boats. As was foreseen, it was in vain.

An hour later, the last wisp of day had faded. The ship was making its way again towards the Mediterranean and the cool, life-giving winds of the North. Night covered the unstirring face of the waters.

31

DOUGLAS motored over with Alden to Kanthala. It was Alden who went in to Findlay first. He came out in a few minutes, and beckoned.

"Go in and speak to him. He's magnificent, of course, the greatest chap who ever lived or ever will live. But he's broken. He doesn't realize yet what's happened; but it'll come. I'm staying here when you go back."

A little later, when the three men were together, Alden said to Findlay: "You'll leave me to run your show, old man."

"You'll get away," suggested Douglas. "Jacks and Alden and I will manage everything, while you have a change. You're run down."

Alden, who knew his man better, shook his head. There was nothing that *could* be done, nothing at all. One could only wait for time to do its work. But time does not change things essentially. As some one has observed, it merely runs up a rough culvert over which the daily traffic of life can pass. The waters of wretchedness are still below, and suddenly, in a moment of time, they can rise and sweep the footway from beneath life. Nevertheless, Alden vaguely felt that the woods would be kind to his friend; whatever healing there might be for him in the world was there. In the woods and in the people. Findlay chose the people.

"I'll get about my jobs," he said. "Only—Alden—Rob—you'll stay with me."

The tide of his sorrow rushed over him; he flung his face upon his hands, and sobbed at last. "I'm sorry," he said. "I'm ashamed of myself. But you chaps have been wonderful to me. I'll never forget it, Douglas."

After Douglas had returned to Vishnugram, Findlay took up the day's work. All day long, till dusk had fallen, he fronted the jostling, stricken crowds, and listened to their appeals, adjudicated, fed them, cycled from station to station, tested the stones they had broken. Alden was with him, silently by the presence of his love and distress upholding his suffering mind. The day was endurable, there was too much to do for any thinking to be possible. And all through the hours with tiny, trying tasks—so gratefully welcomed and accepted—Findlay built a wall between his mind and himself. But in the night control gave way. Alden heard him, and was at his side in a moment, his arms beneath his friend's head.

"John, old man," he said, "just let it rip. It's awful, it's horrible; don't hold it in. It'll help, and it's the only thing that can."

Two days later Alden, waiting for breakfast, was

prowling about a veranda, when a car entered the compound. Nixon would not stay to breakfast, but returned to Vishnugram almost at once. He left Hilda Mannering behind.

"I'm taking over all I can of this famine business," she said. "I got a woman in who'll do all that I was doing for Frances, and more."

32

SLOWLY, but perceptibly, the cold weather came seeping in, bringing jubilation. Colleges, schools, offices closed, staffs and students dispersed for the *Puja,* "the Bengali Christmas." The trains moved with laughter and jest, on their noisy crowded way to Calcutta, to Benares, Puri, Allahabad. Little girls welcomed home their hero-brothers, parents and relations and friends gathered for festival. Images of Durga appeared in doorways and courtyards, hung with tinsel and glitter. Goats were selling, as turkeys would be in Britain a couple of months later. Plantains and blood-hued hibiscus flowers were being plucked, for adornment and for offering.

The mornings were cool and glorious. The sals were covering themselves with red new leaves, the jungle wore the appearance both of festivity and of utter peace, after the tense agonies of summer. The world holds no more exhilarating feeling than that which comes to the man waking in India in mid-October, to revel in the fresh, chill breezes and the astounding newness with which the first rud of dawn sprinkles and splashes the glimmering jungle.

Over at Kanthala, the wild *sephali* groves were

carpeting the forest paths with their tiny orange-hearted horns of fragrance. The creepers were draping the dull green drabness of the *kurchi* with a glorious lace of white filmy leaves. The liquid, quickly turned dulcimers of the orioles sounded in the mangoes, and the golden bodies flashed from tree to tree. The air was a lavish wine, spilt and sprinkled by the winds. Hilda Mannering, walking through the morning's splendour to her famine-relief station, marvelled that men and women of her race should have lived and worked in this despised Bengal, year after year, and yet have carried away nothing but bitter and disdainful memory.

She had been three weeks with Findlay now. Alden stayed on—Douglas had taken over his work during the last two weeks of term, and now the students were all away for the *pujas*. Alden and Findlay arranged the one still habitable portion of the old *dak*-bungalow for her occupation. They were far too conscious of what her presence meant to them not to accept it; without her, Findlay could hardly have gone through those first terrible days. His weary eyes roved over that crowd of broken humanity, emaciated and shrivelled to bone and hanging skin, a crowd in which lepers came led by little children, and old hags in the last dreadful stages of decrepitude's lingering pilgrimage. Then his look grew restful as it rose to her.

In the evenings, when the long after-dinner talks had finished, the two men would see her across the compound to the old bungalow. Their lanterns swung their rays across the rustling dry leaves, here and there catching a jackal's blinking gaze, where he fed on the fallen figs of *pipal* or banyan, or surprising a

viper whip-like gliding over the grass. The land in
its quietness grew friendly to her; and her presence
was the peace of God to her companions.

She got to know the night sounds. She remembered
well the first time she learnt the note of the little owl
that is the steed of Lakshmi, the gracious and lovely
goddess. That was the first time that Findlay had
laughed.

From an oleander-thicket came the crying, "Oh-o!
Oh-o!" "Show a lantern on the veranda, John," said
Alden, "and get the goddess of luck to come this way."
He told Hilda the legend of the Queen of Beauty
and Fortune riding over the darkened city that on her
festival night was regardless of her, and how she
guided her owl to a thin glimmer far in the forest,
the home of two who remembered and had lit their
lamp of welcome. Hilda, reaching for a lantern that
was keeping the mosquitoes from her ankles, pushed
it forward to where it shone between the bars of the
veranda railing. The teak-trees had tossed down their
great untidy leaves, scorched by the sun into a crinkled
brown paper. They lined the road to the gate; and
thousands of toads were slowly stirring them, as they
climbed after their prey. In the mighty *simul* beside
the well, fireflies had hung innumerable lights, and
made a vast fairy-lamped Christmas-tree between the
house and the crescent moon, peering through its
leaves. Hilda rose and looked out.

"No chance of Lakshmi," she said. "The elves have
stuck their home full of fireflies for her. She won't see
our one poor lantern."

Then, listening to the leaves scuttering under the
toads' halting limbs, she asked: "What's that?"

Her brother-in-law dreamily removed his cheroot. "Tigers," he answered nonchalantly. Unthinkingly, Hilda jumped back. Then they all laughed, as Alden cowered under his hands, while she boxed his ears. Findlay assisted in the punitive measures.

"What a shame, Rob, to lie like that!" he said. "Don't you let him frighten you, Hilda. There hasn't been a tiger in this district since the year 1864. That's official. It's in the *Gazetteer*."

"What about the man-eater last year?" asked Alden, emerging cautiously.

"He doesn't count. He didn't come nearer than a dozen miles. You know that. And you know he's finished, too."

"Tell me about him," commanded Hilda.

The tragi-comic tale was unfolded. A tiger had paused midway on some trek between Orissa and Midnapur, and ravaged the district. A reward of five hundred rupees was put on his head, but he continued to be elusive. "As you know"—Hilda did not know, but she nodded; they were happy to have got John talking freely—"a tiger covers enormous tracts in a night; thirty or even forty miles. And people just went on disappearing. The sub-postmaster of Barh Gaipur, an old pal of mine, was never seen again after one night when he was cycling between here and Surya-konda. They found his cycle, but not a scrap of *him*. Then one day they got *khubber* that the creature had killed an old woman at Simuldanga. So our sub-inspector, who fancies himself as a shikar, went there with a policeman, to sit up above the corpse."

"Do you mean they used the old woman's body as bait?" asked Hilda, horrified.

"Well, the tiger was bound to come back to it," said Alden.

"They'd hardly climbed into the *machan*," Findlay went on, "and it was still daylight, when the tiger strolled on to the scene, and just looked at them. Looked at them—didn't even bother to roar. 'Whereupon,' the sub-inspector's official report ran, 'I ordered my constable to fire and shoot that tiger.' But he didn't; they both dropped their guns in terror. The tiger walked off again. But they sat up in the tree for twenty hours, and didn't dare to come down till after noon next day."

"Didn't anyone come down from Calcutta to kill it?"

"Shoals and shoals of people—we were simply mobbed. But they never got within sight of him. I was after him myself; so were Alden and Douglas. Douglas might have got him, for the brute walked right under his *machan*. But it was a hot day, and Brother Douglas was tired after a long tramp through bad country——"

"*And* a most excellent breakfast," added Alden.

"And he was fast asleep. It was a great shame, after all the difficulty we had had in getting anyone to beat the jungle. That was the only time anyone could have had a shot at the tiger. He must have had a first-rate intelligence department. Sahebs hung about for weeks, and went back swearing the tiger was a myth. It was a huge jest in the Calcutta papers. It wasn't a jest here," Findlay added grimly. "I shan't forget how carefully we shuttered our doors at night, or how wretched I was till I came home and found Joan and Marjorie all right."

He was silent, remembering. Alden hastily broke silence, to lead his thoughts back.

"I always marvelled that you carried on some of those night trips of yours," he said.

"I marvelled myself," said Findlay. "I get back the eerie feeling now, when I think of cycling those jungle paths in the dark and wondering if the next nulla would produce Master Stripes. When my blood thudded in my temples, I used to imagine it was the tiger padding behind me. I don't know what the world's record is for a push-bike through Indian jungles, but I know I've got it, easily."

"You had no business to do it," said Hilda. "Think of what might have happened to you—with Joan and Marjorie at home alone!"

To the end of her days Hilda never understood how she spoke these words, the unhappiest that ever left her lips. Findlay relapsed into tense silence, thinking as she suggested. And that thought which he was keeping at bay, to stave off the madness that was closing him round, leapt in like a wild beast of the night. If he had not simply loved his wife and child, but had lived for them and watched over them—instead of dreaming that he had a mission to these thousands who were none of his, neglecting his own to save alive the pleading wretched faces that now were all that was left to him of his own life—then he might not now be the most miserable of men, with his wife and child in the depths of that sea. He had thought he was serving God and humanity—but was there any man anywhere who would not think him both fool and cad?

Hilda caught the indignation in Alden's voice as he

broke in. "John didn't do those trips for fun. If you're out here, with these thousands of grown-up babies all round you, you can't lie snug at home, even if a tiger is abroad. I know any other chap would have done it, but John isn't any other chap. Sometimes you've *got* to go abroad, whatever the hour. Someone is dying— or *thinks* he is dying"—said Alden with contempt—"or there's sickness or some danger."

But Findlay remained silent.

"A woodcutter killed the tiger at last," said Alden desperately, dragging them back to the theme. "It leapt out on him, and mauled him so that he died afterwards. But the chap had pluck—all these jungle folk have pluck, any amount of it. He saw to it that the brute went off with his ax fixed in its brain. No one ever saw it afterwards."

33

THE weeks passed. Findlay, with mind too miserable to endure its own loneliness, knew what he owed to these friends who took on themselves all of sorrow that can be taken. And Hilda more than ever felt that men have made an unfair world. Here was a companionship of work and suffering endured in silence, of story and discussion, such as they never shared with women in drawing-room or ball-room.

"How on earth did you ever come to know so much about the jungles, Rob?" she asked Alden one day. "I thought you had always been at the College."

Alden and Findlay laughed. "In my bachelor days," said Alden—and a wistfulness came into his voice which perhaps it was just as well that his wife could not hear—"John saw me for many a week-end. I used to cycle through, and drop in on him on Saturday night. Our dinner was always the same—a roast *murghi* each, sometimes with bread, sometimes with *brinjals*, occasionally with potatoes, more often with none of the three. And afterwards we had a rat-hunt in John's *almiras*. What have you done with the bonny boys, John? He kept *huge* rats in those days—the size of Belgian hares. We used to see their dark shadows gliding behind the crockery, as we sat at dinner."

"I had a tame *dhaman* that cleared them off," said Findlay. "They haven't come back since. But we did other things besides rat-hunt, Hilda. Rob's been to pretty well every village that I go to, and he knows the district almost as thoroughly."

Findlay saw nothing of Hamar now. He had unobtrusively taken over Alden's famine work in Vishnugram, and was working with Douglas, whose enthusiastic gratitude was not less than Findlay's had been. At Kanthala they were too busy to think much about him, but he flitted into the background of their minds from time to time, and Findlay often mentioned him. One evening Alden criticized his attitude towards Indians, and Findlay in his eagerness strode up and down defending him. Hilda made a pretext of arranging newspapers that had been flung on the floor, and rose to hide her face in the task of collecting them together again.

34

THE *pujas* ended, the College reopened, Alden returned to Vishnugram. Hilda refused to go with him. "If we had fifty people here, there'd be more than enough for them to do," she said. "I'm not going. I'm too happy. It's the first time since I came to India that I'm some use."

So Hilda stayed. There was a new constraint between her and Findlay, now that Alden had gone; yet, Findlay was aware, in that very constraint was a fresh glamour. A hundred times a day he would look up and see her there, working beside him, and with the sight labour lost its dusty monotony and became a dew-burnished woodland. She was picking up the language fast, and was capable of running a relief station alone now; and in all those pressing thousands there was no one who would have questioned her decisions. So Findlay, after seeing the work commence, could cycle off to the other stations, to see his helpers there. But he spent the afternoons with her, for he knew that her spirit would let the body break before it owned to weariness and overstrain. He was not going to repeat the mistake of neglecting the one nearest to his blood and thought, in discharge of any imagined duty elsewhere.

At twilight they would pack up together, and then return. He was anxious to be with her then; she should see the beauty and peace of this land, but its ugliness must be kept from her.

She questioned him about the enormous mobs of people they saw, dotting the country-side. "Some sort of *puja*?"

"No. Cock-fights. If you've never seen one," he added quickly, to repress the curiosity that flashed into her look, "be careful never to want to see one."

"Why?"

"It's no sight for decent people. I've seen five cocks dead within five minutes."

"Dead! But how?"

"If you saw the steel spurs they fasten on the birds, you'd understand. It's the crudest cruelty in the world —not the worst or cruelest, but the crudest. The people are crazy about it."

Once the sun-dappled shade beneath a *sephali* bush quivered with a tremor of brown and pale-yellow mottle; the head of a panther was thrust towards them, and withdrawn again. Turning round, they saw him in mid-glade, staring after them.

"Fearless, cheeky beasts," commented Findlay. "They love to hang about villages."

Hilda's hand, which had unconsciously gripped his arm, remained there. "But surely they're very dangerous?"

"Ye-es. In a way. I'll be bound I get a deputation asking me to settle this gentleman. A leopard won't bother you if you ignore him; I've met them heaps of times. But sometimes one meets a woman on her way to the tank. She just drops her water-pot, lets out a yell, and runs. And the leopard, being a sporting beast, can't resist the temptation to pull down anything that runs away from him. But bears are more dangerous, really. They knock into wood-cutters in the cubbing season. I have people brought in every spring in a shocking condition, all torn and bitten and clawed."

The leisurely after-dinner discussions were at an end now. When the meal had finished, and while the servants were still on the premises, the prying eyes of that populous compound saw the shadows of Findlay's lantern swaying to and fro as they made their way past the darkness and possible snakes of the way to her room. Two minutes later the lantern was swinging back. Then Hilda would read for a while, but the days left her too worn out for much except sleep at their finish. Findlay, the day's comradeship over, lay awake; and knew that the sea swirled hungrily beneath this thin crust of daily consciousness that he had built out of trifles—out of trifles and Hilda Mannering.

The first Saturday after the College reopened, Hamar motored Alden through. He was silent and preoccupied; this was put down to the Conspiracy Case, now worming its way through a deal of hard lying. The magistrate's preliminary investigation had sent up a number of accused to Hamar's court. No one in the province doubted that they were all guilty, but it was difficult to see how any one of them could be convicted. The men realized this, and felt how much depended on the case for Hamar. Their manner expressed their sympathetic thoughts; he and Alden were good friends now, and Hilda felt a throb of pride at the swift frank kindness with which Hamar and Findlay greeted each other. A woman can never rid herself of the feeling that a man who has loved her in some way belongs to her and is of her household for ever.

Findlay and Alden went inside the house, leaving her and Hamar together on the veranda. "Excuse us a second, Hamar," shouted Alden. "I've got some rubbishy mission business on which our chief told me to get John's opinion."

Hamar, alone with Hilda for the second time in his life—for that momentary vision by the river-bank did not count as interview—found himself troubled with happiness that was almost agony. He was alone with the goddess whom he worshipped, and she was passing irrevocably from him. Meantime he was wasting the precious moments in silence. No, not wasting; for he knew that every line of that slender, maddening loveliness was limning itself on the tablets of unfading memory. Fifty years hence, when he, Vincent Hamar, old and with all other vision erased from the dying stuff of his mind——

Hilda was speaking to him. "Mr. Hamar, I wonder if you'll ever know how we feel towards you for all you did for John. You helped him through this awful summer of famine. Without you, he would have broken down utterly when his trouble came."

"And you," said Hamar, "now? A lady who was made only for happiness and to give happiness——" His voice stopped, and Hilda turned away, half in hope that Alden and Findlay would return before his control gave way. She knew now the tides of feeling that swept this man when in her presence. "*You*, killing yourself here! What are these people, what is Findlay, what is anyone, that you should be allowed to do this!"

"There is only one thing to do now," she said. "We must keep John's mind from being alone with itself, until time has had a chance."

Hamar thought that there was no sorrow that the world has ever known which a man could not forget with Hilda at his side. John Findlay had been made rich, and she must know it—must know, too, that his own hopes were going out in blackness. Alden, entering with Findlay, saw her face; startled, he saw that Findlay had noticed also.

35

THE Vishnugram Conspiracy Case, as everyone knows, came to a sudden finish.

The police had flung their net widely, and a good many fish were in the meshes. Some of these had to be released almost at once, a circumstance duly noted, and unduly exploited, by the nationalist press. Then came the struggle to land the larger fish that remained. As the trial proceeded, racial excitement grew more and more acute. The Indian public delightedly saw that the biggest coup of the two centuries of British dominion was going to be carried off successfully. An enormous arsenal of weapons had been secretly gathered, undoubtedly the presence of a vast underground plot of war and assassination had been laid bare, but the evidence—well, what was the evidence? Out of weeks of skilled and desperate mendacity not enough solid soil emerged on which to rest any convictions that mattered. O-ah, yess! A few quite unimportant pipple would go to the jail, no doubt—for a few weeks at the most, mark you! But as for the leaders of our nation! They lay snug and undiscovered. The two or three that had been caught must certainly be set free, without a stain on their characters. And the Anglo-Indian public raged. Everyone *knew* these chaps were guilty—hang it, those guns and bombs didn't *walk* there of themselves!—and it was all in the hands of that fellow Hamar, a pronative and a fool! If only Seward—or Wilkinson—or any sensible chap—were in charge!

And then, one day, the police intercepted a sum of twenty thousand pounds sterling, sent from Shanghai to the leading accused, the two Chatterji brothers. This belated gift, by astounding stupidity, was sent by the hands of a Chinese shoe-maker of the Calcutta New Market. Unwitting of anything that had happened during the last three months, the Celestial had made his leisurely way back to India, after holiday abroad, doing "business" in North Borneo, Rangoon, Mandalay, Singapore, and Chittagong. No one ever knew how he had missed tidings of recent events. In face of this evidence, it was maintained that the sum was a genuine tribute of appreciation of scholarship— it was sent, the defence maintained, for the two brilliant sons of the elder Chatterji, to further their education in England, after they had finished at the Presidency College. Even so, the sum seemed excessive for its purpose. So it was asserted that the police had manufactured this absurd piece of evidence; after being at the pains to bring together a sham store of revolutionary arms, they would not stick at this trifle. The assessors found the principal accused *not guilty*. But Hamar had decided otherwise. He pushed the opinion aside, and sentenced them both, to eight years' transportation apiece. Minor punishments were meted out to the lesser offenders.

Then the storm broke. The Anglo-Indian press conceded, grudgingly, that Hamar had "done his job," though with less severity than the shocking circumstances demanded; and of course he could hardly have had the face to let the accused off, after he "had seen the stuff with his own eyes." Still, though the sentences were inadequate in view of the enormous offence involved, the intention to plunge a province, if not all India, in bloodshed, it was dimly felt that he had

R

taken his own line, when it involved great courage
to do so.

But all the pent-up chagrin and outraged national
feeling of the opposition burst on his head. In a
moment he seemed to have lost all his Indian friendships; and these had come to matter to him tremen-
dously. In those months of work with Findlay and,
later, with Douglas and Alden, he had found common
ground with many a subordinate official and with
College professors and school teachers. They who had
come forward from the apathetic mass to save the
poor and outcaste of their land knew that this English ruler cared also, and that his will was iron against
any indulgence to his mind and body, so long as work
remained for him to do. And now they were aloof
and sullenly respectful, and some were afraid to be
seen with him. He was surprised to find that he felt
lonely, still more surprised to find that he cared.
Before, at the time of the Lambertgarh Case, when
he had been acclaimed as "a Daniel come to the judgment," the one pure spirit in a naughty service,
he had been simply that not uncommon person, an
Englishman without a shred of sympathy for any
alien mode of thinking but with a passion for absolute, abstract justice. But now—when he had been
mingling with this people daily, had been seeing their
patience and their courage under adversity, that gentleness of theirs which goes with bravery of a kind
different from the Englishman's, but nevertheless as
admirable—he was hated and distrusted, a tyrant and
an unscrupulous perverter of the law. He had had
his ready-made opinions overturned by intercourse
with the best of Alden's students, seen by him when

at their most attractive—for every Bengali instinctively rallies to suffering, at any rate in sympathy, and lacks nothing of willingness to work, uncomplainingly and without rest, once he has been pulled out of his initial inertia. And now, when he realized a thousand subtler things, and had begun to catch, by flash and glimpse, knowledge of how this race felt and thought, that he should lose his friendships with them! He was aware that other lands had known revolutions, and that expulsion of foreign rulers has never been accomplished by rose-water methods. He knew, too, how much history has been willing to overlook, when rebellion has proved successful. He was under no illusions that imputed exceptional turpitude to Indians who collected arms; they were doing only what Bruce and William Tell and Washington had done, with the full applause of later ages. Still, with an increasing number of his countrymen he held that there was open to India another way to independence, one unstained by the bloodshed and misery which these men were seeking to bring about. They knew nothing about war; he, who had seen a regiment lose four hundred men in five minutes, knew that open violence stood no earthly chance against his own well-armed and warlike countrymen. As long as the Raj existed, its business was to prevent violence, and its laws had to be enforced. It was unfortunate—he had sympathy even with the Chatterji brothers—but—as long as he was judge, he "had to do his job." He had done it, with a heavy heart; and he wondered that Indians should resent it. "Sane, reasonable Indians," that is. But Hamar forgot that when national feeling is roused, there are no sane, reasonable Indians, any

more than there are sane, reasonable Englishmen. He
reinforced his mind, when it wavered, by recollection
that these men—the Chatterjis, at any rate—had
sought alliance with that monster, the blood-stained
bolshevism of Russia. That, in itself, settled the matter for every right-thinking Englishman.

He opened his perplexity to Alden.

"Well, you see," said Alden, who felt by no means
sure that Hamar had done right, though he had no
doubts about the man's genuineness and his motives,
"it's partly a matter of different ethics." This was a
favourite statement of his; Douglas was felt by listeners to a recent argument between the two to have
scored quite neatly when he asserted that Alden
meant nothing by it but to gain time under cover of
which he could find out what his opinion really was.
"We think first, second, and last, of doing our job;
our favourite virtues are justice, firmness, integrity.
To us mere kindness, as such, is weak sentimentality.
But Indians don't give a bean for *our* cardinal virtues.
To them any sort of harshness seems infinitely worse
than the worst lapse from absolute justice. Oh, I
know they often *seem* to assent to our code, and to
accept it. But they never do. Take our rigid standard
—by the way, *is* it as rigid as we persuade ourselves?
However, that's by the way—of truth-speaking. Now
there's nothing that Indians resent so much as being
called liars."

"That's because they know they *are* liars," said
Hamar bitterly, fresh from two months of unmitigated law-court.

"I don't think so," said Alden. "It's because they've
at last got an inkling of *our* attitude on the matter,

and they wriggle because they feel *our* contempt for the liar—that is, for certain kinds of liar. It's just resentment of what they feel to be unmerited contempt."

"Unmerited?"

"Yes. Because they don't accept our ethics in the matter. If you could get to the back of the best Indian's mind—and I'm thinking of one of our Christian ministers—he's a saint, a man I admire immensely—but you won't admire him, you won't do him any sort of justice, if you insist on looking for British virtues in him. He's a better man than I am—but in a *different* way. And if you were to get to the back of his mind—though I don't believe he ever tells a lie himself—I *know* a lie seems differently to him than to us."

"What the horns are to the buffalo, what the paw is to the tiger, what the sting is to the bee"—Hamar began to quote Macaulay.

"Cut Macaulay out," said Alden impatiently. "Macaulay was a fool, if ever a man was. He spent five years in India, and he never saw it for a minute. No man, not even another Englishman, ever took less away. He wasn't a man, he was what Sydney Smith called him, 'a book in breeches.' He just sat in a Calcutta office, and read his fellow-books."

"Well," Hamar began.

"It comes down to this. They would rather tell a lie than give pain; we would rather give the pain. We worship Themis, they Charis. Hang it all, the world wants a shrine where both statues can have a place. And you, Hamar, have chosen to be just, when the circumstances gave you abundant loop-hole to be kind.

You've proved true to type, and once more blood and heredity and training have aligned you where you belong. Indian nationalism, which was never wholly persuaded of you, resents this, and its knife is out for you."

"But will they *never* see our point of view?"

"Oh, they're seeing it now, seeing it only too fast for their comfort of mind. Be sorry for a chap like Neogyi. He's been stripped of his own code of ethics, and he's trying to administer ours. He'd have done what you did, in this trial; and they'd have murdered him the next night. Yes, Hamar, he'd have done what you did, though he knew he was signing his life away. *That's* the kind of courage it takes to serve the Raj and be straight. You know what the Deogharias do."

It was an unhappy illustration, and Alden's face showed that he was cursing himself for the reference.

But Hamar had consolations in his perplexities. Colonel Henderson drifted into Vishnugram for the annual shooting tests, which he arranged to hold earlier than usual, as he was being transferred to Central India; he explained that he wanted to see the station again. Findlay came in from Kanthala, but—to Henderson's disappointment—without Hilda. The visitor was amazed at the readiness with which Findlay and Alden assumed that she was all right, an English lady alone in the wilderness. "Why," said the former, "she's become a goddess. And who's going to touch a goddess? She's saved a thousand lives this last month. And she's alone only for this noon. I shall be back before nightfall."

The soldier wavered. He could not go to Kanthala unless some member of the station drove him; and the request would make both Miss Mannering and himself conspicuous. He wavered; the topic changed, the chance was lost. He left Vishnugram, wondering if he had missed his destiny, by lack of the last touch of courage which risks even wounded self-esteem and the esteem of those we care for.

Relief mingled with Hamar's disappointment. He had not forgotten—how should he forget?—the last time he saw Hilda and Henderson together. That glowing comradeship of hers, so unstintingly given to the man who was with her, would have been more than he could have borne to witness, especially since rumour had joined her name with the soldier's not three months ago.

Henderson turned to Hamar, as they went towards the butts. "I followed every minute of your case, Hamar," he said. "No man ever had a more ticklish job. If you had let the fellows off, no decent man anywhere could have blamed you. If you don't mind my saying it, your action was the pluckiest thing I ever knew."

36

FINDLAY, returning to Kanthala, found the land an estranged face, and unfriendly. Its iron bonds had burst, and the tide of release was swelling, a foam of green and red and white. The awakened wood-gods were tossing wide the spray of new leaves, the lusty blood-flushed emerald of mango, the delicate pink of young sal; their silent, invisible shuttles were weaving the lace of the creepers. But Findlay, with self-loathing in his spirit, hated the happiness around him. It was for this land that he had, "like the base Indian," thrown away "a jewel richer than all his tribe." Himself, yes—there was no indulgence he would have kept, no pang or toil that he would have shunned, to help these people. But, while he thought he was sacrificing himself, he had only been sacrificing these others, in their weakness and their love dependent on him and on what he did.

Immediately there swept up before him, like a vision, the remembrance of missionary meetings that he had attended in England. He saw again rows of semi-intelligent, excited faces, he heard hymns—ah, they served their purpose; Jesus Christ has made it clear that there is no place in His follower's mind for intellectual intolerance, for the cheap scorning of anything that helps men and women to forget weakness and failure or nerves them to effort and hope. The hymns should pass, then. But what of the speakers? He heard a famous preacher encouraging "these brethren who are going for us to the frontiers of the war, to the far-flung battle-line of Christ's mighty Empire." There was too much of the Roman Empire, Findlay thought fastidiously, in the way Christendom dreams of itself, too little of the Athenian republic. Well, whose fault? Paul's? No! If the rabbit-brained and idly fluent chose to misunderstand that gallant spirit, the blame was theirs. Still, had not Jesus spoken of "The Kingdom of Heaven"? Yes, but that Kingdom was not of this world. It was within you. It was not within Findlay. He was destitute, afflicted, tormented.

The speaker was now talking, earnestly, eloquently, with arms upraised, about the "sacrifice" our "brethren" were taking upon themselves. That sea of rapt

faces looked as if for the moment it had been hyp-
notized into belief that such sacrifice was entailed. In
their normal moments, Findlay knew, its members
were sceptical of its existence. So was the speaker,
once you caught him in the frank cynicism of a
preachers' after-service, after-supper Sunday night
symposium. Neither he nor his hearers knew where
the sacrifice lay, or dreamed how bitter and terrible
it was. Their minds—and Findlay, in such revulsion
as he had never imagined he could know, loathing and
scorning his fellows, wondered what word any language contained that could fit the thing these were;
he found none, and continued, reluctantly—their
minds were thinking in terms of palm-trees and black-
coated men under them, an open Bible in the right
hand, the left hand pointing to Heaven as witness.
Or some of them had gathered enough of recent
missionary jargon to visualize "the foreign force" as
soldiers in some vague "firing-line" or as sappers and
miners beneath the walls of heathenism. But what
"sacrifice" is there in that? Of the real sacrifice, the
price paid in the spirit and the body, they knew nothing. They never *could* know anything, any more than
the fools at home know of the life that survives the
nightmare of the trenches. Findlay thought of cases
he knew—of missionaries who had flung their lives
away early, not heroically, not effectively, but wilfully,
idiotically; and their widows had paid the price, in
illness and overwork and miserable anxiety, years
after the glow of enthusiasm had faded and they had
first wondered why they had ever given their young
womanhood and all its promise and beauty to a fool.
He thought of missionaries' children he knew—some

were pitifully satisfied with themselves and with the very meagre outlook that life had brought them. "Thou sayest, I am rich, and increased with goods, and have need of nothing; and knowest not that thou art wretched, and miserable, and poor, and blind, and naked." There was nothing, he reflected, that so blinds the eyes of the mind as the religious life. John Wesley had said that the world was his parish; and his followers had somehow got it twisted into the notion that the parish should be their world. Findlay thought of other cases, where early neglect, by parents too occupied with the task of doing good to others, had sent into manhood and womanhood children physically, as well as mentally, undeveloped, or neurotic or half-witted. The real sacrifice came here, long after the real fool had gone to his own place. And he, John Findlay, had been such a fool.

He reminded himself that he that saves his soul shall lose his soul. But that did not mean that God wanted a man to marry a woman and leave her to a long drudgery, or to beget children who had no childhood, no start in life or future or prospects. Why should a man, strong and with the choice of what all their lives should be in his hands, save the heathen at the price of—not *his* blood, *that* he had a right to dispose of—but theirs? He had let Marjorie and Joan go through those years of growing weakness and pain, which had ended in death and the madness which leapt into death.

It was growing dusk, and his road was touching the outskirts of Trisunia. The hill-top was far—five miles or more. But he must find some help somewhere, for he felt insanity closing on his brain. If anywhere, then on that cool mountain crest, with its whispering leaves and singing waters, he would be comforted and strengthened. Why had God forsaken him?

He left his cycle under a tree, and swung into the wastes. He strode along, looking neither to right nor left. He leapt across the nullas, he scrambled up the ravines, he was heedless of snake or wild beast or gathering darkness. Suddenly a sweet, ethereal fragrance came to him; and, mingled with it, a fouler taint. He knew where he was now. Those tall, intertwisted trees were the grove of Padalsini, the jungle she-demon. They were a rarity, no others of their sort grew for twenty miles round, and they had been dedicated to the wood-queen. But that fouler taint was of blood, of the goats that they slew in her honor.

Then Findlay's mind broke. The terror and wrath that had been besetting him took shape. This was the land that had fooled him, the false deity for which he had flung away his jewel. Its sweetness, all that glory of blossoming sal and *neem* and autumn-flowering orange-hearted *sephali* that had intoxicated him, was stained with blood, it stank and was vile. And the land was living, it was a demon, it was here, its home was in that thicket. He saw dimly the crude clay horses and elephants clustered round the grove, the steeds on which the hateful spirit rode abroad in the darkness. She was seeking him now, she was persecuting him. God had forsaken him, he was delivered into the hands of the Hosts of Evil. He had played with them, he had loved their land—how he had loved it!—he had tried to see, kindly and with sympathy, why men worshipped these things. When he should have been as the prophets who cut down the high places and slew their priests, to whom Baal was merely a stone to be kicked aside with contumely! Those pentecostal missionaries whom he and Alden scorned were right. He should have taught that every word in the Bible was true and righteous altogether, that the scriptures of the heathen were nothing but malignant and deliberate lying, that everyone who died unbaptized would go to hell, the eternal victim of a Just and Holy God whose wrath was on all who knew Him not, even if no opportunity of knowing Him had come their way. Findlay was mad.

And Padalsini was seeking him. That dark place in the thicket was her demon-body, that gleam in the branches her teeth; her eyes were following him. Through the forest she was stalking him, his soul and body would be hers. And his gallant spirit, that had never cried for help before, cried for it now. But there was no help for him anywhere; his earthly help he had tossed away, it was dead, dead, he would never see those faces again; and God had given him over. But had Christ? Would Christ ever forsake a man who had loved Him, who had trusted Him as he went through the wilderness, his life in his hands? Findlay felt that he could not trust God—what right has God to be trusted, as men and women have trusted Him? What has He done, through all the ages, to win and deserve our confidence? But he could trust Christ. God had forsaken Christ, as He had now forsaken Findlay; He had left both the Just and the unjust. Well, since he must die, he would die calling on Christ.

And as the night took visible, menacing form, and

towered above him with burning, unpitying eyes, Findlay called out. But there was no answer save the surging blackness that overwhelmed him. His mind darkened, his body grew sick and faint. Trying to flee in the wilderness, he stumbled, and felt the hands of the jungle across his flight. The demon-queen had caught up with him, she was lying in his way, and had gripped his foot. He cried again, terribly and despairingly. Then he fell, and all was blankness.

37

ALDEN, in reply to Hilda's telegram, was at Kanthala next afternoon. Findlay had been found unconscious in the jungle, by peasants crossing the wilderness to their work. He was lying in bed now, and had recovered consciousness. But he refused to say anything. He had had an accident, and would soon be all right; that was all they could get out of him.

Hamar, who had motored Alden out, took them all into Vishnugram. At least, Findlay could be cared for here, and made to rest. His mind seemed to be all right, except for an unreasoning, unfathomable misery which was beyond their reach. He was soon up and about again, but he shared in neither conversation nor games. He was alone, for all that his friends could do.

Christmas came, bringing its grave, quiet revels. The Nixons had guests, and a tennis tournament was arranged for the station. There were also the usual shooting-picnics. Famine relief slackened. The Christmas rain fell this year, and with unusual abundance.

Some sort of cultivation was possible in the district, which in good years produced a meagre crop of spring rice, as well as the main autumn crop which had failed this year.

By the ironic juggling of Fate, Jacks was Hilda's partner in the tournament, and the spectators had renewed opportunity to admire her pluck and self-control. Hamar saw little of her. Her time in India was drawing to a close; her sailing, originally planned for the autumn just over, was now fixed to take place in April.

Findlay, a silent, uncaring figure on the edges of their pleasures, disquieted them, and the station were glad when he went back to Kanthala. Even his friends were glad, for they knew nothing of what had happened that night in the wilderness, and they supposed that he was pining for his work and his own people. He insisted on going; Alden, Douglas, Hilda, Hamar, all tried to keep him a while longer. But he just shook his head, and went.

Hilda did not return with him. Her sister had been back in Vishnugram for some time now, and she felt that she wished to spend her last weeks with her.

The New Year came in, bringing the Feast of Cakes for the children of Bengal. The mango groves were one vast censer, steeping the winds with fragrance; the big black bees were riotous in their boughs, the *kokils* were shouting all day and—so it seemed—all night.

One morning Hamar heard Alden's voice on his veranda. Without ceremony Alden tossed up the curtain and strode into the bedroom. Behind him dawn was beginning to sweep and counter-sweep the sky with light and colour.

"Still swigging tea, and in bed! No! On my soul! He hasn't"—he shouted to someone outside—"even touched his tea yet. Still asleep! Throw a *dhuti* over you, and come out. I've fetched Neogyi with me. He's been transferred to a vile hole in East Bengal, where Deogharia's intention is that he shall die of drink and malaria. We're going to have one last revel; and you're coming with us. Which car? His or yours? It doesn't matter which. Choose."

Hamar began to make objections, which were firmly set aside. He was told that Neogyi had already sent a message to his office in his name, giving them a holiday for the day. This deed of defiant lawlessness convinced him that Neogyi was certainly leaving the district. He liked Neogyi.

So in ten minutes—no, fifteen—Hamar was shaved and dressed. All through this expeditious performance his companions cursed and harassed him for a slacker. He was flung up into Neogyi's car, and found himself whirling away in the direction of Kanthala. For the first time for years (it seemed) he gave himself up to happiness.

The exultation of that spring dawn lit his veins to dancing fire. This endless procession of people going by, to market and to their day's work, filled him with bliss. The earth was spinning onward on her course, interchanging hot and cold days, summer and autumn and winter and spring, rains and dewy season; and she was spinning away, as on a never-pausing loom, his own fleeting days, and the days of these countless unknown men and women, his brothers and sisters.

But these days, while they raced to their finish, were scattering beauty and happiness and, most precious of all, comradeship. Why should he, Vincent Hamar, who had known the perils and boredom of Sannaiyat trenches and of the desert where man's spirit is naked, be an official? Or an Englishman? Damn it all, because God had placed him on an island in the midst of the seas, he wasn't bound to keep an insular soul and a ragged, ugly, beastly little mind. Look at these people on the road! They were his own flesh and blood—he repeated it in ecstasy, and he longed that somehow his love and good will might reach them and make them also happy. The same Mind—he was sure this morning that it was Mind that had blossomed into the courage and beauty of man—that had flung its passion for loveliness into the poise and glory of Hilda Mannering, had expressed its patience and heroic endurance in that withered woman going past, her shrivelled breast and the taut spare body beneath her whitened, meagre hair witnessing to the record of struggle and motherhood and semi-starvation that was nearly finished.

"Where are we going?" he asked.

"What?" shouted Alden back. The car was going at a terrific pace, now that it was free of the crowded city. Hamar repeated.

"Alden is going to continue what Nixon calls his researches into sedition," answered Neogyi, who was driving.

"When did he say that?" asked Alden. "That's rather good for Nixon."

"When you went off to Santiniketan for the weekend, just after old Rabi Babu had been saying beastly things about some Government arrests. But this time it's *worse*. We're going to see Jayananda Sadhu. That'll finish your reputation, Hamar."

"Does Alden know him?" asked Hamar in surprise.

"Know him?" said Neogyi. "Don't you know that Alden *is*—in his very person—*the* Revolutionary Party? Hasn't the Calcutta press told you that? He's the chap whose indecipherable signature is scrawled at the bottom of those glorious pronouncements that we find stuck up on our office boards."

"They get stuck up on the College boards, too," said Alden.

Hamar joyously leapt into the buffoonery. "Ah, that's just your low cunning," he said. "But I *am* shocked to hear that you are a pal of Jayananda's. Ought I, a Government official, to be associated with such an expedition?"

"You've had no choice," said Neogyi. "We kidnapped you."

"Does Neogyi also know the ruffian?"

"Neogyi?" said Alden. "Why, Neogyi *is* Jayananda Sadhu. Wait till you see him suddenly change into tiger-skin and ashes!"

"No speed limits on *these* roads!" chanted Neogyi. "Who dares arrest the Magistrate Saheb Bahadur, even if there were? Out of the way, you wild elephants and leopards and all you jungle beasts!"

The car had crossed the dry Gandeswari, and entered Findlay's territory, the once enchanted wilderness of *mahua* and sal. It sped along recklessly— Neogyi was evidently prepared to smash tires and car to pieces. Then it switched off from the Kanthala

s

road, and rattled along a boulder-strewn track till it
reached Khamadhi.

"Change here for Seditionpur," shouted Alden, as
Neogyi jerked the car to a standstill.

They ate the zizyph berries, as they sauntered over
the heath that led to the Sadhu's abode. These were
ripe, and spiced the air with winy fragrance. "India
in spring," said Alden, "is like one vast pub. These
berries and the unformed jack-fruits that tumble off
prematurely all ferment, and it reminds you of cheap
beer at home. It's exhilarating, Neogyi. Just look at
Hamar; he's treading on air."

The Sadhu was sitting by his lake, which was aglow
with red lotuses. "Jayananda," said Alden, making no
ceremony of their meeting, "this is Hamar. Don't
pretend you haven't heard of him, for we know you
have. You know," he added quickly, seeing that
Hamar misunderstood his words, "what a brick he
has been all through this summer. And there won't
be any C.I.E. for *him,* nor any Kaisar-i Hind either,
not even a second-class one. Your old school-chum
Deogharia has annexed the little loot that was going
for this famine *biznai.*"

Deogharia had become K.C.I.E. in the New Year
Honours; and Alden's remark had been an instinctive
anticipation of the suggestion that Indian critics
immediately make when an official does his duty
magnificently, that he is after a decoration. But the
remark was clumsy and silly. He saw this; he had
almost seemed to suggest what no one present would
have suspected for a moment, that a Government
ribbon had been in Hamar's mind. The Sannyasi
looked puzzled.

"Deogharia?" he queried.

"Is now Sir Radhagobinda Deogharia, K.C.I.E. But no one cares an O.B.E. what happens to him. When decent blokes forgather, why should they discuss the criminal classes? I'm sorry to have mentioned so ill-omened a name. The present business before the meeting is: Brother Neogyi has been transferred. He wants a last chat with his spiritual adviser. And we both want you to meet Hamar."

The four men sat on a mound of up-flung gravel. Alden, his gaze wandering, began flicking the lake's surface with pebbles. "Sadhuji," he said at last. "Hamar has been wondering why on earth he wasn't assassinated over his case. Shall I tell him? You know, you *have* been wondering, Hamar."

"Well," said Hamar, "why was it? I got a chit from Headley, warning me. Headley doesn't get the wind up for nothing, does he?"

"By no means. I'll tell you, if the Sadhu has no objection." Jayananda made no sign. "It's thanks to that superstition which I and my colleagues are so busy trying to uproot. *There* is the reason!" He pointed to the Sadhu. "Everyone knew that his curse was on the man who raised a hand against you. But for that, you'd have been a dead man weeks ago."

"But why should the Sadhu interfere to save me?"

"Oh, you shall know that too. I'm keeping no secrets after to-day. None! A Christian missionary came to the Sadhu, and made him swear to save the English Judge Saheb who had sent the Sadhu's own folk to jail."

"A Christian missionary?"

"Even so. Are not my words clear? John Findlay

came here, and asked that a Sannyasi's curse might go abroad."

Alden's excitement was over; he subsided, and resumed his slow, thoughtful pebble-chucking. Hamar and Neogyi turned to the Sadhu.

"I did nothing," he said. "Nothing. My people know that there is a curse on murder. I did but remind them. And it needed no persuasion by Findlay. You had saved my people, you had done what I longed to do but could not. I have left the ocean of doing, and I dared not return."

Alden grew restless again. "Sadhuji," he said.

"Yes?"

"Oh, what's the matter with us all? Why are we so damned futile? *You,* for instance? We know what you were to this people." He paused; he was asking the question that Findlay had asked. Perhaps, till the end of time, the Western saint will ask it of the Eastern. "Why——"

"Why did I not join Findlay?"

"Yes. Why didn't you? For I *can't* get away from the feeling that there's something inhuman in sitting tight meditating on the Great Silence, when men and women are dying by the million in the midst of—shall I say the tiny noises? Dying from helplessness and ignorance and stupidity. Oh, not only in famine time. And you, Sadhuji, could have helped. No one could have helped so much."

The Vairagi was silent. "I felt so myself," he said at last. "And I all but flung aside my hard-won peace of victory, and entered that ocean of deeds once more. But there could have been no return. Once I had appeared among men and women, toiling for them,

listening to them, perhaps—oh, yes, it might easily
have happened—losing all patience with them, I
should never have regained this shore of quiet. Every
Indian has a Sannyasi in his heart; but I, Jayananda"
—he seemed to stress the title, with perhaps uninten-
tional sarcasm; the "joy of victory" had vanished from
both his eyes and his heart, and he was the troubled
figure that had lived and worked with Englishmen
twenty-five years ago—"have a demon also. That
demon of disquiet once drove me hither and thither
and men's lives were destroyed because of the sparks
that he scattered from his blazing torch. I have driven
that demon out—with how much prayer and struggle,
no man knows! No man *could* know, unless he were
your Christ, who spent long nights on those uplands
of his Galilee. I *dared* not return!" The Sadhu was
speaking swiftly, almost desperately, not to Alden,
not to Hamar or Neogyi, but to himself. "Yet—
I will not say that the freedom of your Findlay is
not a greater freedom. I longed to join him when I
heard that he had thrust aside the terrible pain of
his own heart, and continued to serve others."

The Sannyasi, Alden mused, knows nothing of Findlay's state now. Why should he know? How could he
know? The man who saves others cannot save himself.
All day long Findlay's spirit must meet the demands
of those who came to him; but there was not one of
them to suspect that his own spirit was in any need.
At the Last Day the Englishman may be saved after
all, because in his loneliness he has carried on, asking
nothing, expecting nothing. There may somewhere be
a gospel for those who "do their job," a gospel hidden

from the Gentiles who never dream that there is any job for them to do.

"And if a man could serve others, and be busied with the works of every day, and yet had that peace——" Alden paused.

"That peace which the workers never win," said the Sadhu. "Yes, if he could do that, then he would show men that which combined our peace and your energy, and transcended both. I will tell you, Alden the *padre* saheb, what it is that we have not seen. Through these three centuries countless Englishmen have shown us courage, honour, justice. We are not forgetful of this, though we will not acknowledge it now. But hardly one, whether missionary or official, has shown——" the Vairagi hesitated, then continued with a gentleness amazing to his hearers——"the grace of the Lord Jesus Christ. And until you can show us your peace, we will not believe in your victory. It is not energy that proves holiness. A child or a mad dog can rush round and round. Your *padres* pray——I have heard them, when I was in England——that the grace of their Lord Jesus Christ may rest upon them and those who have listened to them. But that grace does not rest upon them——it never has rested on them."

Hamar had been silent, listening. Now he spoke.

"I'm not a religious man, Sadhu," he said. "But I feel what you say about our restlessness. There's no peace for the man who has to get things done. It's only the dreamers and the boys in the universities who can think there is. All day long and every day it's just one round of jobs, one thing after another. A bit of excitement at the start; and then——dullness to the grave."

"All the same, Hamar," said Alden, "it needn't be. I *won't* give in, I *won't* accept the wearisomeness as inevitable. If we were suddenly placed, by some magic of the Sadhuji's, in the midst of an Athenian day, we should be bored stiff with the mistakes of our slaves and the women's chatter about the price of olives. While all the time Æschylus or Socrates had passed us in the market-place, or the news of Platæa was about to fly through the city! Yet to us, in after-time, every hour of all those days has a light upon it, and we dream of it as wonderful. Even so, some day, men and women, discontented because life is so dull and unheroic, will look back across a century, two centuries, ten centuries, to this day we four men are spending in India, and they will see it as in a dream. No, they won't have heard of *us,* of course, but they'll imagine the lives we have lived. Look! the light on those waves, the glitter through those leaves, that hoopoe treading a minuet with his own dancing, lovely shadow! And here are four ghosts exchanging thoughts they care about. I'm hanged if I'll be beaten, or if I'll admit my life is dull."

38

NILKAMAL had brought fruit and water. The Sadhu said: "Alden and Hamar, let me introduce your suppliant. Nilkamal, behold the United English Nation."

Alden stared. "Is *that* the chap?"

"It is all right," Nilkamal assured him. "I am now receiving my clothing and fooding regularly from the United English Nation."

Alden was perplexed. The Sannyasi did a most unsannyasilike thing; he laughed.

"Aha, Alden Saheb, there are some matters, then, that your Intelligence Department does not report. I will explain," he added, as Nilkamal left them again. "Findlay has taken on the job of being the United English Nation."

Alden outlined for Hamar and Neogyi the story of Nilkamal's meeting with Findlay. "The poor chap's wife and child had died of cholera," he said.

The Sadhu looked on, silent. At last he said: "You believe in a God, Alden?"

"I believe in nothing else, Vairagi."

"Then you are a Hindu, *padre* saheb—a fact that my people have long suspected. And also, I think, some of your colleagues?"

Alden laughed. Jayananda continued: "This God in whom we believe is a jester. He mixes scraps of absurdity with our tragedy. Nilkamal was a clerk in Calcutta; and from time to time he still remembers vaguely that he was employed by some firm of Englishmen. Their dress and features have all merged, and they are just the United English Nation to him now."

"I'll dare bet his employers were Scots," grumbled Alden. "The United English Nation is a myth—it's merely the world's biggest and most long-suffering scapegoat."

"I don't see how it can be *both* those things," said Hamar.

"I'm not thinking of Nilkamal," said Alden.

"What *are* you thinking of?" asked Neogyi.

"Something quite irrelevant. The way my people obsess the thought of the whole world. I'm sick of the way everything is put down to us. Vairagi, have you noticed *this?* Whenever an Englishman does a thing that strikes the rest of the world as the outside edge and red-coloured limit——"

"Alden," said Hamar, "you manage to get as close to swearing without actually using recognized bad words as anyone I ever met!"

"Shut up, Hamar. I'm fighting your cause as well as mine, and the cause of the whole misunderstood United English Nation. I tell you, the man I'm talking of is always a Scot or an Irishman or an Ulsterman. But the whole world curses *us,* from San Francisco to Peking. No one ever curses the Irish or Scotch. On the contrary, they are everywhere regarded as picturesque, poetical little peoples, shockingly oppressed by the brutal English. And *we* have to carry all the villainy they do."

"All this," laughed Hamar, "because poor Nilkamal wants to raise a fund from us!"

"Yes," said Jayananda. "He remembers that he was entitled to a small pension from his firm's Provident Fund. And he can't understand why it doesn't come in. Once he went to the Bealda Police Station to draw it. A sergeant there was a bit of wag, so drafted a document by which Nilkamal became the property of the United English Nation, in exchange for his keep. Findlay has made himself responsible, and Nilkamal has lost his grievance. He's a very great man, is Findlay. He understands all that your psycho-analysts make such a fuss about, as to the necessity of digging these complexes out of people's minds."

"If he'll let me," said Hamar, "I'd like to become

paymaster to the United English Nation. I've more
money than Findlay."

"You can fork up complexes from some other
Indian's mind. Our mental clay's overrun with them,"
said the Sadhu.

Alden had been rumbling on discontentedly. "I've
got another grouse against you folk," he said. "You
pretend to be highly moral about violence; but you
know, you *do* rather admire ruthlessness. I'm taking
risks now, Vairagi. But you and I know too much
to be able to stop short of absolute frankness. I've
been reading a proscribed book on the Mutiny."

The Vairagi nodded. There was no emotion in his
eyes.

"The writer's a *beast*," Alden continued. "I'm not
blaming him—*I* should be in his place. But he is. He
revels in the butchery of our women and children.
But that isn't all. He can't help showing admiration
for folk like Neill and Nicholson, whereas he half-
despises the decent men, such as Henry Lawrence. I
sometimes think that your cursing the United English
Nation for what our Scots and Irish and Welsh and
Ulstermen do isn't genuine indignation but just a dirty
political game. Your enemies are right when they say
you admire the strong, brutal ruler. Most of you do.
Our ethics are a whole heap better than yours, in some
ways."

"Worlds better," the Sannyasi conceded cheerfully.
"But we are changing. And here's a thing that you'll
never get the rest of the world to believe—they know
nothing of England and India's relations from the
inside, they judge only by propaganda. But, you know,

we like the individual Englishman, when he gives us a chance. Gandhi likes him, you know."

"I do know," said Alden.

"Neogyi likes him. I like him. Alden, if you don't continue to drift my way, you'll find me on your College veranda during one of your Scripture periods."

"I suppose," said Hamar, "three hundred years together does make two nations something like a family. And a family often behaves very badly in the home."

"It's my turn," said the Sannyasi. "And I'm going to question Alden. I want to ask him what annoys him most in Indians."

"I can't say offhand. There's so much," said Alden. The others burst out laughing. "Backbonelessness— they wash their hands and cringe, instead of behaving like men. No. I think I'm more annoyed yet by the way they keep bragging. Your people never forget if a foreigner praises you. You still quote some silly thing that was said in 1826 by a fool of a major who didn't know a word of any Indian tongue, except——"

"Except enough to order drinks," Hamar suggested.

"Exactly. And yet considered himself entitled to say that Hinduism was a far deeper and finer religion than Christianity—and this at a time when you were burning a thousand widows a year in Bengal alone! Please don't think I'm wantonly dragging up the past. I know all about my own folk in that benighted age. Or he said that some obscure Indian poet was far better than Shakspere or that some florid daub put Raphael in the shade. And——" Alden lifted his hands in horror, a favourite action when he was excited—"You—damn silly blighters—go on quoting

the moron! As if his opinion came to a row of beans!
Why, the man was a *known* ass when alive; and he's
been dust this seventy years! And then the number
of silly European and American women you quote!"

"We do. Have you ever thought why?"

"Oh, yes, I *know* why," said Alden impatiently.
"You're a new firm, and you've got to bounce and
swank and advertise. We're old-established, the world
knows what our goods are, it doesn't matter an O.B.E.
whether anyone praises us or curses us. *We* don't care;
and we're the only nation extant that doesn't. There's
no merit in our indifference. It's easy enough to be
dignified if you're Lord Curzon or George Wyndham.
The world has been made for you, and it gives you
full marks for every copy you show up, you don't
have to shout or push or pull strings. If Burns and
one of those chaps came together, which would do
the bragging? Burns, of course; he'd behave like the
vulgar, grousy, discontented peasant that he was.
Shakspere bragged and behaved like a cad; he knew
it, and was wretched about it. I say, down with these
self-made authors! They spoil the sweet dignity and
peace of the world. Now, Vairagi, it's your turn. What
vexes you most in us?"

"Your nobly moral airs. The way you have persuaded yourselves that the Empire is just a magnificent
philanthropic institution, disinterestedly run for the
sake of an ungrateful world. That's where *your* brag
comes in. You don't brag about your poetry—or your
men of science—or your martyrs—or any of the things
that really exist."

"What's wrong with us both?" Alden's hands went
up despairingly.

"Second-hand opinions. Ours come from books— you've had wit enough to notice that."

"I know," said Alden. "The way of the publicist who writes about India is made easy for him; his stuff is all ready and in a common store. He just shuts his brain and writes about the parrot babu who has memorized Burke and Macaulay and 'no taxation without representation.'"

"And *your* opinions," said the Sadhu, with resentment in his voice, "you get from chatter among yourselves. But it's second-hand opinion in both cases. Once a man sees that, he's lost to the orthodox parties. That's why our nationalists are splitting, with huge gaps and fissures in their solidarity. Your papers see it, and cheer."

"Not seeing," said Alden, "the crevasse that's opening under our own feet."

"Opening in fifty places. Even your missionaries are throwing up heterodox members who've ceased to be patient with the stuff they get from their leaders and their magazines. When I was a nationalist, I used to hunt up your religious papers, and they made me angrier than anything else. I know now they don't matter. Our books and your talk are both wrong. Once you get among facts and people, you never want to get back to the books or the clubs."

"The clubs are people," said Neogyi.

"They are *not*," said Alden. "They're just *faces*— screwed up round cigars and above pegs and billiard-cues. People feed there, they are social there, they agree with any rot that's said there. But the world outside, if you want to keep a brain in your skull!"

39

ALDEN was working himself up to another pitch of excitement. He could sit no longer, he paced up and down.

"That's what I told Gandhi," he said, "when he was doing one of his fat-headed fasts. He was shutting himself up *with himself*—my hat! what doleful company for any man! Sorry, Vairagi! I forgot you were doing the same! But it's hard to take your sannyasi-ship seriously, after all the times I've looked in here, just to say 'Damn all things' to you. Douglas tells me he once played cricket against you—says you were a shockingly sticky wicket to get. It sounds absurd!"

"No more absurd than an Indian Governor turning *padre*—which they tell me *has* happened."

"Well," said Hamar, "is it good enough to have all the parsons men who've never had a decent contact with life anywhere? I think it's going to help that we have sannyasis in the jungles who know what the word 'cricket' means to Englishmen. Perhaps that's why I haven't had a revolver-bullet in my brain. Has Gandhi ever played cricket?"

"I think not," said the Sadhu.

"And *why*," asked Hamar irrelevantly, "does he call us Satanic?"

The adjective has rankled queerly in the English mind, stirring it half-amusedly, half-resentfully. Alden took it on himself to reply.

"It was the Government that he called Satanic. And I guess he was thinking of one province most of all."

"Still—*Satanic*!" Hamar made a gesture of disgust. "It's a bit thick!"

"Because Satan is the only chap who never apologizes, never admits he has made a mistake." It was Alden still speaking. "The rest of us from time to time are prepared to own that *some*thing we have done is not quite perfect, comes short of absolute wisdom or fairness. You can even suggest this now with most Government departments in India, and not be torn to bits. But hint it about the Punjab, and see what happens! Letters in the heaviest type in *The Times,* wordy raging of ex-officials, endless and sickening apologias and articles in monthlies! Thank God! Satan's been such a damned fool that he's lost his case. He's been a bit *too* successful in the courts of this world. No, listen to me, Hamar"—as Hamar tried to speak— "I know I've been swearing. I intend to do some more. It's all rot, our belief that Indians have only one mind about everything. They've as much anarchy and variety of opinion as we have, on *every* subject. But there isn't an Indian in all India, whatever his creed, whether official or supporter of Government or out-and-out extremist, who hasn't made up his mind about certain notorious events. And they see a section of our people continuing, year after year, to get official or legal pronouncements in our favour in that controversy. Well? We've been remarkably successful. We've collected as many chits and testimonials as Henry the Eighth would have done. And *still* we remain—unsatisfied! What's the result? India says the attitude is Satanic."

"The Punjab," Hamar began.

"I'm going to be kind enough to tell you what's wrong with the Punjab. Its curse from the very first, and all along——"

Hamar interrupted him angrily. "Oh, swear and have done with it! I never knew you could be so heavily serious."

"Has been, and is, self-righteousness. I guess the average Punjab district officer is as sick of it as the rest of us. There are too many folk loose in India who imagine they are God Almighty. It's a delusion the climate and people both foster."

"I'm not satisfied with Alden's exposition," said Hamar. "Is it the answer an Indian would give?"

"We haven't analyzed our annoyance so far," said the Sadhu. "I think the Mahatmaji merely wanted a term of sounding abuse. And *Satanic* is magnificent!"

Hamar accepted this. "And he wants us to have a change of heart," he went on. "Is it possible—with anyone?"

"Hasn't yours changed?" said Neogyi.

"Ask your extremist press."

"We prefer not to waste our time. You're ten times the friend of India that you were when fools were garlanding you."

"I suppose—things have changed my attitude."

"And they'll change the attitude of any man who gives them a chance," said Alden. "If our men-folk could be left alone in India for five years, we'd get our change of heart. I never yet met a *man* who was a solid reactionary through and through. Facts have always beaten him at some one point. Get close to the smuggest business-bloke in Calcutta. Let him blather on about these wicked natives. But agree with him. And you'll find him admitting that *his* office babu is all right, and as straight and reliable as need be. If all natives were like him!"

"And in the War," said Hamar, "when Indians were first given the King's commission, we all went in at the deep end about it. I did myself. But the 51st Nagpurs were unanimous that their old *subahdar*-major was every bit good enough, and a sight better than half the ribbon-sellers in the so-called New Army. If all Indians were like him, the commission would be all right. And the 85th Satpuras were sure that their Parsi doctor—who had got a rather fine M.C. at Es-Sinn and who drank and played cards and did his job like a white man—was first-rate."

"Of course those were exceptions," said Neogyi, who was under no illusions as to the executive ability of the general run of his countrymen.

"Of course," Alden agreed. "But it's over the exceptions that the principles get conceded. The exceptions are the point of the ram before which the wall goes down. And it's because you can't mix with other people without your wall being smashed somewhere that you can't run Empire Leagues without a nucleus of idle, sheltered women."

"I suggest that Alden be put under arrest," said the Sadhu.

"I should *think* so!" said Hamar. "I'm a sound Empire man, and I won't stand for such sedition. But Neogyi's been saying nothing."

"I've been thinking I must get back," said Neogyi. "I'm off the day after to-morrow, and I'm not going to leave anything not in order. Meanwhile I've been letting the two protagonists have it out—the United Indian Nation against the United English Nation. I've learnt to be a good listener. An Indian has to. But now——" He had risen to his feet; Hamar and

T

Alden rose also. "Good-bye, Vairagi. *Namaskar*! I'm being sent to a swamp near Mymensingh. Deogharia's doing. Well, if I die it won't do Sir Radhagobinda any good! He'll find me waiting for him when he comes to hell himself. *And I shall know the ropes by then*!"

The Sannyasi had risen, and was accompanying his guests to the borders of his *asram*. "Fie on you, Kamala," he said, "to be going with such vindictive sentiments! I must shake off the contagion of these evil passions. But I shall see you all again? You, Hamar? Remember, I was in your service when you were a schoolboy. You, Kamala? Alden, I know? When I'm arrested and put on my trial for sedition, I hope it'll be before you, Hamar. I shall get a heavy sentence, no doubt." Like most Indians, he pronounced the word "doubt" as if it were a large plum in his mouth. "But a *most* sympathetic hearing. And, as Alden has so eloquently reminded us, it isn't your ruthlessness that Indians mind so much as your unimaginativeness. Neogyi, if you don't visit me at least once every six months—I don't care how far away you are—I shall write Deogharia an anonymous letter. He is greatly influenced by anonymous letters."

"He's no longer my Commissioner," retorted Neogyi.

"But no man has greater influence with the Government, whether here or in England," said the Sannyasi.

He stood aside, and his palms were together at his forehead. Neogyi stooped swiftly to take "the dust of his feet." The other two were already ahead on the path, but were looking back and calling: "Good-bye, Vairagi." "Good-bye, Vairagi," shouted Neogyi, as he joined them. "Good-bye. You'll see me oftener than once in six months. You'll see me whenever my mind goes altogether bad"—he said these words in Bengali—"and I feel that I *must* find some one sane to talk sedition to. Then I shall come here. Good-bye."

And so Neogyi passes out of the story.

40

FINDLAY was reading a letter from Alden. The latter, ever since he had returned to the College, after the *puja* holidays, had written regularly and often, and his letters—as Findlay knew well—were his deliberate contribution to the task of keeping his friend's mind sane. The last year had changed Alden greatly. The childish foolery and irresponsibility that annoyed his staider colleagues, often with good reason, now flitted only rarely over the surface of his conduct. But in writing to Findlay he called back the old mood. Anything that showed up in relief the absurdity of everything was a gain, carrying thought through another space of time, further away from sorrow. The jests were sometimes poor enough, but they limped as friendly cripples might, whose presence was the only help they could offer. Findlay was smiling as he read:

Referring back to what you used to call the "licensed buffoons" of our Mission, I wonder that you overlooked Gurucharan Babu. Perhaps in his case baboon would be correcter than buffoon. Anyhow, though he has long departed from Vishnugram, we owe him a debt of gratitude for all the joy he gave us. I was reminded of him last Sunday. I had a sort of Boy-Scouts parade at the morning service, and the boys had chosen "Stand up, stand up for Jesus" for the first hymn. You can guess my astonishment when they started singing the hymn to the tune of "Oh, who will o'er the downs so free"! That was the reverse

side of Gurucharan's effort when he trained them in day school
to sing "The stately homes of England" to the tune of "Stand
up, stand up for Jesus," but you will recognize the association of
ideas. I am thankful there were no others present who could
appreciate the jape, or I might have found it hard to refrain from
showing my congregation that I felt they were doing a highly
successful humorous turn.

Lately I have been too much in the "maggots in the brain"
condition that you used to talk about to be alive to all the extant
beanos. One of the penalties of being alone in a hole like this
is that you have no one to share a jest with; and one needs
laughter about as much as oxygen. Douglas has never seen a
real binge in his life; he's one of those men who don't even
smile when they see themselves in the mirror in the morning.
And dear old Jacks just keeps on shaking his head at the abysmal
darknesses of the paynim mind. To him, laughing at these folk
is like giggling when the trumpet has gone for the Last Assizes.
Hilda has shared many a laugh with me; but she's in Calcutta
for the week, worse luck! So yesterday I rampaged about the
place behaving rather like a madman, and only recovered after
I'd been out with the Scouts in the afternoon. When we had
done prancing about the jungle, we sat down in an open space
near the *beel* where you and I used to snipe-shoot, and we had
a camp-fire yarn, though without a fire. I was talking about the
various parts of the Scout law, and in talking about animals,
etc., I asked them what they did if they saw a bird's nest. Almost
at once I got the reply in chorus from them, "Throw stones at
it"; and when I asked *why*, the answer was, "to knock it down."
A pretty sort of rule of life! It reminded me of your yarn of
the fledglings being taken home for the cat, but here there
wasn't even the excuse that the cat had to be fed. I must confess
I got a bit of a shock, though as in the fledgling yarn there *is*
something funny about it somewhere.

41

FINDLAY put the letter aside, and looked out to the
forest. It was the same scene that he had watched a
thousand times; over which he was looking when

temptation came to him, and Marjorie had drawn him aside from it. Her spirit seemed to be calling him. He was a beaten man, with everything gone except the indomitable will that continued to serve. Life's radiancy, life's peace and hope, had vanished, his skies and his earth were void of God. Only—even though God had forsaken him, still he was resolved to serve Him—well, then, if not Him, his fellows. By this religion he would cling to the last. It might be that the light would return. If not, no matter. He would get his job done, for this is the religion of the English.

It is Christianity, too; or else the gospel of our common-sense chaplains, our virile clerical school-masters, and all our purveyors of "straight talk" is somewhere at fault. Our Lord desires us above all else to be manly and brave and vigorous; we must not let others down, we must not day-dream or moon or be sentimental. Only so can the United English Nation attain its perfect ethic of four-square efficiency in an inefficient and disorderly world. "Unto this promise our twelve tribes, instantly serving God day and night, hope to come." Findlay the Englishman, alone in the wilderness and amid childish minds, life's meaning and happiness vanished for ever, was now standing and being judged for that hope.

And even the Enemy of mankind, watching with Padalsini's brutish eyes, must have found something not ignoble in a courage so enduring. He had seen such valour before, in lonely, broken lives in every age. It was not merely the faith of the English. It had been St. Paul's faith as well. In Findlay's weary brain were ringing the words, "I have fought the good

fight, I have kept the faith, I have finished my course."
What was that but the unconquerable tentmaker's
triumphant repetition, "I have done my job, I have
done my job"? Findlay the Englishman could not be
expected to have at command the Oriental's picturesque and stirring imagery; we win our battles in drab,
desolate fashion. But Findlay's was a harder courage
than Paul's, for he was forsaken and without hope.
There had been neither glamour nor peace in the year
of labour that had gone by—nothing to keep him
going but an inexorable will that would not fail itself.
"Shall such a man as I am flee?" Every saint that the
East has ever produced would have told him that this
was not religion—it was egoism, it was masterfulness,
it was Puritan self-deception, it was nothing that God
would own. Every saint? Well, no; perhaps One
would have said otherwise.

And now the utter emptiness of this grey bungalow,
so long a centre of light and love and joy unutterable,
was closing down on his mind. The sun was crushed
out, clouds were massing—he must fight, he must
strike out, somewhere, anywhere, or he would go mad.
Outside the glorious light breezes of early March
were moving in the trees; he knew that sun-flecked
wilderness, so warm and so comfortable, with its tiny
wisps of coolness mitigating the growing sun. The
Eyes of the Forest twinkled. The whole world without
was a challenging face set his way; and it was calling
him. Yes, he would go.

He remembered, it was an unfriendly face now.
But, even as he shuddered with remembrance of that
night of terror and felt, even in this bright daylight,
madness about to blot out the lamp of his mind, he

resolved to risk all. Once, two years before, he had visited Burma, and the engineer of a river steamer had asked him to swim with him. Findlay was aware of the Chindwin's reputation, and he was weak after malaria; but, faced with the choice of "being a fool or a funk," he had chosen to be a fool. There was forty feet of water where he dived, he had gone too far down and an under-current had gripped him. It had taken every ounce of fight and strength he had to regain the ship; and as he climbed on its stairway, through his whole body swept revulsion, as he looked down on that dark, serpentine water. Never again, something deeper than his surface consciousness swore, would he risk himself in such a river. But in the very moment of exhaustion and physical fear his will had taken hold, and had commanded him to conquer this enemy in the moment of its arising. He had dropped back into the stream, and swum round the ship. The engineer had never known that anything had been amiss.

Outside his home, he paused, looking back. It was forbidding, bleak, an expanse of white-washed wall and open veranda. There were pots of dreary crotons and hateful evergreens. But the fairy image of his dead child flitted through its drabness, and he knew that no place since the world's beginning had ever been so beautiful. His wife? He remembered her patience, her love, her perfect trust in him, their comradeship. His heart filled as if it would break. He grew dimly aware of the long weeks of wretchedness that had gone by; they had no shape or form, they were twilight and aching only. And then, suddenly, they brightened, their darkness became a starry happiness. He saw Hilda at his side, as day followed day; his mind wondered, opening out to a wild hope. He remembered Marjorie, and all faded again. He cleansed his thoughts, fiercely, passionately; and he strode to the wilderness.

The morning was but a few hours on its way; and Findlay felt that to-day nothing could tire him. He had duties, he knew, duties in abundance; but, for the first time in his life, they seemed not to matter at all. Had he stopped to listen to his English conscience, he would have acknowledged that he was sinning. But that conscience for the time being had been dethroned, some unknown power had swept it ruthlessly away. He knew, without knowing, that he could do no other than he was doing. He was possessed; and he must put as much space as he could between him and his old self.

On the high *bund*, the narrow nose that interposed between the twin Eyes of the Forest, he lingered, watching the myriad-twinkling glitter; a flock of wild duck sprang from the reeds, and hurtled overhead. The banyans, with their grey, feeling roots hanging and swaying over the crevices in the *bund*, seemed like the brooding ascetics to which Indian poetry loves to compare them. They were his friends; that smiling water, in whose cool waves he had swum and fished, knew him. But his heart was still bound; and, though he knew that a sky and earth of infinite beauty were about him, they were uttering their language to one who could not hear.

He made his way down the *bund*, and over the marshy margin. The air at his feet quivered in a score of places, and whitened into the wings of a covey of snipe. He knew that they were here always in winter; he had spent many a morning tramping after them with Alden. But he had forgotten all that; and to-day it was nothing to him either way. From their swift wings some tilt of momentary buoyancy may have touched him; but it was gone. He stooped to look at a patch of sundew, and saw that arrowhead was flowering, freely as beside a Fenland stream. Then he plunged into the forest. He made his way along a ravine, where the laterite thrust redly round the ebony, snaky roots of the *kurchi*. The nulla's sides were glorious with the flower that is like a fuchsia, the *dhaiphul*. *Woodfordia floribunda,* that was its Western name; Findlay could not help smiling, as he felt how we have killed loveliness with our heavy names for it. Who was the Woodford whose style had been set on the flower? He had never heard of any Woodford in these wilds. The last berries were shrivelled on the zizyphs, the Saviour's Thorn, the scrub where the partridges run—they were whirring up from his feet now, as he scrambled up out of the nulla. A mongoose perked the moist blackness of an enquiring muzzle at him; and hardly bothered to withdraw it again. It was only Findlay the Englishman, Findlay who knew these wilds as he knew the back of his hand and had a right to be here. The *somalata* had tossed its mesh of silvery fragrances wide over the thicket. *Shyama* was vying with it in white delicacy and gift of sweetness—*ichnocarpus frutescens,* thought Findlay, and his bitter mind laughed again. Their flowers were fading. No matter; here was a copse of *mahuas,* and it was candle-brilliant with the white waxen blossoms.

Insensibly the oneness and unity of the world was flinging its comfort about him. Everything was white —colourless, if you like. There was no splash or glow of colour, except the bright redness of the new leaves of sal and mango, and that was passing, as *simul* and *palas* had passed. The *dhaiphul's* beauty was merely a faint rosy flush amid its grey-green leaves. Everywhere it was white—the springtide's brief glory of red was evanescent, like the five minutes' splendour which followed upon the whiteness of dawn and scattered again before the sun's all-conquering whiteness. And now day was at poise of noon; it would journey to its finish over these jungles, to the last far-spreading radiance that he loved so passionately. Light, air, space—the infinite earth, the infinite sky. His spirit was a desolate pilgrim walking their vastness.

Already the *mahuas* were undergoing the hardly perceptible change which makes their flowers fruits. A party of bears were busy, greedily gulping down the blossoms. Findlay gazed at them fearlessly, and walked through their midst. He knew the risks of meeting them now, when their cubs were feeding with them; but his mind had passed beyond all thought of dread—safety or peril were matters alike irrelevant to him. And, since he did not heed them, the bears ignored him. He all but brushed by a mother to whose back two cubs were clinging, and stopped to break for himself a spray from the mauve, mottled orchids that were making the trees glorious. He had to spring into the lower boughs to reach it; he did this, coolly and unobserved. It was past noon; he would rest here and watch the bears. He did so; and he feasted with them on the flowers of *mahua*, a sickly, sweet inadequacy—but perhaps the manna of the Israelites was nothing better. When one is in a wilderness, hunger can find a feast in the dryest of husks.

After a while, he continued his journey. As evening drew on, he found himself in the foot-jungles of Trisunia; he must have walked nearly twenty miles, so stern had been the travail that urged him on. His way had been circuitous, he had not known that he was being driven in this direction. He walked up to the grove of Padalsini, and across it; he determined that he would return this way by night, the very path and period of her power. He pushed up the hill-side, by slipping gully and grassy waste, and he reached the summit, to see the sun hanging like a golden-red ball suspended by an invisible thread before it was dropped into an unfathomable abyss. Away on the plain he could see the eternal sights of India, the dust fuming and fussing behind the bullock-carts, the whiteness of that peaceful west, the children playing round their huts or bringing home the buffaloes. The air was clear and tense, and sights a dozen miles away seemed near at hand. He sat down by the old idol. Some one had turbanned its head with fresh marigolds. An invisible god was busy in the sal-tree above him, and was showering down, in delicate gust on gust, the sweetness with which the Indian spring was dying. Another god was guiding the brook's melody; a third was playing upon the rustling forest a music as lovely and as faint. A man must listen with his whole mind, or he could hear nothing of all this. Findlay's mind was not listening, and it was not till afterwards that he knew that he had heard.

He knew now the thought that had been knocking

at the door of his will, through many months. The temple was empty, the shrine was swept and ready; but the deity was gone. And Findlay remembered what gracious loveliness had made the months of anguish endurable. Alden had been a friend—his heart welled up in gratitude—had any man ever known such a friend? But the most radiant lady of all India had given him companionship. His heart bounded with the thought that he might win Hilda Mannering to take the place of the Dead in the temple of his worship. Hilda Mannering! Her very name made him happy. He would fight this question out, now.

But even as he dwelt upon her amazing dearness, the magical sweetness of every word and action, he recoiled from the thought of trying to win her for his own, as from a suggested wrong. No man but the one that could give her most had the right to become her lover. She must have not only the deep fires of a man's affection, but the leaping glory of a young man's imagination, the glamour that surrounds his thoughts of woman and that can be, though it rarely is, brought to the one goddess who gains his love. Findlay knew that he could love Hilda—how easily and how greatly! But who could not? And he knew, also, that, though much remained, more had vanished for ever with the Dead. Yes, Hilda must go to the man, whoever he might be, who could give her most. Hamar came into his mind, and he remembered when he had found them crimsoned in each other's presence. Let Hilda choose. He would not wrong her, by thrusting his own lesser gift upon her, if Hamar could bring a greater.

Night was closing down; its sounds and its silences were beginning. Findlay remembered the first time he had ever come to Trisunia. There was a ruined bungalow at its foot, deserted thirty years since by a German company who had tried to quarry stone here. He had meant to sleep in it, after preaching in the village at the hill's foot. It was a night wretched with mosquitoes, and he had lain awake. About ten o'clock he saw torches along the hill-side, and went out to see what they were. People on the road told him that a party was out trying to spear a pair of leopards that were vexing the village. He had joined them, and had spent the night beating through the forest with flares. He was reminded of this now by the quick glimmer of the fireflies in the blackness of the spinneys. Leopards? Yes, there was a rumour again that a pair were haunting Trisunia. He liked leopards. Still, leopards in a wilderness in dense night were a different matter from leopards glimpsed in a noonday glade. But what was this that the Hindus say, that no beast will touch you unless you first get in *your* mind the thought that he and you stand in the mutual relation of destroyer and victim? Nonsense, of course; he had posed them with the question of how the theory applied to sharks and crocodiles, that pulled down bathers who were unaware of their presence. Still, sannyasis spent the night in forests where tigers and leopards wandered. They had done this for milleniums, and who ever heard of a sannyasi being harmed by wild beasts? Jesus had spent nights alone on the Galilean hills; there were leopards there. There was no shadow of misgiving in Findlay's mind. He was alone; but he was safe. What beast of prey would strike at a life so poor as his?

Alone? No, a thousand times, no! Suddenly the

Love that had all day long been offering its strong
arms of comradeship drew him to Itself. In a moment
the long months of sorrow were swept from his mind.
Findlay had never dreamed that in the whole world's
multitudinous processes was any wave that could have
swept away a deadness such as his. Yet it came. It
came, mantling from the forest's rim, by slow—no,
swift—steady encirclement from the edges of Trisunia.
It came, gliding from the sky that twinkled with the
innumerable eyes of God. Everything, the winds that
rustled past, the dead leaves that shivered, the living
leaves that whispered in dry talk together, was hurrying to help and save John Findlay, the man of God.
He was talking now, and his friends were with him.
Marjorie was standing by him, and Joan was with her.
His terrible anguish gushed out in a rain of tears, as
his dead child flung her arms around him.

"Daddy," she said, "we've been with you, we've been
with you. And oh, Daddy, you couldn't see us! You
didn't try to see us. But we were with you, we were
with you. And we shall always be with you."

Findlay was sobbing, as he lay on the ground. And
then he found his sorrow going. He was able to
speak. But he did not wish to. Without voice, he had
been talking to them, he knew, and he had told them
of all his misery and weakness since they left him.
He said but their names, and was silent again. "Marjorie! Joan!"

He had loved them more than everything else that
life had held for him; and now, he knew, nothing,
not even Hilda Mannering, could be taken into their
empty shrine. That temple now belonged to every
living creature; he, John Findlay, was the servant of

all, and his body should be the dust of every road along which man goes in lonely pilgrimage. He would lighten everyone's burdens; his own sorrows had been taken from him that he might bear the sorrows of every man and every woman that he met. This was to be his lot, to the end. He, John Findlay, had been wretched beyond all, that he might become happy beyond all. This was joy—why was it that the religion he had learnt and taught said so little about joy?—to be one with every leaf and bird and human creature, to have a heart as free and infinite as this sky that was his friend, this earth that was his mother. Hitherto, his service had been vile, hateful, unworthy—he had given it grudgingly, given it because he was a Christian man, was a missionary. He had been a professional servant of God and man, he felt that his service had gone for naught.

Dawn was breaking, and the heavens were a scurry of doves. In the deep nullas that fissured Trisunia jungle-fowl were crying, peacocks were screaming. Findlay sprang up, and his veins thrilled to the ecstasy of the day. The planet was spinning forward to its destiny of happiness, and he had joined the pilgrim host of eternity. Time had fallen from him, a threadbare garment. He was neither young nor old, neither Indian nor Englishman; he was of one age with the absurd stone idol before him and with the green leaves of this spring. The *neem*-tree above his head shook to the radiant dance of parrots, as they clung to its boughs, screeching, and raced away and back, away again and back again. He stepped up to the lion *devata* of the hill, and patted the grim, silly head. *"Namaskar, bhai!"* ("Greetings, brother!") he said, "many thanks for protection through a jolly night." He placed a rupee between the stone paws, for the next pilgrim who came. He was going to get rid of all his rupees; everybody here needed money more than he did.

He went down the hill-side with great bounding steps. He stooped to pick up stones in the boulder-strewn gullies, and for sheer joy of health and life and oneness with the world about him, he chucked them hurtling through the bushes. "Marjorie! Joan!" he called, as one wild with an ecstasy beyond the touch of time's finger. The sun began to lift a cautious shoulder in the east. "O Lord, my Father, my Friend!" chanted Findlay, "I thank Thee for my brother the sun. I thank Thee for my brother this hill, for this glorious jungle, for this ridiculous stone idol, for this golden world that Thou hast made! I thank Thee for my brethren the children of men, whom I am striding to meet!" A leopard peered round a rock, startled by the leaping of a stone that Findlay had tossed. Findlay clapped his hands joyously, and the face vanished.

Here was Padalsini's grove. He had forgotten her; and now he cared nothing about her. She should have a greeting, though. Crash! a chunk of rock was tumbling in her branches.

To John Findlay, resting on his midway journey, beneath a wild mango, came the Sannyasi, striding like a giant, the glimmer of noon encircling his ashy-grey limbs. Never had that tiger-skin been seen on their paths before, and men marvelled as at a portent. Findlay hailed him with a shout; and Jayananda, gazing in that glowing face, bowed swiftly before the Englishman could stop him, and "took the dust of his feet." The eyes of a country-side were on these men; and the action was published over a province.

"Seeing thy face, Brother," said the Vairagi, "no man need ask. Thou hast found the bliss of victory; and I need no other witness than the same the ascetics found who came to the Lord Buddha. Henceforward thy home is in the universe, and thou and I are one. I serve the Lord of the Ascetics, Siva the Naked, whose dress is the Ten Directions and the Four Quarters of the Sky."

"I follow my friend and master," said Findlay, "who walked the shores of a lake, and whose days and nights were spent at His Father's side. His home was in upland fields of lilies, and where the glow-worms shone beneath the olives of a garden."

Findlay's chains were broken indeed. He no longer felt that he must produce a knowledge of God at all hours, and at any notice or at none—that he must preach and pray as the time-table dictated, that he must give comfort and exhortation whenever his profession demanded. He was free to wait till God came; and if He came not, still—He was there. He was free to walk the roads and jungles, and where he found himself, there he slept. In the Rains, there were caves; and he knew now that no living creature would hurt him. Or there were huts; and the poorest were places where men and women, his own kindred, dwelt, so they were his home also. In the fiery heats there were the mighty trees and the sheltered sides of the steep cracks in the forest. And always, always, there was

U

the mind's inner glow, composing the body and its cravings, so that all discomfort fell away, unheeded and unnoted.

42

THE Bengali year was ending. Again the Great God massed his war-clouds, and a racing tempest scoured the exhausted air. The lightnings stabbed, the thunders burst, the huge red faded bowls of *simul* blossom tumbled heavily down, the leaves were rent from the trees, the black clouds strode majestically through the sky.

The first storm caught a group in Alden's compound, assembled in the hope of tennis. They huddled on the veranda, cursed it, and watched it.

"I wonder if Findlay's out in this," said Nixon. "They tell me he's turned sannyasi; hardly ever sleeps at home now. The whole place is full of it. Douglas, your folk ought to stop it. He'll be dead in six months. Besides, it lets the saheb down."

"It lets the Christian religion down, which is much more serious," said Jacks.

"He was bound to go out of his mind, after all that he suffered," said Mrs. Nixon. "I can't understand how your Mission ever let him stay out here."

Douglas did not know whether to take the criticism seriously. "Alden manages John's affairs," he said. "I told him Findlay ought to go home; and Alden said he *had* gone home. What were you driving at, Alden? I meant to ask you."

"He's where his heart has always been," said Alden. "He's one with the people. Their homes are his, their thoughts are his."

"But their thoughts are so *dark*," objected Jacks. "How *can* a Christian want to live with them—especially a Christian clergyman?" He shuddered.

"Oh, well," said Alden, light-heartedly "if the heathen's ways get on his nerves, he can always go off in high dungeon again."

As soon as he had spoken, he shrank guiltily before his wife's glance. He felt ashamed of himself, when Douglas was such a thoroughly decent chap and colleague. Luckily Douglas noticed nothing; on the contrary, he seemed to think both sentiment and expression unexceptionable.

"Yes, he'll soon be coming back to normal ways," he agreed. Lofty incarceration, Douglas implied, was a thing tolerable only in small chunks.

"Why doesn't Miss Mannering *ever* come to tennis now?" Mrs. Nixon asked.

"It's her last fortnight in India," said Alden; "she wants to be in the jungles and villages all she can. She's gone off to those old temples. I'm not worrying about her. Hilda has always followed her own will, and she can't be far from shelter, with all those buildings about."

The storm had a sudden intermission. The courts were flooded; since the clouds plainly intended a renewal of their favours, the company seized the opportunity to get home first.

Vincent Hamar, however, did not go home. With one eye on that threatening horizon, where the storm-demons were dancing and brewing their spells, he went towards the buried city. Every step of the way was haunted; this had been the way she came, and this dust was shining ever since. Here, that morning, he had met her face to face, when she was radiant with the spring breeze and the gladness of movement and mastery. There she had ridden quickly from his sight, that sudden bend had caught her away. He was striding now beside the Red Tank. He had forgotten Mrs. Nixon, he hardly troubled even to notice the mound from which he and Nixon had come upon the guns and bombs. Here was the place of the Great Burning; but he had no time to linger among forgotten agonies. The present was tense with life and hope. The present was Hilda Mannering. He reached the temple where he had told her that he loved her. She was there, and underneath the *neem* where they had spoken that morning. As she faced him, he saw that she knew why he had come. Her hands started, instinctively, to hide her face; but he caught them, and drew her to himself. There was no wooing; she had given herself to the hunger in his gaze, before ever he could speak.

"Hilda, Hilda," he cried. "I never dreamed I had a chance. I knew—or thought I knew——"

"You knew nothing," she told him, "or you would know that a woman gives herself to the man who wants her more than anything else in the world. She knows that it is not safe to do anything else. At least, that is what a woman like myself knows. Why did you take so long to come and claim me?"

The advance winds of the approaching storm began to blow; a gust snapped in two a bough of blossoming *neem* above their heads. As it swayed and fell, the wind that had broken it shook out its heart of fragrance, in shower after shower. The splendour of that earlier morning brightened through the dusk, the gloom was the twilight of the first dawn in paradise. As they ran for the shelter of the temple, the tempest broke, and the last showers of blossom were stripped from the forest. Spring had passed, in that fierce spasm of thunder and rain that swept the land; but its sweetness had gone into their hearts for ever.

Glossary

Achchha....... All right
Ahimsa........ Non-violence—a main plank of Gandhi's platform
Almiras........ Cupboards
Badal......... Cyclonic storm
Bagh.......... Large beast of prey; tiger, leopard, hyena, wolf
Baisakh........ April-May; here personified as a form of Siva the Destroyer
Bhadra-log..... Respectable people, gentlefolk
Beels .... Wide shallow lakes
Bibikhana...... Women's (harem) apartments
Bilait......... England (Blighty)
Boxwalla...... Commercial traveller
Brahmo Samaj.. The famous Hindu theistic society founded a century ago
Brinjal........ The egg-plant
Budmashi...... Rascality
Chaprasi....... Office servant
Choop........ Silent
Dak-bungalow.. Government Rest-house
Danga......... High ground
Deshabandhu... Friend of country
Devata........ God
Dhutis........ Clothing of men
Durga......... The favourite goddess of Bengal
Durwan....... Door-keeper
Gowalla....... Milkman
Gurudeb...... Teacher-God
Hookum...... Order
Hural........ Wolf
Jao........... Go
Jeldi.......... Quickly

Khubber....... News
Lota.......... Brass pot
Machans....... Shooting-platforms in trees
Maidan........ Public and open space
Manasa-puja.... Snake-goddess festival
Mantra........ Incantation
Mela.......... Fair
Mohur........ A tree with an abundance of red blossoms.
             The mohur was a gold coin originally
Munsiff....... Subordinate judge
Murghi........ Chicken
Nekrebagh..... Hyena
Paramatma..... The Supreme Soul or Self
Prayaschitta.... Atonement
Samadhi....... Death; used for tomb. Some sects of
             ascetic are buried, not burnt
Seristadar...... Record-keeper
Sikander....... Alexander the Great
Tat tvam asi... "Thou art that"—the message of Hindu
             pantheism
Terai.......... Forest strip at the foot of the Himalayas
Thana......... Police territorial unit; also the police station
Vahan......... Vehicle
Vairagi........ Ascetic
Zoolum........ Oppression